"What about our affairs here, Mr. Hoskins?"

The man who had seen his father safely through two financial crises, whom Murray counted upon now to deliver the undressed truth, shook his head with slow finality.

"It is done here, Murray. There can be no denying that this change in your family fortunes comes most opportunely. We have had no word from your father for more than a year. Were he to walk into this room at the moment, he could not hope to meet the obligations of his firm. It was in hope of saving something that he went east. But I am now most happy for you both. What Mr. Trews suggests is the only sensible course of action. I tell you frankly, boy, the Lyons have no future here."

"That western land—" Murray made his last protest.

Hoskins' swing of the head was deeper, his broad face mirrored concern.

"That, too, is gone. Now there is nothing to hold onto. Though I am sorry to say this, knowing your feelings, my boy, your future no longer lies here."

He had slammed the last door.

STAND & DELIVER

BY

ANDRE NORTON

A DELL/EMERALD BOOK

Published by
Dell Publishing Co., Inc.
1 Dag Hammarskjold Plaza
New York, New York 10017

ISBN: 0-440-08233-1

Printed in the United States of America
First printing—March, 1984

For Robert Adams—not a tale of the future but at least one of the adventurous past.

Contents

Prelude: Yankee Lyon—English Starr

To Murray Lyon the stale fug of the inn room formed a fog to catch at the throat. He sent the small casement scraping open with an impatient shove of his weather-browned hand; outside a drizzle laid an oily, freezing sheen across the greenish panes. Stubbornly he stared into that free world, presenting only his buckskin-covered shoulders to the two men at the mid-room table.

It was the brooding silence outside which wore on him. Where those streets had once rung with the clatter of wheeled traffic, the normal buzz of a thriving sea-port, there was now only to be heard—at too long intervals—the rumble of a heavy country cart. That unnatural quiet spelled the plight of Baltimore in this late winter of 1807.

The Embargo—mere mention of that unpopular decree was enough to turn men either red or white with rage, and made shipping-conscious New England ready to break from the young American union of states—had already squeezed most of the life out of the nation's sea trade, the trade on which this city and all the others up and down the Atlantic coast had been founded and had flourished since the Revolution. A few more months of such dry rot and Baltimore might well be a ghost town. That had been the major cause to bring Murray here today.

His forest-trained ears caught the crackle of heavy legal paper. To be followed by that hiss of in-drawn breath which preceded any word of weight from John Hoskins, a patient man who had been laboring so mightily to save something from the business wreckage of Lyon and Company, Importers.

"I think we have provided a sufficiency of proof, sir?"

That had not been addressed to Murray, but to the third man in the room. Murray, refusing until the last possible minute to be involved, stayed where he was, unaware that he was the object of a searching appraisal. He neither knew nor cared that to that third man he was as strange a sight as a Cherokee painted for the war path.

Francis Trews, late of London, had never before been faced with such a client, and he remained uncertain as to the best method of handling—not the difficult situation in which he found himself embroiled—but this young man upon whom so much of his own future depended.

The Londoner's fingers beat a soft tattoo on the table, until he was conscious of that self-betrayal and thrust his hand out of sight. He continued to examine his quarry with an intentness approaching a rude stare, marveling at the exceedingly great difference between this new viscount heir to Starr and that other Lyon with whom he had had none too happy dealings in the past.

He answered Hoskins' question hastily: "You have been all compliance and assistance, sir. Now if his lordship will but—"

Bead-heavy fringe glinted in the candle light as Murray swung away from the window. With a cat's—or a woodsrunner's—soft tread he came to the table, his hand playing with a long knife at his belt, clicking it up and down in the sheath. Every detail of the barbaric designs ornamenting his hunting smock, the leggings molding his legs and thighs as tightly as fahionable inexpressibles did those of a London buck, the moccasins on his slender feet, were alien and therefore slightly offensive to Trews. "His lordship"—what a way to address this wild young man. It was ridiculous; the words rang hollow in the air.

Murray Lyon, Viscount Farstarr, heir to the new Earl of Starr—Trews could accept this new Lord Farstarr as long as he kept his eyes on the papers before him, concentrating on facts. But the physical presence of the man those facts and papers represented was something else.

It was far easier to think of this lank, leather-clad young man with his beads and fringes, his angular, wind-browned face, his thatch of black hair, as a forest savage—a role he had played in truth. And before his years as first a captive and then an adopted son of an Indian tribe, what had he been? An unlicked, unpolished colonial cub, a boy born and bred in this dying provincial port—just Murray Lyon, son of Fitzhugh Lyon, himself an unregarded and unacknowledged kinsman of lordly Starr.

It was Murray who now broke the silence with a question:

"What of my father?"

To Trews that held something of an accusing ring, his resentment stirred. But he refused to allow this woodsrunning barbarian to see his irritation, admitting to himself alone his bafflement.

As far as the Londoner had been able to discover, the Lyon pockets on this side of the ocean were to let, decidedly so. In fact, if this youngster's father, the new Earl, had not departed to China on one of the last ships to clear before the Embargo sealed the ports, he might at present be cooling his heels in a debtor's prison.

Yet now his son acted as if he had been handed a regular facer instead of an assured position in the best society in the world, a higher place than any provincial-turned-merchant could dream of gaining. Ten thousand a year to play the fool with—which he would do if the usual Starr blood ran hot in him—and more to come. His present reluctance could only be the result of pigging it with those western savages, Trews generously made that allowance. Five years such constraint—as a captive and then one of them—happening when the lad was scarce into his teens (Hoskins had given him all the preposterous details before their meeting this afternoon) would do little to elevate the spirits.

So now Trews kept a curb on his temper, schooled himself to smile as he answered:

"Officials of the East Indies Company having factories in the Hong ports have been advised of the change in Lord Starr's fortunes, m'lord. They have pledged themselves to appraise him of the news. He may at this very moment be on his way to England to assume his proper rank. In the state of disorder now existing about the world communication and travel are both subject to hazards and delays. But be assured, m'lord, we are making all possible efforts to reach him. You have no notion of the various expedients we are able to employ in times of necessity. And now, m'lord, when will it be *your* pleasure to go?"

Murray shrugged, the gesture rippling light from beads and dyed quill embroidery. "I have been back here but a scant week, sir. And, as you have doubless been made aware," a quirk of amusement curved the disciplined line of his mouth to remind Hoskins fleetingly of the boy he had once known so well, "during the immediate past I have been otherwise engaged."

He spoke slowly, almost as if he translated from another tongue.

"Give me space to come out of the woods. The world has been radically altered for me twice within six years. I returned to Baltimore hoping to find my father, to resume a life I knew. Instead—'' he spread his brown hands and Trews took swift advantage of that pause.

"Instead, m'lord, you discover that in a general way your fortunes are much altered for the better. I can readily believe that this is bewildering—since, in a manner of speaking, it was also upsetting to those of us who were in charge of the Starr estate in England. After the death of Mr. Burnette, your great-grandfather's man of business, and the employment of my own father in the same capacity by the late Earl, your father's cousin, there was never any openness over private family matters. Many papers and much vital knowledge were deliberately withheld from us. I am not losing my proper sense of discretion when I inform you that the late Lord Starr was inclined to secretiveness, he was never in the least open, even when that quality of trust was needful for the satisfactory conduct of his own affairs. It was not until after his death that we were advised of the existence of your father. Then I reached Baltimore, only to discover that the new Lord Starr was two years out of this country, supposedly in China, and that his only son, on his way to visit his kin on their holdings in the west, had been taken by the Indians and was now on his way back—'' He smiled a little wearily.

"And now, m'lord, please believe that in no way do I wish to be unaccommodating, nor do I want to urge on you a course of disagreeable action. On the other hand, the state of war now exists between England and France, and this nation is engaged in maintaining a shipping embargo—

which has not only grievously embarrassed your
father's affairs, but tends to imprison most Ameri-
cans on their native shores. Our speedy return to
England is an imperative matter, though we may
be forced to a roundabout route through Canada—''

Murray's lower lip was caught between his teeth.
''In other words, sir, since nothing remains for me
in Baltimore, we'd best be on our way. What
about our affairs here, Mr. Hoskins?''

The man who had seen his father safely through
two financial crises, whom Murray counted upon
now to deliver the undressed truth, shook his head
with slow finality.

''It is done here, Murray.. There can be no
denying that this change in your family fortunes
comes most opportunely. We have had no word
from your father for more than a year. Were he to
walk into this room at the moment, he could not
hope to meet the obligations of his firm. It was in
hope of saving something that he went east. But I
am now most happy for you both. What Mr. Trews
suggests is the only sensible course of action. I tell
you frankly, boy, the Lyons have no future here.''

''That western land—'' Murray made his last
protest.

Hoskins' swing of the head was deeper, his
broad face mirrored concern.

''That, too, is gone. Foreseeing the possibility
of his involvement, your father assigned his title
there to George Hawtrey, so that the property
could not be seized by his creditors. Should you
attempt any claim there, it might be swept away
with all else. We may be able to pull some pieces
together after the storm, but now—no, Murray.

Now there is nothing to hold onto. Though I am sorry to say this, knowing your feelings, my boy, your future no longer lies here.''

He had slammed the last door. Whether Murray willed it or not, he was to be Lord Farstarr. He stood frowning a little at the candles which made so pitiful a fight against the gloom of the room. Just as he had learned to walk warily in one strange forest—and keep his hair safely on his skull—so must he begin again, in an even stranger maze of men and manners. His hand came away from his knife hilt and he spoke crisply:

"I am at your service, sir. When do we go?"

Trews arose with a relief he did not trouble to conceal. "This day if you wish, m'lord."

Again that fleeting, rueful smile curled Murray's lips. "Nothing is as I wish it, sir. But that is not of your doing. So—we'll go."

That stung a retort from the Londoner: "M'lord, one would believe that you went to your hanging—"

"And not to everything a sensible man could wish to obtain? But—" the amusement deepened, "—I have had strange schooling, Mr. Trews. Perhaps I have not come out of it a sensible man—"

He stopped short. Lord, he thought, he was spouting like a fool! But there was something in the Englishman which brought out stiff manners. He turned more happily to Hoskins, making his farewells and thanks warmly.

As the coach bowled them out of town some hours later, swaying and dipping along the rain-softened road, Trews continued to study him. A deucedly queer fish, this young provincial. What would London make of him? They'd have to get in a bear leader to smooth him—manners, clothes, all the rest. He was the rawest sort of material. Trews fell to considering the proper social mentor. What *would* the polite world make of the new Lord Farstarr?

But he never asked himself—what would Lord Farstarr make of the polite world? Nor did he even speculate at the thoughts behind those now half-closed blue eyes, watching him covertly with just as exacting an appraisal as his own.

1

Encounter on the Bath Road

"Now why a *mummy*?" Murray Lyon held a bronze candlestick into such light as was able to seep through the heavily curtained windows of the Starr House Book Room. Supposedly it was summer, supposedly it was mid-day. But the chill of the big room was such that he had ordered a fire for the hearth, and the gloom so pronounced that he was meditating the stripping of the high, narrow windows.

Candlesticks in the form of mummies, tables

legged by enigmatic sphinxes—they were all the height of ton, to be sure. But—his shoulders under their tight peel of blue super-fine cloth moved in a half shrug of bafflement.

"I'm wanted, Brooke?"

The new Lord Farstarr had not turned his head to glance at the opening door. However, the man who had entered was not surprised at his greeting, nor did he permit his irritation at this familiar trick of his employer to ruffle him. Viscount Farstarr's hearing was either supernaturally acute, or he had invisible eyes in the back of his head—as his staff had come to learn. He was always aware of a new presence no matter how softly one footed it across any carpet, and also, invariably, he greeted the newcomer by the right name before he saw him.

"You are dining out, Farstarr?"

Murray set the bronze mummy on the desk. "I believe that I can now say your efforts at introduction are successful, Brooke. It seems that in spite of London being out of season, I am engaged to Sir Arthur Rogsberry today. We are to visit the Pair of Fives and enjoy the triumph of Rogsberry's new cock, taking dinner there to celebrate its certain victory. So thanks to your efforts at our meeting at Tattersall's I am launched upon a social career at last. But does this interfere with some duty?"

He spoke with a soft drawl, which might have been either affectation, or the care of one speaking a foreign language, and now, behind his back, his fingers twisted together. So far he had managed to keep the tight control he had so painfully learned as a safeguard when confronting a new and, well, possibly dangerous situation. Just as the tribal elders of the forest world had impressed customs upon the young, so did this other life have narrow trails he must follow. But some day Brooke might take a leveler he wasn't expecting. Two more days—just two more days— and then this paragon of all the social virtues would be on his way north to visit his parents. To think of Brooke playing the dutiful son was a bit daunting in itself. However, with him gone, Murray would be free to breathe full-lunged for a space. He had had rigorous training in curbing all emotions long before he landed on these shores, and it was an excellent thing that he had.

Now he thought he could guess Brooke's private opinion of him. Murray had assumed the outward lacquer of the class to which he was told he now belonged. His black hair was teased by a master's touch into the proper fashionable disorder, his strangling coat was the needle work of Weston. An intricately creased, starched neckcloth fretted his throat until he could hardly keep from tearing it to bits. His feet, used to the freedom of moccasins, were cramped into Hessians polished with champagne to achieve the right glitter. He had kept his mouth shut and his ears open until he had absorbed enough of the idiomatic speech to be inconspicuous. But in Brooke's eyes he must be far, far from the finished product!

Luckily he rode well—so his inability to manage either a phaeton or a curricle could be forgiven. He could shoot, an exhibition at Manton's Gallery with the pistol had established that firmly. To a Viscount Farstarr some crudities might be forgiven.

He had made a few mistakes, but none of them for the second time, for he had never been the unlicked cub of Trews' superficial judgment. Some years' enforced residence among Creek warriors, Murray decided wryly soon after his arrival in England, was excellent preparation for any society.

Only Brooke, impecunious cousin of an earl, made Murray always conscious that he was a bizarre outsider who, by some quirk of unfeeling fate, had fallen into a well-feathered nest which belonged to one better able to fill it with grace and distinction. Brooke had never displayed that feeling, of course, and he had proved an invaluable tutor during the past weeks when a woodsrunner must be speedily turned into a viscount. His position was nominally that of secretary and he had stated frankly, upon their first meeting under Trews' auspices, that he had political ambitions he expected the Starr influence to further. All he had done was make Murray inwardly unsure and very unhappy, feeding his secret loathing of the shell he had had to build about him. However, Murray's control was so much a part of him no one ever suspected that shell nor the very sensitive core it concealed. But he longed for the hour of Brooke's departure most fervently.

"I have no intention, Farstarr, to comment upon your personal plans."

Pompous fish! Murray allowed himself the small pleasure of that inward sneer. Outwardly he tried again to conciliate. He missed the companionship he had known in the lodges more than he would ever have believed possible.

"I take it, then, that it is not my dining in or out

which interests you, Brooke. But surely you have
no objection to the jaunt with Rogsberry. He's a
rattle, to be sure, but I don't intend to be pockets
to let, no matter how he cries up that red pyle of
his.''

"I wish, Farstarr—'' Was there a trace of heat
in that? "—that you would not always take it that
I am censoring your actions. There is nothing
farther from my mind.''

Murray bit down the observation he longed to
make and said colorlessly: "Your temper is always
uncommonly good, sir. I sometimes wonder that
you bear with me so patiently.''

Brooke did not rise to the bait and Murray
marked up another test point in their eternal fencing match.

"There are some other matters touching your
tour of the Starr estates which may be discussed at
your leisure. Mr. Trews also desires you to ap-
point a time to meet with him.''

Murray came alive. "Has he heard from my
father?''

"I'm afraid not, Farstarr. And there is a sad
legal tangle which will ensue should Lord Starr not
arrive soon. Your lacking a year of the legal coming of age complicates matters.''

"Well, I know very little of Starr affairs anyway.
The sooner I learn more, the better. But you had
some errand with me?''

It was odd for Brooke not to come directly to
the point. As he studied the other more closely,
Murray noted unmistakable signs of unease. Brooke
had taken up a bronze mummy in turn and was
weighing it in one hand absently. It was almost as

if for the first time in his well-ordered life, Harvey Brooke was at a loss for the proper opening.

"You spoke of Tattersall's just now, Farstarr. It was when you were there last Monday—"

"Buying under your direction," Murray prodded impatiently as he paused again.

"You may have remarked at the time a certain person who was so ill advised as to recommend to you that bay gelding—"

Murray laughed. "I may be counted a flat come out of the wilderness, Brooke, but I do know horses and I'm not cod headed in that direction! The bay was showy, but had no bottom. Yes, I remember the fellow who talked it up."

"He is a Captain Lionel Whyte."

"So?" Murray tried to recall the Captain, since it seemed to be of importance. At the time he had been more intent upon making additions to his stable, on the necessity of proving to Brooke that that was one facet of a gentleman's knowledge that he did possess. Tattersall's, the center of the horse-dealing world—the courtyard with its fountain center—the parade of "smooth-goers" led out for display, the snap of the auctioneer's voice. They had been breaking up the stud of a certain Sir James Beal who had backed his own mounts far too well and needs must drastically retrench. Captain Whyte—

"A dark-jawed cove," he fell into the cant idiom affected by young Rogsberry and his friends. "I'd be surprised, though, if he ever sniffed gunpowder for all the handle to his name. But he was accepted, he was there with Hawksley and Manners."

"With them, no, about them, yes," Brooke made the distinction with some force of tone. "He's a toadeater in search of a new patron."

Murray was alert to that accent on the word "new."

"Then he's suffered a loss in that direction? Who was the Captain's last patron?"

"The late Earl of Starr found his services useful upon occasion."

Murray smiled. "You are under the impression, Brooke, that he may seek now to make himself a legacy, self-bestowed, upon Starr?"

"He had the impertinence to call here yesterday. It may be that you will encounter him outside this house where it is not possible to avoid his company. For, as you have noted, he has acquaintance in good circles where he makes himself of use."

"But this is to give me a warn-off?"

"Exactly. I believe he will try to presume upon his connection with the former Lord Starr and force himself upon your attention."

"How close was his acquaintance with the former Lord Starr?"

"I have no idea. Neither does Mr. Trews. As you know, the late Earl led a somewhat irregular life."

Murray laughed. "A polite way of putting a bad matter, Brooke! I have heard tales to the hundred about his unpleasant activities. But I shall keep clear of the Captain—he'll have to look for his pull elsewhere—thanks to your warning."

He might dislike Brooke to a high degree, but his good sense made him recognize the other's worth as a guide in this new wilderness. The only trouble was he had to be grateful to the fellow. Maybe they'd be better friends if it were otherwise, he thought, as he headed the powerful black, his first choice from the Beal sale, toward the meeting with Rogsberry. But Murray pushed both Brooke and Whyte out of mind as he came into the countryside with hedgerows instead of walls about. He was in the open, it was a fine day, Murray lost a fraction of his feeling of constraint. London was a cage, and these narrow, well-drilled fields were only a little better. There was no width, no stretches of untamed land to be seen here.

He rode up to the Pair of Fives well within the appointed time. There was a goodly assortment of phaetons, hacks, and curricles waiting in the stable yard to show a company assembled. Passing under the sign with its two massive fighter's fists threatening the sky—The Pair of Fives—Murray was ushered into a parlor filled with the babble of sport fanciers.

"Long" Legge, who had once come within battling distance of the champion belt for all England, his silver punch spoon now thrust through his belt as a badge of office, his broad face beaming good-naturedly in spite of its battered, off-center nose, greeted Murray. Then Rogsberry hailed him, pushing his lanky young person through the crowd as Murray made determinedly for space by the window where some modicum of fresh air might be had.

"—can promise you a proper go, Farstarr. He turns to scale at four pounds and a little," half of his host's speech had been lost in passage. Sir Arthur's snub-nosed boy's face was flushed with enthusiasm and his words tumbled over each other, "He's scarce three weeks and more. I tell you Grafton's grey is a pitiful piece of feather work to face up to him, he's ill advised to challenge at all! You may say what you like, but Jack's in a sad case if he sports a pony on that grey as a fighter!"

Murray grinned. "All right. I'll be guided by you, Rogsberry."

He glanced at the room over the other's shoulder. This was indeed a distinguished occasion, it would appear. There must be a draw of more importance than the meeting of Rogsberry's cock with Grafton's to bring out Lord Alvanley, Sir Henry Mildmay and Charles Standish. Though "Long" Legge was a prime favorite with the sporting set, and the inn he had bought since his retirement from the ring was a well-known meeting place, equipped as it was with a cock pit and a discreet place for a mill where a pair of ambitious youngsters could display their form in the hope of finding a patron.

Rogsberry left, to nail another of his wide circle of friends with the latest news of his pyle, and Murray was allowed to nurse a bowl of Legge's notable punch and retire into his chosen role of spectator.

His attention was caught by a dark-faced man displaying the profile of a crafty eagle. His neat, muscular figure, a trifle below medium height, was well set off by a coat of vaguely military cut. Save for dark stains under the alert eyes and a certain slackness of mouth, he was a handsome, even striking person. Murray drew back into the window alcove. Captain Lionel Whyte!

At the moment, the Captain was talking animat-

edly with a couple of bucolic squires to whom this
assemblage was plainly a breath of the great world.
Murray wondered just how much cash would flow
from their pockets into the Captain's before their
association was ended. He continued to study the
other. The man had good address, his manners
were commendable, he wore the shell of the world
in which he moved. And he would doubtless be
excellent company when it suited him. Only because he himself held a vast contempt for what he
had heard of the late Earl of Starr and all his works
and company, was Murray content to accept
Brooke's advice and keep clear of the Captain.

Rogsberry returned to sweep him on to the pit,
finding them both places on one of the benches
ringing it in. Below was a platform of carpet
crossed by a mark of chalk. While a chandelier
had been rigged directly above for clear lighting.

There was an announcement of terms—five guin-
eas a battle. But along the benches and among the
standing spectators swept a brisk wind of wagers,
offered and met, which had nothing to do with the
size of the purse.

Murray dutifully admired Rogsberry's bird, having been solemnly assured that it had been hatched
out in a magpie's nest to insure fighting spirit.
And he nodded amiably when the merits of its
opponent, a duck-wing grey, were cried down.

Put out by the setters, the birds ogled one another for an instant and engaged. Though the grey
was game, feathers flew under slashing work with
spurs hooked well inward on both birds. He was
floored but came up—only he was shy of a new
meeting until the pyle locked in a crash which took

the aid of both setters to loosen. Warily then the birds stood apart while the time keeper counted off seconds and a mutter of impatience arose from the audience.

"Set 'em—Set 'em!" The mutter became a chanted order as the time keeper reached fifty.

As each setter caught his bird and brought him to the chalk mark beak to beak, Murray became aware of someone shoving in beside him. He swung partly around, half affronted and ready to protest. But a glance told him that the new seatmate had no attention for him. Nor, it seemed, was he bemused by what was happening in the pit. It was his strange detachment from the battle which riveted Murray's interest.

The newcomer was an undersized young man, showing a thin face under a mop of red-brown hair only partly concealed by a shabbily smart sugar-cone topper. At first inspection, because of his slim frame and smooth face, he might be judged a boy in his early teens, but a second scrutiny of that firm chin and mouth, the knowledgeable eyes, added a good five years to the estimate. His brown coat, worn but well fitting, the belcher handkerchief tied in place of a complicated stock about his throat, suggested a would-be buck with a slender purse and a taste for the stable.

Murray, perhaps because he himself was a stranger in this world and so alert to small differences, was sure he was not of Rogsberry's easy-going circle of budding bloods, neither did he bear the stigma of Whyte's breed. Here was no imitation gentry. Yet on the other hand he was no stable boy nor groom thrusting in cockily where he did not belong. He had an air of independence which no servant nor countryman could so unconsciously wear.

Murray continued to watch him covertly. The fellow's glance was flickering restlessly along the benches, sometimes fastening for a second or two on one spectator or another. He could be in search of someone. As he studied the eager sportsmen he whistled a draggle of tune, a trickle of notes hardly above a whisper. While with his left hand he massaged his right wrist where it rested on his knee, his fingers, thin enough to be termed bony, moving round and round in a turning bracelet.

As the birds engaged for the last time he gave them a single raking survey before returning promptly to his study of the crowd. The whistle ended almost in mid-note, the fingers stopped, tightened as his whole body tensed. Then he was gone, off the bench, melting back into the crowd where Murray could not pick out his drab clothing.

Murray looked down the sweep of the benches in the same direction the other had been facing. Three of the shouting men there were known to him by sight, another he had been introduced to. The fifth was Captain Whyte, his eagle visage flushed as he mouthed encouragement to the fighting birds. Which one of that group had given his late companion such as start? That it had been a start, Murray was confident. And his attention fastened on the Captain, who was on his feet now, plainly well pleased with the outcome in the pit.

The red pyle had upheld his master's belief in him, bringing the grey to grass. Sir Arthur, his face a bright red from excitement, his voice reduced to a squeak from the vehemence of his shouted encouragement, swung Murray around in an impromptu war dance of joy before going to see his champion safely bagged. So that when Farstarr was able to eye the milling throng he had lost track not only of the young man in brown, but Captain Whyte as well. Perhaps that was all to the good, considering that he had promised to avoid the latter.

Neither did he sight either one again in the course of what turned out to be prolonged evening. They lingered over an excellent dinner, joined by a young army lieutenant, Arthur Mosby, who had had the good fortune to lay his wager on the pyle and so was well in the pocket and in the best of spirits. And Rogsberry invited this new acquaintance to share his curricle back to town, since Murray was riding.

They were still well away from London's limits when Murray's black went lame and Rogsberry was forced to pull up.

"This ain't the place to come it slow," he called. "The Mounted Watch rides the beat all night, but they can't cover every strip of the road. Do you want the Barker to put his pops to your head, man?"

Murray laughed. "If any highwayman takes me for the picking, he'll suffer a sad shock. I don't ride plump in the purse to satisfy such gentry. And look at the moon! Lord, it's near as bright as day. Don't tell me your Barker is going to risk a ploy in such light."

Rogsberry's pair were fretting at the pull-up and now he burst out:

"Confound it, Farstarr, I'll have to let these tits out or they'll grind us into the ditch. Come along at your own pace then."

The curricle bowled off and Murray watched it round a curve. He was rather glad to be alone; Rogsberry's high spirits could be more than a little wearing when taken in large doses. At night the prim fields, the ordered hedges had a new promise of wildness which in a measure satisfied his craving for space and freedom. He was in no hurry to get on.

It was easy to locate the stone wedged in the black's shoe. And the moon gave light enough for him to pry it out with the knife which slipped easily into his hold. He weighed the blade, tossing it up and catching it when he had finished the job.

The weapon was fine steel—maybe tempered long ago in Moorish Spain. Someone had taken it overseas and it had passed from hand to hand for perhaps a hundred years, working up from the Spanish settlements until it had come to Red Hawk—to be a parting gift to an adopted son of another race. Murray swung back to the saddle, the knife tucked loosely into the front of his waistcoat, his mind several thousand miles to westward.

He trotted the black along the grassy verge of the road to favor the bruised hoof. And his passing made little sound, so that he came around the bend to face a fantastic tableau.

The curricle was backing and skidding on the loose surface of the roadway as Rogsberry fought to control the nervous horses. His companion sat with hands well elevated into the air. While on a level space to one side was a horseman, the moon picking out very clearly the gleam of the pistol he held in plain sight.

"—shall bring down one of those precious nags of yours, sir," he was threatening as Murray came up unnoted in the shadow. "Toss over your purses and drive on, or I shoot. Surely a few roundboys ain't worth losing one of them bloods, now are they, guv'nor?"

Evidently Sir Arthur agreed, for with an oath he tossed his purse to the ground and the lieutenant lowered one hand to follow his example. It was then that Murray moved. Silver flashed through the air, a streak of light, there was a startled gasp from the highwayman as the pistol thudded to the ground and went off.

The roans bolted, tearing the curricle and its occupants out of the picture. Before Murray could spur forward to close the gap between them, the highwayman jerked the blade from his forearm and hurled it from him. There was a hulloo of shouting from down the road, and the thief wheeled his mount, taking off in a leap, to be swallowed up in the shadows of a copse.

Murray was left to scoop up the knife and both purses, adding the pistol as spoils of war. He had no intention of pursuing the other into strange thickets. At any rate, the fellow would have a scar to remind him of this night's folly. As he cantered on after Rogsberry's runaways, Murray was puzzled by a feeling that he had missed something important—but he had no idea what it could be.

2

Birth of a Reputation

"—the Devil to pay and no pitch hot! Stuck that pop at us cool as if he were cupping a wafer at Menton's. 'Stand and deliver!' he says, and rare fools he made us look! If it's the last thing I do I'll have that neck-or-nothing rogue snabbled and up before the beak at Bow Street—" Murray could hear Sir Arthur's voice carrying across the countryside in a furious hound's bay. Rogsberry had his pair under control and was striving to turn the curricle when Murray came up.

"First you'll have to catch him, Rogsberry," he said. "And from what I saw of the way he took cover, that won't be the easiest task in the world. After all, you're not out of pocket. Here, catch!"

He tossed over the purses one after another and the lieutenant caught them eagerly.

"That was no triumph for him. He's lost his barker as well as the blunt." Murray displayed the trophy he had gathered out of the road dust. "And he has a slit in his shooting arm into the bargain. Put the Mounted Watch or the Runners on his tail and you may fry his fish for good."

"*You* threw that knife?" Rogsberry sounded incredulous.

Murray laughed, he had not felt so carefree and at peace with the Murray Lyon who used to be since his meeting with Trews in Baltimore. "I'd been a poor woodsman if I couldn't mark him at that distance and in this light!" He brought out his adopted father's gift, balanced it for a moment, and then again steel whirled through the air, sinking cleanly into a fence post some yards ahead.

"A knife—" Lieutenant Oldham was as wide eyed as if he were once again faced by the Barker. Murray sent the black ahead and leaned from the saddle to retrieve his weapon.

Rogsberry had his temper under control again. "We're for Bow Street to lay a complaint—unless we raise the Mounted Patrol on the way. I want that hang-gallows boy in the dock. Shoot my steppers, would he?" There was a greater threat against the highwayman in his tone now than there had been in his louder ravings of a few minutes before.

"Well enough." Murray restored the knife to concealment. He realized that Sir Arthur's usual good nature was soured and that the young man was aroused to a point of anger of which he would not earlier have believed him capable.

Granted that the attack had been a startling shock, and that Rogsberry must be smarting at his own helplessness, still his present fury seemed out of proportion to the result of the encounter. But perhaps Murray's own close acquaintance with violence, with dangers Sir Arthur could not possibly visualize, had toughened him to the point where he looked upon this as merely an exhilarating adventure. At any rate he was perfectly willing to accompany Rogsberry to Bow Street—that Magistrates' office which, with its twenty celebrated "Runners," was one of the most famous law enforcement bodies in the world.

The visit to the Bow Street esablishment and court was an experience worth having, he decided as they found their way, under the flickering oil lamps, along the city streets to the center and brain of the only well-organized police force in England.

Oldham was entrusted with the curricle, staying to walk the roans up and down as they grew restless, agreeing to keep an eye on the black, which Murray turned over to a ragged horseholder before he followed Rogsberry into the crowded outer hall of the building—the late hour, seemingly, having little effect upon the volume of business to be brought before the magistrates.

Sir John Fielding, the "Blind Beak", and the brother, Henry, the novelist, had laid the foundations of this organization, taking over from the

chaos of an earlier day. The system they had built
had survived the blind fury of the mob during the
Gordon Riots which had emptied the prisons.
Though the rioters had gutted the court itself and
looted and destroyed irreplaceable records, Bow
Street had continued to uphold the might of the
law against continued official cheese-paring and
obstruction through the lack of funds, as well as
the hatred of the criminal worlds. It had kept
grimly to its task of proving that only in a central-
ized and trained force of law officers was there
any hope of controlling the anarchy of London's
underworld. Now Bow Street was tolerated by a
suspicious government, and feared—in a very
healthy way—by those outside the law.

The hall was crowded and the smell of the
waiting room was a thick combination of a hundred or so odors, none of which were allied to
scent or spice. Chairmen, lounging hangdog fellows without any outward sign of any honest trade,
frowsy women—it was a seething spectacle of a
side of London Murray had never thought to explore,
had hardly known existed.

He listened with only a quarter attention to
Rogsberry as the latter spilled out his indignant
tale of their encounter on the Bath Road before a
man who was either the redoubtable senior magistrate, Sir Sampson Wright, or his confidential clerk.
This inner chamber was less crowded than the hall
and in much better order, but it still was a cross
section of a brawling, alien city.

Several well-muscled men in inconspicuous dress,
who bore themselves with a quiet self-confidence,
he judged to be Runners—those champion thieftak-

ers who raided the stinking morass of the London
slums to emerge a surprising number of times
victorious, with guilty men manacled and safely
delivered to the cells—spending hours patrolling
streets to bring the weight of the law into places
where it was bitterly resented. They were a hard-
looking lot, not far removed in dress and air from
the prey they sought.

But there was another man, sitting on a stool
against the wall. He supported a board across his
knees, intent upon some scraps of dingy paper he
held fast to that unsteady desk with a broad left
thumb, while he made marks from time to time,
pausing to read and shape each word with his lips
as he wrote.

"Stukley!"

At that call from the magistrate, the seated man's
head came up. He stuffed his bits of paper into the
front of his rather threadbare coat and stood the
board against the wall as he got to his feet and
came forward, with a crooked gait caused by a
shortened left leg.

"Aye, sir?" His voice was oddly soft and mild,
in contrast to the rough bumble used by all but the
upper officers of the court, and he caught at the
edge of the clerk's table to steady himself as he
came to a halt before the bench. He might still be
on the right side of forty and his features were
regular, almost handsome, save for a scar running
from the edge of his right eye to vanish in his thick
mop of rusty brown hair.

"Stukley, it would appear that the Barker's out
again. If you would be so good as to run through
your account once more, Sir Arthur—" The man

on the Bench inclined his head toward Rogsberry, who, so encouraged, rattled off his story of their meeting with the highwayman.

Before he had done, Stukley was nodding. "It's the Barker, right enough, sir. But he's usually not one to give up without poppin' in a good one. Didn't shoot your cattle, guv'nor? Lord, you is a lucky one, to be sure! He ain't put lead in a man yet, but he's one as will shoot be he pushed to it—the Barker ain't cow hearted. He knows how to use that snap of his and he's never been prigged—a regular smoky one, he is." Stukley shook his head in rueful admiration. "If it wasn't that he plays in such luck, he'd have cocked up his toes 'fore this. Two years he's been a bridle cull, and Lor' bless you, that's a lifetime for the road! It's past time to cast up his account, so it is! But you're the first, guv'nor, what rode away from the Barker without payin' his toll—"

"Oh, Lord Farstarr came up behind us—and threw a knife. Caught him in the arm and he dropped his pop—"

Stukley, keeping one hand on the table for support, edged part way around. Murray found himself observed by a pair of ruddy brown, strangely compelling eyes, in which the pupils were distended as if their possessor demanded that they register every point of air and appearance.

"A shiv now, m'lud, that's somethin' out of the ordinary, ain't it? Got the Barker in the right arm—bad, m'lud?" he ended hopefully.

Murray shook his head. "I don't believe so. It surprised him into dropping his weapon and he'll carry a mark to remember it by, but not a bad hurt, I would say.''

Stukley sighed. ''More's a pity. We might have traced him the sooner had he had to lay up with a real rip and tear. But the Barker, he ain't no common bridle cull what's good on a horse and with the pops, but thick up here.'' He tapped his forehead. ''He uses his think-pan and don't just try to mill his way out of a row. The man who lays hand on *his* shoulder has got to be uncommon lucky, too—or the devil of a pusher with his own noodle! Want I should publish him on the Hue and Cry, Extraordinary, Sir?'' he asked the magistrate.

''Do that, Stukley. In the meantime, Sir Arthur, we appreciate your prompt report, and once published in the Hue and Cry there will be eyes out for him all up and down the country. Someone may claim his forty pounds for turning him in. Do you have anything to add to the account, m'lord?''

Murray described the Barker's swift disappearance into the woodland and his own idea that the Barker was very familiar with the country, an idea which Stukley agreed to. The small man took notes, listening intently with his rough head on one side.

When Rogsberry turned to leave and Murray made to follow him, the crippled man was still examining him with a very thoughtful expression on his scarred face. He spoke softly as to himself:

''A shiv now—a shiv, mind you!''

Some hours later Murray lay on the wide bed in Starr House staring up into a darkness broken by bars of moonlight. He was frowning, trying to understand what had happened just at the end of his exciting evening. Rogsberry's attitude had been almost curt when they parted. And Oldham very aloof. Odd.

Or was it? Sensitive to any change in this new atmosphere Murray began to speculate. Was Rogsberry flustered because he had not been able to best the highwayman on his own? Did he think that Murray's action in some way reflected upon him? Murray rolled over and tried to think of something more interesting.

Stukley—at least the whole affair had introduced him to Bow Street and the Runners. To Murray the little lame man was the most notable character he had met in dreary weeks. Stukley might be worth cultivating as an escape from the stifling correctness of a Brooke-dominated world.

Thoughts of Stukley led Murray back to the Barker. Where was that enterprising rogue lying up to nurse his slit arm? Once more he was plagued by the feeling that his forest-trained eyes and hunter's skill had overlooked some important point. He rubbed his throwing hand along the smooth sheen of the linen sheet. That had been as neat a cast as he had ever had cause to be proud of. A good thing for Sir Arthur he had spent those hours of practice almost half the world away.

The pale-yellow and blue-green walls of the Egyptian breakfast room—their gold designs copied faithfully but with little discrimination from the decoration of mummy cases—he found a depressing sight the next morning. None of the ultra-fashionable decor of Starr House was particularly elevating to the spirits: asp-armed chairs, bedsteads with gilt palm trees for posts, black Wedgwood vases perched like funeral urns on marble-topped tables, busts of Roman Emperors in niches along the halls, deep purple wallpaper. Murray munched cold beef with an appetite and meditated on the pleasure of sweeping all this elegance into discard. Brooke came in. After one glance at the other's face, Murray dismissed the serving footman and made a brisk foray into enemy territory:

"Just the man I wanted to see, Brooke," he lied blandly.

"Farstarr, what is this? You were stopped on the Bath Road last night?"

Murray was relieved that no sin of omission or commission was to be aired.

"So that is already known? Where did you pick it up? I thought that I kept such rudely early hours that I should be able to tell you myself. There is nothing to be in a pucker about. This Barker thought to lift our purses. He came off without his pistol and a hole in his arm into the bargain!"

Brooke did not match his grin. "In that you *were* in luck, Farstarr. Though these rogues seldom stand up to determined opposition, yet the Barker has the reputation of doing so. But this other discreditable story—I had it from my own man this morning, Farstarr, and there is no telling how far the calumny has spread. Ownes told me that the fellow was put to route by a knife, a knife thrown by you! Naturally I ordered him to speak most sharply to those spreading such a nonsensical story. But I fear it will be all over town by nightfall."

"That is also true, Brooke. The throwing of knives is an art I do understand—oddly enough."

"Art!" Brooke seated himself at the table. He unfolded his napkin with a snap of the wrist and inspected the viands before him with an interest which exiled his employer. "Indeed, m'lord." his voice was entirely toneless.

Murray pushed back his chair. "I take it that my method of intervention is not to the popular taste?"

"It is one which will cause, is causing, a great deal of talk. Knives are not used except by gypsies and low persons of such kidney."

"Is that so? I am beholden to you, Brooke, for the warning. So it is better to let a rogue confront you with a pistol and do nothing to discourage him, than to defend yourself to the best of your ability? And gentlemen do not use this." He slid the blade from beneath his waistcoat. Then with a fluid movement he tossed it. The point quivered in the center of a curving oak leaf on the door. "A very great gentleman, of the Blood Royal of his race, taught me how to do that, Brooke. And it's a useful trick, whether it is acceptable in polite company or not. It may even have saved more than two purses last night. Also, I dare say, it gave an arrogant thief a set-down he won't forget in a hurry."

Brooke displayed no signs of thawing; his displeasure was complete. "It is fortunate you leave town this week, Farstarr. By the time you return the story will be forgotten, if it is given no after addition."

Murray, retrieving his knife, looked back over his shoulder at the self-satisfied young man at the table. Then he sighed inwardly. To carry on a wrangle would avail him nothing. To mentally picture Brooke dropped down in Creek lands to survive was palely satisfying to one's esteem, but useless. He left the room with a curt farewell.

More to get away from Brooke than for any other reason, Murray went out of Starr House and headed back toward that section of the city he had seen for the first time the night before.

"Stukley, guv'nor?" echoed the first of the men hanging about the Bow Street office that he ventured to question. "He's off to th' Bow an' Bells. Want I should fetch 'im?" A glance at Murray's dress had planted the suggestion of at least a tenner in return for services rendered.

"The Bow and Bells—where's that?"

"Down th' street, guv'nor. You duck into a cellar like. I can fetch 'im in a minute. Who'll I say wants to clack wi' 'im?"

Murray spun a coin into the waiting paw. "Thank you. I'm my own messenger today."

He found the Bow and Bells, recoiled from the first meeting with the steamy vapors which curled from its area door like the fumes of the nether regions, and then resolutely invaded the half-lighted, busy underworld. The smell of boiled meat and cabbage, and less pleasant odors, the cackle of voices which seemed to Murray to be speaking an entirely new tongue, the lack of all light except a dull grey murk—kept him blinking by the door for a long moment. Then his eyes and nose adjusted somewhat, and he caught a passing waiter by the arm.

"Mr. Stukley?"

The lanky boy stood gaping at him slack jawed and wide eyed. Flash culls did not ordinarily find their way into the Bow and Bells. Then, sensing Murray's impatience, he closed his mouth and used an unclean thumb as an indicator to the far side of the room where a shoulder-high partition of aged and dirt-blackened wood made a small corner of isolation for the "Bow Window Set" of patrons.

Murray threaded a path to where the man he sought sat alone on a bench. As he came Stukley looked up, his surprise, almost as graphic as that the waiter had shown, changing quickly to something else as he got awkwardly to his feet.

"M'lud," he greeted Murray in a low voice, and then glanced behind the younger man as if seeking some bodyguard. Seeing that the other was alone, his slight frown became pronounced.

"Mr. Stukley," Murray returned. Now that he was here he knew some embarrassment. What had begun as a gesture of defiance now appeared to have little motive. He was at a loss as to any reason—except that he was interested in Stukley and wanted to annoy Brooke—for meeting the man.

"M'lud, this is a smoky business."

Murray froze. He had had to take one set-down from Brooke, he certainly did not intend to take another from this stranger.

"The word's out, m'lud. There's those ready to do you a mischief. Yet here you be a-walkin' right up to their kens, as it was, so any ramshackle sort o' cove could give you a wristy tap on the brainpan—or paint a peeper for you—you never knowin' who'd made cold meat o' you! I'd take it kindly if you'd cut line and go 'fore just that there happens."

Murray tried to translate and made a guess. "Do

I take it that the Barker has friends ready to avenge him? I'll be all obligation to you, Stukley, for the straight of this."

"Very well, m'lud. But not here. There's them what has their tongues hung both ends loose between their choppers, and their ears fannin' hearty in the breeze. We'll get us a snugger hole to scaff and raff this over. A cull can be as game as a pebble, m'lud, but if he ain't up to the mark in takin' caution here and there, he's apt to find his noodle goin' round like a miler at the track, along of a good crack on it!"

Somewhat lost in the maze of that warning Murray allowed himself to be herded out of the Bow and Bells. He noted that the cane Mr. Stukley used was no dandy's slender stick, but a stout cudgel, and that those ruddy-brown eyes swept from one side of the street to the other with the raking regard of a trail runner in enemy territory when on the war path.

They passed over two blocks, Stukley setting a brisk pace in spite of his lurching limp, and found themselves in a different type of neighborhood, one of small respectable shops and dwellings. Now Stukley walked more slowly and when he turned into another tavern he had almost ceased to frown.

It appeared that Mr. Stukley was also recognized in this establishment and that recognition got them the use of a small bar parlor, exclusive, at this hour. It was not until refreshment stood on the table between them that Murray pressed beyond civilities once more.

"You are a Runner, Mr. Stukley?"

Stukley swallowed and made a rather precise

business of setting down his mug again. "Not now, m'lud. I was that. But then I was cracked up in the way of business. Now—I makes meself useful to the beak, 'cause I remembers," he tapped his forehead. "Here I has more memories of a lot of peevy culls than they knows. I still has me ears hung straight and wide, and me ogles workin' good. With me stick in hand, I ain't too easy to give the push to. Does some cull want a bit of peerin' and pryin', some respectable, law-abidin' cull, that is—all for the good, you understand, m'lud—then I peeks and pries and finds out the needful for him. But I ain't never on the old lay, nor goin' to be. Only ears, and ogles, *and* a good memory for a bad 'un—they comes in handy, m'lud."

"A private inquiry agent," mused Murray.

The other grinned. "Just so, m'lud. Are you desirin' of some private inquiries now?"

Murray laughed. "I would judge that I might need a bodyguard more, if I understood you rightly a few minutes ago."

The other was sober in an instant. "Don't you believe that I was flammin' you any, m'lud. You did more'n crease the Barker's arm with that there shiv o' yours—or so I'd say it. A shiv now," he broke off to eye Murray with open curiosity, "a shiv ain't the sort of weapon you'd think a gentry cove'd take to natural. Meanin' no offense, m'lud."

For the second time that morning Murray produced the knife and Stukley examined it with the critical detachment of an expert.

"Nice bit o' steel that, m'lud. And old, I take it. Family piece, eh?"

"No. It was given me by the man who taught me to use it—so!" Murray did not resist the temptation. Stukley's attitude was warming after the scene with Brooke. Steel curved through the air to stand point deep in the door.

"Very nice, m'lud. Aye, I can see as how you were able to come it over the Barker, 'specially when he warn't expectin' none of the sort. But it ain't goin' to keep you up and movin' when the word's out. They tell us how the Barker has said he'll tend to you. But there's those who'd take that trouble offen his hands to get his good will."

"What!" Murray, who had gone to pull out the knife, turned to stare at the other.

"You see, m'lud, the Barker's top cove in his lay. And bridle culls, they's top men of all lays. But the Barker's got tongues clackin' 'bout him now. There's them who'll pull him down iffen he shows shy. Also there's them what'll run his errands. If he wants a flash cove ruffled up some to be taught a lesson, well, should that cull stay in London, there's coves as want the Barker to notice 'em kindly and will rough up that buck—even if he's a lord with half a hundred footmen and such to see him safe to bed at night. Do you want to mince 'round with guards at your heels, m'lud?"

"No!"

"Then I'd advise a little trip into the country for awhile. Let Ned Stukley nose about here and there and get the news for you. Then maybe we can lay the Barker up for fair and all!"

A second warning that he was better out of the city, but Murray did not feel the same resentment over this one. Stukley might only be trying to

make a job for himself. But it seemed that everyone agreed Lord Farstarr was better on his travels.
In the end he gave Stukley a commission to lay a
watch on the Barker's volunteer henchmen.

Brooke departed northwards—reluctantly Murray believed—undoubtedly fearing some disastrous
outburst from his charge during his absence. My
Lord Farstarr began his grand tour of the Starr
estates. But he refused to share the first steps of
the route with Brooke and head northward. Instead
he picked the Cornish manor of Garth Holme as
his goal, the farthest he could find from his mentor's
road.

It was none too auspicious a morning. Mist
curled in the hollows. The chaise slowed to pass a
coach on a steep hill, the passengers walking, the
blowing horses reeking with sweat. That night
Murray lay at the George, and it was well into the
next day that they rattled past a churchyard in
which ancient yews were clipped into fantastic
shapes, then down a village street straggling to a
sea cove, and last of all turned between gates
where a woman bobbed a curtsey, before more
clipped yews walled a drive in gloomy, dark green.

3

Country Visit

Perhaps it was because he came upon it in the afternoon of a dull, overcast day that Garth Holme overawed Murray at first sight. The small manor made a solid impact of the past such as he had not met before. Starr House in London, with its cold, fashion-dictated magnificence, placing show above comfort, had inspired him only to sweep it all out and start afresh. However, Garth Holme was so sturdily rooted that, short of leveling it to the green earth, one could make few changes. It re-

mained unique as it had been constructed almost
four hundred years earlier.

Murray climbed from the chaise to stand staring
at those walls of herringbone brick and hewn oak,
towering into four great peaks from which windows made open eyes to watch a somber expanse
of lawn unbroken by any flower beds—giving root
space instead to scattered yews which had been
disciplined by careful shearing into a weird zoo.
Murray was not the first, nor would he be the last
visitor or homing Lyon, to be startled by two
monster green elephants, each bearing a howdah,
who flanked the outer wall of the side terrace.

The front door, huge, studded with nails and
banded from side to side with iron hinges of half a
palm's width, was opened for him, giving Murray
to wonder for a moment about the peaceful nature
of the neighborhood, that portal being more one of
a fort. The hall into which he was ushered was
breathtaking. Some forty feet long and rising thirty
feet or more to the roof beams, it dwarfed everyone within. As if for no other reason than to
display Garth Holme to the best, the sun broke
through day-long clouds to make a rich tapestry of
color across the floor boards as it shone through
windows blazoned in wine, blue, gold and purple
with the arms of kings and lords long gone.

"Clagget, and Mrs. Clagget, m'lord." Murray
was snapped out of his wonder at Knapp, his
valet, having arrived efficiently ahead of the young
master, discreetly directed his attention to the couple standing before the gaping hearth. The black
silk, jingling key basket, and discreet show of
good lace identified Mrs. Clagget as the house-

keeper. She was a tall woman, overly thin in spite
of the bulk of skirts a good twenty years behind
the current styles. Her hair, a pepper and salt
mixture strained up under her cap, gave a severe
cast to her angular features.

Clagget, plainly her co-ruler here, was a fit
match in rigidity of spine, cragginess of feature,
and the impression that nothing could be found
amiss in any pantry, cellar, or household department under *his* supervision.

The staff of Garth Holme, drawn up to welcome
the new master, could not rightly be judged, when
ranked against that of Starr House, a large one.
There was a line of print-frocked maids in a prim
row marshaled by Mrs. Clagget. On the other side
were three footmen and some unidentified under-
lings which Murray never set eye upon again, as
well as the grooms and the gardeners.

Clagget and his wife marched Murray down a
short passage and up a flight of stairs to another
hinge-bound dungeon door. Mrs. Clagget pushed
this open and gave a snap of the head, first right
and then left, as might a drill sergeant review lines
before an officer arrived for inspection.

"The Justice Room, m'lord."

Murray fronted a diasied bed, clearly out of an
earlier and more stately age, and intended, one
might suppose by the size, to serve for the slum-
bers of an entire small family. From a carved
canopy of fat Tudor roses and unnaturally plump
vines fell hangings of a melancholy mulberry on
which stiff heraldic embroidery had been muted by
time to hardly distinguishable patterns.

''The Justice Room?'' he echoed, unable to remove his eyes from that loom of bed curtain.

''The hanging beam, m'lord—'' One of Clagget's bony fingers pointed roofward to a beam surely of uncommonly sturdy girth even here. ''The lords of the manor held court here, m'lord. And they had the right of high justice as well as the low.'' He rolled the words about in his mouth with open pride and relish.

''Old day, old ways, Clagget!'' For such an outwardly thorny dame Mrs. Clagget had a soft, almost musical voice. ''That be far past, m'lord. Don't you be a-thinkin' on it. Old houses all have tales—and without much truth in the pack of 'em, either! There's no troublin' in this one, nor never was!''

Having been so exhorted, Murray was left with no possible protest. The justice room was the master's bedroom at Garth Holme. And if there were any uneasy ghosts lingering there, the new Lord Farstarr would have to put up with their company or explain his distaste to Mrs. Clagget. Of the two prospects Murray was already convinced that the former would be the less daunting.

Further explorations, before shadows drove him into the great hall and a limited measure of candle light to be found there, convinced Murray that in Garth Holme he had stepped from his own time into an earlier century. He was agreeably occupied with thoughts of secret passages, priest holes and other romantic discoveries which might be made.

However, he found a newcomer before the fireplace, a stocky man with faded straw hair, who bowed jerkily to Murray.

"Patrick Furth, at your service, m'lord. I was detained by a bit of trouble down at the cove or I would have been here to welcome you rightly." He spoke very fast, with a rising lilt in his voice, as if he were a small boy trying to get out an excuse before authority pounced with retribution.

"Good evening." Murray experienced his usual inward awkwardness in his unaccustomed role of young master. The Lyon establishment in Maryland had not required the services of a bailiff, and whether Furth ranked as a semiequal of Brooke's standing, or whether he was in Clagget's class, was one of those vexing little problems which always arose to plague him, since he was also painfully aware that Furth would be offended if he were overvalued socially just as quickly as if the mistake were to be made in the opposite direction. He took momentary refuge in a question.

"Trouble at the cove? Of what kind?"

"The Searchers, m'lord. They will have it that free traders are running in cargoes hereabout—over Holme land. This new man who has come over from Portsmouth— Hurrell, he calls himself—is all set to clear them out, and speedily." Furth's honest countryman's wind-reddened face was clouded, he twisted one of the broad silver buttons on his coat.

" 'Free traders'—you mean smugglers?" Murray poured a glass of wine from the decanter set out on a small table, and offered it to Furth. He recalled his father's tale of his own youth. The Lyons of Maryland had good cause to look upon the "gentlemen," the "free traders" of the English coast, with favor. Fitzhugh Lyon, an escaped prisoner of war some twenty-five years earlier, during the Revolution, had been helped along by the "gentlemen," a service which might have saved his life.

"Aye, smugglers, m'lord. This Hurrell will have it that all hereabout, gentle and simple alike, are of the same set of company. There perhaps he has the right of it to a part. Cornishmen, m'lord, they look upon the trade as a way of life, apprentice their lads to it, they do. Lord, it's been going on hereways for three-four hundred years or more. You ain't going to pull it out root and branch so easy. Hurrell busies himself hunting out all the shore caves and such, causing those who have better business elsewhere off to watch that he doesn't do any damage with his prying and poking. He can't be trusted to keep the line like his fellows, and is forever at some night ploy—thinking he can catch some innocent body stuffing tea into his haystack or some such nonsense." Furth's eyes twinkled over the edge of his glass. "Were he to sample some of your lordship's kind hospitality—which the good Lord forbid—he'd doubtless be pressing as to what duty this paid! What with keeping one eye on Hurrell and another on the village where he ain't, as you might say, relished, I have a wearying time of it."

Murray lapsed into the cant of Rogsberry's circle. "It's a wonder some enterprising soul doesn't give him a ding on the canister. Or does he come it too strong to be hopped?"

Furth laughed and relaxed. "Should he linger here long he might be in difficulties at that, m'lord. But not on Holme land—*if* you please! You have no idea what a bargle that might add up to. Nay, let Mr. Hurrell meet with uncivil handling anywhere but here.''

Under Murray's urging and his own open pleasure at being invited to share Lord Farstarr's dinner, Furth expanded upon the subject of Preventive Men, their annoying snooping, and the countryside's frank opinion of the same. In the process he provided Murray with a fairly clear picture of the village of Tregarth, its inhabitants, and their general state of cheerful and oddly respectable lawlessness.

Not to be found here were murder and robbery as part of the activities of the smuggling organization, as had happened so often in Sussex and Kent, where the people were terrorized by powerful gangs. But, as Furth had said, along the Cornish coasts ''free trading'' was a recognized business, providing a backlog of income for the fishermen. In fact it was considered a respectable occupation, with apprentices following their elder relatives aboard the channel luggers. Sailors who were highly trained pilots had proved to be even more skillful at outwitting His Majesty's Preventive Officers.

Murray listened to a wealth of amazing tales concerning swift sailing luggers with false bottoms and hollow masts for the storing of profitable cargo, of tobacco coiled into ropes among the ships' extra gear, of hams hollowed out and stuffed with lace, of brandy kegs sunk beneath the surface of the water to be towed along by innocently empty boats which could be safely searched at will by the suspicious revenue officer. Master smugglers flourished on the grand scale, contracting abroad for cargoes to be run in on a regular schedule, landing in coves where trains of ponies waited. Brandy, tea, coffee, lace, playing cards, silks, were ferried over from Middleburgh, Flushing, Ostend, Dieppe, and other French ports. Murray wondered a little wistfully how one could make contact with the "gentlemen." A voyage across and back might be amusing. Since he had thrown a cloud over his social standing by his ungentlemanly ability with a knife, he might as well enjoy being an outcast.

However, when he embarked upon a few guarded inquiries, Furth became evasive. Murray was his employer, but he was also an outsider. While the bailiff undoubtedly did not lead a line of nags down the moor on a moonless night, or flash in some cargo from the shoreside, he was enough in sympathy with those who did (as were most of the inhabitants of the countryside, including several justices of the peace) to cover up just when Murray wanted to learn more.

He slept sound enough in the Justice Room, though he discovered in himself a disinclination to raise his eyes to that sinister beam overhead. And he assuaged his lively curiosity about the manor and the village by riding out with Furth to visit the estate tenants, so learning not only the lanes, but a hidden path or two from the seashore cliffs to the inland moors.

It was on the fourth day after his arrival that there was a break in this somnolent routine. Murray was breakfasting in the small parlor giving on the inner court, a room which, Clagget had obligingly informed him, had served as a guardroom during Cromwell's troublesome rule. And he was attacking a slice of excellent home-cured ham when Clagget himself appeared with the post sent down from Starr House.

There were a scattered number of useless invitations. It would seem that his social disgrace was not as complete as Brooke had feared. The newspapers and a journal were put aside for the evening. But a last missive intrigued him into opening the sealed page at once. He read the few lines and refolded it thoughtfully.

So Captain Whyte greatly desired to wait upon Lord Farstarr, did he? For the purpose of imparting some information of great value to his lordship. Altruistic of him. And the nature of this information suggested the necessity that the meeting be a private one. Oh, it did, did it?

Murray believed he could read a threat into that. Trews had warned from the first that the late Lord Starr had left family affairs in an awkward muddle. Rumor, via Brooke, had it that Whyte had played his lordship's jackal. What did Whyte know that made him such a pusher now? Brooke *had* counseled strict avoidance of the Captain.

But—Murray made a quick decision. Upon his return to town he would at least hear what the Captain had to say. However, that could wait until he was back in London, he had no intention of inviting the fellow to Garth Holme. As he passed through the hall on his way to the stable, he crumpled the note into a ball and threw it into the empty fireplace, pushing the whole matter to the back of his mind.

Today he rode alone, cantering through the village, where he acknowledged greetings with a flourish of his riding crop. The air was crisp and carried the tang of salt—almost Maryland air as it blew from the Chesapeake. He felt keenly alive to a tingle in those toes now covered with stiff, well-polished leather, those fingers dressed in gloves.

He would go up to the beacon on the rise and then come back along the shore. Under his urging the black raised cleanly over a hedge and thudded across grain stubble. Ahead stood a stack of frieze, faggots and tar barrels—eight wagon loads piled up together. Already birds had made it their own with a nest or two near its summit. Let Boney's squadrons hover off shore and that would have the torch set to it, loosing a pillar of smoke and flame to be seen at least two miles away—a signal to be passed from beacon to beacon inland faster than any horseman could spur.

On the slope below, Murray reined up, allowing his mount a breather, and himself a chance to look over the countryside. This morning the neat checkerboard of fields did not irk him so greatly, he was less oppressed by the lack of the wilderness he had known and loved. This coastline was alien to the wooded miles of the forest never touched by axe blade, to the tidewater plantations where rivers served as roads, the two worlds he had known. The strange orderliness of fence and hedgerow, of road and cottage—yet the brisk wind tore at him, and from here the houses were only tree-sheltered dots, the village almost completely hidden by a fold in the hills. Save for a distant grazing cow or two he had the world to himself.

No, he didn't!

A shaggy nag, hardly above pony size, was

footing it at a sullen amble along the cliff edge,
and on it perched a man. Beside the unkempt
mount trotted a dog which set Murray staring. The
hound could be only slightly smaller than the nag
it escorted so soberly. For the giant canine did not
run ahead, explore to the side, or follow any patterns of its species. Instead it paced beside the
rider with a businesslike composure.

Murray headed the black for the odd party, and
as he rode closer saw that the man was no villager,
nor was he a farmer or laborer. His sober coat was
buttoned high, with very little linen showing, and
the hat, crammed well down on his head, was of a
dull grey as if many seasons of dust had become
ingrained in its fabric. With the dark-coated pony,
he made a blot which faded easily into the background.

Nag and hound came to a halt as Murray cantered up, the dog wheeling to face him with a
watchful stance which held no promise of friendli-
ness. It was part mastiff, by its powerful jaw and
dour eyes, but other strains had been bred into its
rough, brindled coat, its flat, wide head. It showed
teeth in a soundless snarl, but made no move.
Murray's grip on his crop tightened, he was suddenly glad of its lead-weighted butt.

"Good morning," he spoke first.

The man touched the brim of his weathered hat
in a gesture which was akin to a military salute.

"Good day, m'lud."

Murray was not to be put off by the other's
sourness and shortness of greeting. But perhaps his
tone became slightly peremptory because of it.

"You are?"

"Jasper Hurrell, Preventive Officer, m'lud."

The ridge of an old scar made a purplish line across his ill-shaven chin, and he had never been a handsome man to begin with. But there was a dogged stubbornness in his eyes, a set to his mouth, which Murray recognized. Yes, this type of riding officer might well set the countryside seething. There would be no covering his eyes with a sovereign or two—"putting bank note spectacles" on him during a run. He was zealous with that dour honesty and grim dedication to duty which had inspired Cromwell's lantern-jawed despots of an earlier day. It was a type the Cornish never suffered gladly.

"And this then is Satan." Murray regarded the dog with wary interest. Legends of the animal were growing fast enough to outshadow the deeds of his master. Satan, the trailer, the monster-hound trained to carry a cudgel or pistol in his mouth for his master's use, known to harry a pony train and set the nags stampeding until the Preventive Men could pick them up, as formidable in a fight as a man armed and skilled.

Hurrell might have meant his answering grimace for a smile, though any geniality was totally lacking.

"Aye, m'lud. That there be Satan. An' a good hound he is!"

"You are on duty now, Hurrell?" Murray asked, to be disconcerted by a sudden glare from the other's deep-set eyes.

"I be always on the trail in this country, m'lud. This be a lawless land hereabouts, it be that truly. But the time is comin' when them as laughs at the King's men will sing small, mighty small." He

gave a small, unpleasant chuckle. Then he stared
over Murray's shoulder, a look of open amazement softening his harsh features for the passing
moment.

"Now—what under Heaven be all that!" he
demanded.

Murray brought the black around and a moment
later shared the riding officer's astonishment.

A loop of that highway which tied Tregarth to
the Portsmouth road ran along the coastlands. Traveling it now came a caravan so utterly fantastic
that with one accord Murray and Hurrell were
drawn forward to verify the evidence of their eyes.

Wagons garish with the brightest of red, yellow
and blue paint, picked out here and there with gilt
which glittered in the morning sun, rolled along,
and marching between them were not only sleek
led horses and well-clipped and groomed spotted
ponies, but other beasts which certainly were not
native to England. Murray's boyhood acquaintance
with a book of prints identified correctly for him
the sneering, lurching camel, led in a solo state
which emphasized its unique value. Three cages
on wheels lumbered by, their canvas flaps thrown
up so that a fat and elderly tiger, something brown
and furry balled in sleep, and some other indistinct
creatures half buried in straw were visible.

Murray read signs aloud:

"Strumper's Famous and Fabulous Presentations
from the Wild."

"Ape-Man from the Forests of Deepest Africa."

"The Noble Civet Cat."

"Tiger from the Shores of Ind."

And, on one two-wheeled, green and red cart—

"Largasso, the Learned Pig. He has perfect
knowledge of the Alphabet; understands Arithme-
tic and Reading, will Spell and cast Accounts—tell
the points of the Sun's rising and setting. The First
and Original Learned Pig."

Unfortunately the curtains were pegged down on
the carriage of this wonder and it could not be
viewed by the spectators. For spectators there were,
gathering along the line of march. Out of what
Murray had, a few minutes before, thought to be a
deserted countryside, children and their elders appeared to spring from the ground itself, to tag
along the route of the vans.

A rider spurred ahead down the line of wagons
to where Murray sat on the black.

"Good morning to you, sir!" The newcomer
swung off his hat, one cocked after the fashion of
a previous generation, and embellished not only
with a liberal quantity of gold braid but a small red
plume. His wide-skirted coat was a brilliant hunter's
"pink," and the horse he bestrode was a showy
white mare with a lot of Arab blood in her.

"Lucas Strumper at your service," again that
flourish of hat. After one survey he addressed
Murray instead of the riding officer. "Strumper's
Famous and Fabulous Presentation of the Wild,
sir. We've horse acts Astley has wished to display,
sir. A man-ape from Africa—a tiger—and two
marvelous beasts first discovered by the renowned
Captain Cook himself."

"Also a learned pig," Murray reminded him
solemnly.

Teeth flashed in the brown of Strumper's mobile
face. "Just so, sir, a most learned pig. The first

and original learned pig, to be exact. But now we crave space in which to show. A pasture will do—a cleared field. Do you know of any such, sir?''

The camel bobbed by at that moment, exciting awed appreciation loudly voiced from the hedgerows where small boys beat a path in spite of prickles, and a few even smaller set up a bawling because they could not catch a clear sight of this marvel. Murray made a decision which sealed his popularity with the major portion of Tregarth people for many years to come.

''Turn into the third gate down, Strumper. You are welcome to the use of the pasture there. When do you show?''

Strumper made a third and last bow and clapped on his striking headgear. ''By this evening, sir. We welcome your custom—''

Again Murray plunged. ''I'm Farstarr,'' and in that moment he knew the first tinge of pleasure that statement had ever afforded him. ''Entertain the village free tonight and send the reckoning to the manor.''

''M'lord, Strumper's is entirely at your service! We thank you and engage to present a most superior performance. This is beyond anything gracious of you, m'lord!''

Murray laughed. ''To tell you the truth, Strumper, I hold my efforts cheap, since I must admit I have never before seen a camel, to say naught of a learned pig! Since *my* education has been so neglected, I shall take steps to see that this sad lack is speedily assuaged. At that age,'' he nodded to the children perched in the hedge, ''it was of all

things what I would have relished most. Perhaps it
still is. Give us good entertainment, Strumper, and
you'll not find yourself the loser thereby.''

"M'lord," the showman touched his hat once
more, "if you are minded to ride with us for a
piece, we can show you, private like and more to
your ease, more marvels than a camel!''

Amused, Murray accepted the invitation. But
Hurrell remained where he was, as if the wonders
of the Famous and Fabulous could never compete
with the claims of duty. And Murray, glancing
back once at man, nag, and voiceless, snarling
hound, thought that, in spite of the brightness of
the sunlight, those three were lapped in a faintly
sinister shadow.

4

My Lord and the "Gentlemen"

Murray was introduced to the camel, a rather moth-eaten grey-brown beast with evil, rolling eyes, and a sneering lip which it curled back in warning from teeth which were yellow and wickedly large. It was picketed by itself at the far end of the field, a good distance from the horse and pony lines. For, Strumper explained, those mounts had a lively dislike for both the smell and the sight of the outlandish desert animal and would become unmanageable to the point of stampede should they be forced into close company.

The circus owner, as he played guide about his collection of attractions, spoke wistfully of the charms of an elephant, until Murray wished he could satisfy the dreams of the obliging Strumper by summoning to life one of the yew monstrosities in the Garth Holme gardens.

His personally conducted tour, taken amid the confusion of booth and tent erection, with all the milling, shouting, and braying attendant upon such a business, enough to deafen the uninitiated, ended up in a line of cages. The "tiger from Ind.," a hoary grandfather that yawned redly in Murray's face, inhabited the first in that line. Next came a collection of monkeys dwelling together with all the amity of human beings, since a fight was in progress in one corner of their enclosure. The fight broke up very reluctantly when Strumper rattled his riding whip back and forth across the bars, bringing the warriors out to scold and jeer at him instead of spit insults at each other.

Last of all was Strumper's chief claim to fame, his darling treasures. The circus owner made a hissing sound between his teeth, such as a groom might use to soothe a nervous horse. One of the two creatures within arose, to sit straight up. The beast's hind legs were massive, on which, together with a broad tail, it reared back as a man might sit on a stool, remaining so at its ease, while shorter forepaws dangled over its lighter belly fur. The head bore some resemblance to that of a doe, the eyes large, the ears tulip. A wisp of green stuff protruded from between its lips and it continued to chew reflectively as it met Murray's eyes stare for stare. Its smaller companion continued to hunt among the straw for other tidbits.

"What are they?" Murray was baffled. His childhood animal book was of no assistance in identifying these.

Strumper beamed with beatific pride. "I bought the pair off an East Indiaman, m'lord. 'Roo, the master called 'em. They hop—like rabbits, so they do. But they ain't no rabbits in spirit, no, sir, they ain't! When we was at Langford, Bargee, he took the male out for a little walk like, and a dog rushed 'em. Me, I thought the 'roo was goin' to be turned up right there; that dog, he was a proper brute. But no, Roo here puts his back 'gainst a wall, see, and sits there on his tail, just like he's doin' now—waiting. There was a rare set-out, I can tell you. The roo, he grabs the dog with his front paws—they maybe don't look so strong but he can hold with 'em! Then he brings up one of those back kickers of his and—" Strumper made an expressive gesture with his hands. "Lor' bless you, m'lord, that there hound never did know what cut his line, it was over with him so fast!"

"You keep them tight now?" Murray did not relish a repeat performance for Tregarth of the scene Strumper described so graphically.

"Aye, your lordship needn't be in a pucker about them here. Calm as a sheep they is, providin' no one tries to do 'em a hurt. They don't like dogs, that's a fact. But men don't bother 'em none. Bargee can do most anything with animals, natural born talent, poor nipper. Takes the place of sense what he ain't got. He's deaf and dumb, you see. Bargee!" The circus owner put two fingers to

his mouth and produced a piercing whistle which
ran in Murray's ears. "That lad now, he can't hear
you shout, but somehow that always brings him.
Aye, here he comes now."

The boy was crawled out from under the wagon
which bore the tiger's cage was perhaps in his
middle teens, though he was undersized. And he
was not ill looking, having none of the dull va-
cancy of an idiot. Instead his eyes were bright with
an odd sort of intelligence, the eyes of an animal
striving to learn some trick in order to please his
master.

Strumper's fingers moved in signs and the boy
nodded. A minute later he had unfastened the door
of the 'roo cage and climbed inside, standing almost eye to eye with the sitting beast. He rubbed
the soft fur between the pricked ears, and then
slipped a collar, attached to a leash, about the long
throat. When he jumped back to the ground the
'roo followed him, as docile as a pet dog. Bargee
proceeded to put the big animal through its paces
for Murray, even freeing it from the leash in order
to display its swift agility in the open. And the
'roo nuzzled against the boy adoringly from time
to time.

"Bargee can scratch the tiger's ears, should he
take a notion to do so," Strumper broke in. "There
ain't an animal livin' what he can't handle. You'll
see him riding in the ring tonight, m'lord. Was he
not wantin' his proper ears and speech, he would
be top o' the bill at Astley's. 'Tis good for the
Famous and Fabulous that he's simple."

Strumper might speak of his handicapped employee as simple, but Murray thought he was in

error there. Bargee lived in a world of silence, but that fact did not mean any lack of reasoning power. And his deft and confident handling of the 'roo, which was almost his equal in size and more than his equal in weight and strength, proved that he had found his proper place in the world.

That afternoon and evening the whole of Tregarth, from the six-weeks-old latest addition, lying on a pillow in its mother's arms, to Simon Gritton, who was well known to be ninety-three and a bit (both blind and deaf into the bargain), turned out to make the most of the unheard-of treat. They were entranced by such marvels as had never come their way before. There was the dancing horse, and the troop of trained dogs with scarlet coats and brass grenadier helmets who, divided into two companies, attacked and defended a papier-maché fort, wheeling a miniature cannon into place to bring down one wall with a flash and a roar.

There was Largesso, at his sapient best, reading and casting accounts—a smug white pig ably earning his rations. The ape-man from Africa, a Negro dwarf further disguised with judicious amounts of false hair applied here and there on limbs and body, used a bow-pipe to shoot arrows at a mark, keeping up meanwhile a chatter.

And the monkeys! Those monkeys would never be forgotten in Tregarth. Clad in silks and caps, some rode a make-believe Derby on ponies—good as seeing the real thing it was, the villagers assured each other. There was a monkey hunt, too, pink coats on the diminutive riders, some of the trained dogs to serve as hounds, and another small dog disguised as a fox who, in the end, leaped

over monkeys on ponies to make a triumphant
escape. A proper do all around.

But when Bargee appeared, transformed into an
elfin figure by spangled tights and shirt, to ride on
the big white ring horses, skipping in mid-gallop
from one broad back to another, turning somer-
saults in mid-air and yet landing on his feet, leaping himself and his mount through a hoop of blazing
flame—Tregarth cheered itself hoarse in a body,
and Murray and the rest of those from the manor
added their voices to the general clamor. Strumper
had been right, Bargee was a master of trick riding.

Outside the main ring of the show were smaller,
more tawdry booths, smoking flares giving them a
limited measure of light. There hoarse-voiced barkers cried up the marvels each housed. A gypsy
wench with bold good looks and a cage of para-
keets on her arm called to Murray of fortunes. And
there was a walker on stilts, a contortionist.

Murray had paused to watch the supple feats of
the latter and to toss a sixpence into the tambor on
the ground, when he almost ran against a young
man not many years his senior, laughing with
infectious good humor at the gypsy he had avoided.

In Tregarth Murray had found few to match his
own inches. But this newcomer had not only
Murray's height, but more brawn than the other
would ever display. And he possessed that type of
masculine good looks which was appreciated not
only by women, but by men as well. Hair the
color of ripe wheat was dragged back, but not so
tightly that its original curl was subdued, into a
seaman's tight pigtail. And he wore sailor's dress,
but of far better grade and cut than those of a

common crewman. Officer of a lugger, Murray guessed, and a successful one, judging by those buttons winking on his blue coat, every one of them a gold piece. He had plainly been sampling the offerings of the village tavern, but just as plainly he was not bosky. That he was not only well known in Tregarth, but also a prime favorite, was proven a moment or so later as a crowd of village youngsters poured out of a side booth to surround him with joyous shouts of:

"Cap'n Broome!"

"Cap'n Max!"

"Do be a-lookin' here, Cap'n Max!"

"There's monkey what—"

The babble arose until the young man clapped both hands over his ears and then whirled one of the youngsters, an amusing smaller copy of himself as to hair, eyes, and fine straight nose, up on his shoulder.

Max Broome! So many of the smuggling tales Furth had spun for the new heir to the manor had centered about the amazing exploits of Max Broome, channel pilot extraordinary and Captain of the Lottery, one of the most notorious and lucky of the smuggling luggers. Captain Broome, for all his youth, his good looks, his hearty, easy ways, was a shrewd buyer and seller in the "free trade." He had contacts abroad which worked smoothly—so smoothly that one of the tales repeated with relish and pride by his fellow villagers was that three times he had been selected by some mysterious power in London to land spies in Boney's territory across the water, afterwards bringing their reports back to England. Which might account in part for some of his continued immunity from Preventive Officers while indulging in his chosen profession.

It had been widely known that it was Max Broome and his crew who had broken open the customs warehouse in Penzance in order to recover a confiscated cargo—leaving a written (but unsigned) excuse that the word has been passed to deliver it safely to waiting customers and that the seller had an honorable reputation for fair dealing to maintain. Only his own cargo had been abstracted and the Preventive Men had philosophically accepted their set-down without fuss.

Rumor had it that in Broome's fertile brain had been born the ingenuous plan which had rid Tregarth of Hurrell's predecessor. When that unfortunate officer and his men had been searching a furious householder's rooms—on receipt of private and secret information—silver spoons had been slipped into his pocket and the cry of "thief" raised by bystanders, all righteously indignant. So that the Searcher had been saved from standing his trial and perhaps suffering eventual transportation only by supreme efforts on the part of his longsuffering superiors.

Yes, Max Broome was already a legend in his youth. But he wore his honors modestly and, with the help of a good sense of humor, kept his head to the original size of his tarred hat. It was Broome above any other smuggler along the coast, Murray guessed, that Hurrell longed to lay by the heels. But in spite of grave provocation, legal proof continued to be lacking.

"Max!" The eight year old riding on the Captain's shoulder was now so far above him as to

be using his cap as a sort of crop to urge his mount
on, "did'ya see the monkeys, Max? And th' horse
what danced? Max, did'ya—"

The Captain was laughing as he faced Murray.
His hand touched his hat brim in salute without the
faintest hint of servility. Max Broome in Tregarth
was fully the equal of any lordling out of London,
and Murray acknowledged that with a friendly
nod.

"Hush your chatter, younguns, you be screechin'
like a convoy of gulls now." Broome's voice held
the soft burr of the district, but it also had a vague
hint of cultivation in it. Broome had more education than most of his fellows, gained through his
own ambitious efforts. "With all your monkeys
and such. Evenin', m'lord."

"Good evening, Captain." Murray held out his
hand, to have it shaken heartily. He was about to
suggest that they both repair to the tavern, having
a mind to know Broome better, when the Captain
stiffened and the laughter vanished. His blue-green
eyes narrowed with the watchful intentness of a
fox who has heard the faintest hint of hound bell
down the breeze.

Hurrell, Satan pacing stiff legged beside him,
had moved into the shadow flung by the nearest
booth. There was an air of triumph about the
Preventive Man, as if he were anticipating some
pleasure to come. Broome shrugged and then
laughed again.

" 'Tis good of you, m'lord, to pleasure the
brats," he raised his voice a half tone, his uncon-
cern did not appear forced. "If you're ever minded

to indulge yourself with a bit of a sail now—well, just you hail the Lottery!''

Murray grinned. ''Now I take that handsome in you, Captain. And I might do just that. It would be beyond anything great!''

''It would that, m'lord. There's some as will speak ill of us in these parts, but they be mostly cod-headed landlubbers and no proper men. Aye, give us a hail on the Lottery, m'lord, and we'll show you some sailin' as 'll make such stub-faced beef boys' eyes start right out o' their misshapen skulls. Now, Tom lad, 'tis past time that you were lashed down in your hammock,'' he said to the boy on his shoulder. But three-quarters of his attention was still on the man in the shadow. ''Make your manners proper to his lordship, and we'll be shovin' off.''

It was a fine night and Murray was tired of the garish excitements of Strumper's and the booths. He swung out across fields, avoiding the roadway, intending to return to Garth Holme by a new route which had intrigued him earlier. The wall which surrounded the inner garden, severing the formal arrangements of geometric beds and walks from the wilder groves of the park, had in one corner a curious series of jutting stones to form an inner and outer staircase. Why it had been so built, Furth could not tell him. But now it offered a short cut to the manor house and, while the thread of waning moon was not too helpful, his woods-trained eyes located landmarks as guides.

Murray had crossed the wall stair and was finding his way through a miniature copse in order to avoid a small stream when he stiffened. There had been no whisper of sound—only the hum of insects, the sleepy twitter of a bird, other noises he accepted as natural to the night and its creatures. However, that odd sense developed during his forest life told him that he was no longer alone, that he was either under observation or being trailed.

He paused only for a moment, then he moved on, but under his tread no leaf crackled nor twig snapped. Hampered as he was by boots, tight coat, choking neckcloth and all the other trappings of a buck, he could still travel with that skill he had learned painfully but well.

But he was not fool enough to venture into the direct light of the open, keeping close to the wall, one hand on its rough surface as a guide along the darker portions of the way.

Here the garden space expanded, the park vanished, so that the wall paralleled the road to the village. A small gate, fastened by night, gave on the dusty lane outside. Murray's hand fell on the top curve of that. As he paused again to listen for what might creep behind, he was startled instead by voices from the lane.

"Smartly now, lads!" That had the ring of an order. "Douse the glim, Hawkins—want to sail in with all flags flying and give the scuts a chance to diddle us?"

Hawkins promptly blew out the lantern, but not before Murray saw uniform coats. Army? Navy? But what—and why? He fumbled at the catch on the gate, snapped it up, and squeezed silently into the lane.

"Down at the Mermaid you'll find 'em, Your

Honor. Good stout lads, all of 'em, trained to the sea.''

Murray caught his breath. He knew that voice; there was no mistaking the rich drawl. Broome! But what was the Captain of the Lottery doing in this company?

"Clap up that tongue of yours, bully boy!" snapped the leader of the party. "This isn't the first time I've been out pressing. The Mermaid, eh? All right, lads, we take six from there—those I tap on the shoulder. And stick the prisoner one in the leg if he tries to make sail, understand?''

An unidentifiable growl from the dark signified that the listeners understood perfectly.

Press gang! Murray moved away from the wall and started ahead through the dark. His father had been picked up on just such a country road, victim of a press gang, when he had been an escaping prisoner of war. Only a happy quirk of fate had saved him from disastrous involuntary service in His Majesty's Naval forces. At no time was the press gang in favor with any American.

What was the gang doing here in Tregarth? Murray's ties with the village were slight, but his indignation was hot. The lord of the manor could take no official part against a naval officer and a party of marines doing their duty. No official part— Murray grinned in the dark. They were heading for the Mermaid, were they? He stopped and stripped off the tight coat which prisoned his shoulders, the length of starched muslin about his throat. Balled together with his topper he tossed them over the wall. This might lead to a proper turn-up. And he could play at bare-knuckles with the best of them, if that was what they wanted.

He sped on, getting into the village well in advance of the press. There was a twittering whistle from the grass beside the lane and he pounced, to clasp a small, writhing body.

"Le'me go—dang your light! Le'me go!" sputtered the captive.

"You're Tom Broome!"

"Le'me go!" He was kicking now and Murray had to dodge those flailing feet. He shook the boy quiet with more force than he intended.

"Listen, brat. The press is out. They've snabbled Captain Broome."

"They ain't!" the protest was hot. "Max's no cod-head. The boys is a-waitin' for him—an' the press—down in the Mermaid!"

Murray relaxed his hold. "Are they now?" That explained a great deal, including Broome's cooperation with the enemy.

"You're Lord Farstarr, ain't you?" demanded his captive. "Be you goin' to stop the fun?"

Murray laughed. "Not at all, Tom. Think they can run the press here in Tregarth, do they? I'll have a hand in *that*. I'm no lover of the press either. So they're waiting at the Mermaid all nice and easy? 'Till Broome leads the lobsters in for a shaking." Unconsciously that old term for the British which he had heard so often used by his father's veteran friends slipped easily from his tongue.

"Aye, m'lord. Me, I'm to pass the word when they's comin'!" Tom's voice was hot with pride.

"Who brought in the press, I wonder?" Murray

let him go. Then he remembered that conversation with the Preventive Man. "Was it Hurrell?"

The sound of Tom spitting was eloquent through the dark. "Aye. 'Twas that old—" he ended with a term which surprised Murray until he recalled his own youthful precociousness in the use of language forbidden in politer circles.

"They're comin'!" Tom's hiss was a warning and Murray ran along with the youngster to the back of the Mermaid. Tom rapped softly on a door which was quickly opened, and Murray crowded in behind the boy—to the astonishment of the proprietor.

"They's comin'!" Tom shrilled. Murray reached for a pewter tankard, a good five pounds weight at least, he estimated by a swing of his wrist. A weapon not to be despised in a melee.

He pushed into the main room and found a stool back in the shadows, hoping—in his shirt sleeves, his tousled bare head—not to be noticed among that select party of male villagers taking their ease.

A hearty tread of issue boots sounded along the short passage from the street, and then the door burst open with the shove of a man's shoulder, letting in fresh air to disturb the reek of spirits and tobacco smoke.

It was the blue-coated officer who fronted them with a call of:

"In the King's name! Who's for the Royal Navy?" His eyes darted from one supposedly startled face to the next, trying to size up the men with a single raking glance, with a pistol in his fist to wave under their noses. Behind him towered Broome, but as the Captain was in turn shoved forward by the marines behind him, he favored the company with a wink.

"Rot you, Broome!" A man at the nearest table was on his feet, knife aflash in his hand, "I'll see the length of your guts for this!"

The pistol cracked and in that same instant the three or four candles which lit the scene were extiguished together. Above the shouts and the confused milling of the marines who had pushed to the fore, Broome's voice boomed in a quarter-deck roar:

"Don't you fire, lads. We be all friends here. Join us and be free of the navy. We'll show you the proper sort of life for a seaman!"

There were cheers, shouts from outside. A crash of glass punctuated the speech as a stone, hurled from without, broke the window. Hands clawed at Murray. In the faint gleam of moonlight he saw the glint of a uniform button and brought down his tankard. The hands fell away.

"Get 'em out—push now—with a will, lads!" Broome was giving the orders and Murray added his strength to the effort of the rest to force the struggling naval party back to the door, through the narrow entry beyond, and into the main street of Tregarth. Murray himself burst out just in time to see a marine, his hat lost, his musket clubbed, attack a tall shape who could only be Broome. The lugger Captain raised his hands, manacled, the length of the chain between them his only weapon, in defense. But the musket landed on Broome's shoulder with a force which brought a grunt out of him and set him swaying.

Murray used the tankard effectively for the last

time and let it clatter to the cobbles with the marine it had stunned. He caught at Broome, steadying and pulling him free of the fight.

"Blacksmith—" Broome panted in his ear, "give me an arm to Joe's, mate. He'll get these danged clinkers off me!"

Murray steered a course by a back lane to the smithy. But he did not go so fast that he missed that shouted threat from the melee behind.

"You of Tregarth! You've resisted and assaulted the Royal Navy in the execution of its duty. The army will be here in an hour. All men under fifty will be pressed. The rest will be fined, imprisoned, or hanged according to the degree of offense. Stay where you are or we'll hunt you down. Royal marines, about face! March!"

"Chesty, ain't he?" Broome chuckled. "Nice to tell us all about what's comin'. Best take to the caves while you can, mate. It'll be scatter and hide out for all the boys."

They reached the smithy, where a lantern on the floor proved that they were expected. And the smith had tools to cut Broome's irons ready to hand. The Captain's eyes widened as he saw Murray clearly.

"You! You was lendin' a hand in that mill, m'lord?"

Murray jerked a dangling tatter of his shirt loose and balled it to throw into the fire. "Yes. D'you think I'd better head for those caves of yours, Broome?"

The Captain laughed. "If you want, m'lord. We'll make you welcome. But I'm thinkin' you have a snugger place to lie up in." He used a broad thumb in the direction of the manor.

"Perhaps. And I'd better be on my way before the navy *and* the army pin me out of it. Can you manage now, Broome?"

"Now I've shucked these here janglers, m'lord, no Searcher nor press is goin' to get in sniffin' distance. And a good voyage to you, m'lord."

Murray waved a farewell and slipped through the discreetly opened door into the welcome darkness of the night.

5

Illuminating Conversation With a Toadeater

Murray shifted his weight as unobtrusively as possible. The worn velvet cushions of the manor's huge box pew had been so flattened by the posteriors of his churchgoing ancestors that little comfort remained to ease his own generation. There was a fair congregation of women and children to be counted in the body of the old church, but very few males between twelve and seventy. Those he did see were employed at the manor or had other excellent reasons for not having to fear the sweep of the press gang. A sweep which so far had netted exactly no profit. Tregarth's eligible men had taken to their hiding places with dispatch and cunning.

Soothed by the drone of the vicar's sermon, Murray studied the roundabout carvings of mermaid, dolphin and whale, most befitting a sea-town church. This was a very old one indeed, with the faint marks of raiding Danish axes yet to be seen on a door frame, incorporated from a still older sacred edifice which had occupied the same site. Besides those historic slots, it had another claim to local fame: a bottled ghost. For a seventeenth-century divine of vast confidence—one of Cromwell's iron saints, according to rumor—had prayed an uneasy spirit into a bottle, straightaway corked it tight, and bricked the container up somewhere above the altar.

Murray played briefly with the idea of resurrecting that bottle and loosing its contents on Hurrell. Surely the ghost would be highly potent from its years of imprisonment and so doubly violent—a fitting reward for a Searcher who the whole countryside was convinced had brought both the press and the soldiers to Tregarth. If he were Hurrell, Murray decided, he would be very careful where he traveled from now on, even with Satan as a bodyguard.

The congregation arose to intone a closing psalm, their quaverings up and down the scale sustained and strengthened by two bassoons, a flute, and a clarinet which the vicar had trained to the business. Murray assumed an air of alertness, which his activities late the night before made it difficult to counterfeit. The vicar would be up to the manor for dinner. In addition Murray had, for the general appearance of things but not for any love of their company, invited both the officer in charge of the press gang and the Captain commanding the force of red coats which had moved into Tregarth shortly after dawn. He would have to watch his tongue while playing host today.

He was crossing the churchyard to the smaller gate, which gave upon the shorter back way to Garth Holme, when a small figure scrubbed and slick as to coat, greased as to unruly hair, sprang out of the ground before him.

"Please, m'lord—"

"Tom Broome!"

"Aye, guv'nor—m'lord." Tom twisted one foot behind the other, jerked at the sleeve of his too-short Sunday jacket in a vain effort to cover a bony young wrist. "The Searcher's Pocket, m'lord—being as how you can get to it without no redcoats on your tail—"

He was gone through a wall of hedge that Murray could have sworn no mortal body could pierce.

The Searcher's Pocket, eh? That was one of the landmarks along the seacliff which Furth had pointed out to him. It was a standing stone, vaguely, very vaguely man shaped—provided the man in question possessed no arms and a minute lump for a head. But it harbored, halfway down the seaward side, a crevice which, according to Furth, was deep enough to contain at times interesting objects. Before Hurrell had arrived to harass Tregarth, most of the local representatives of His Majesty's customs had been broad-minded men.

A suggestion that they visit the cliff and the

"Searcher" from time to time, with a quick dip on their part into the "Pocket," had provided the necessary contact between sensible men. If a Preventive Officer had an extra roundboy in his purse later—who was to ask awkward questions?

It was the next morning before Murray was free to ride up to the cliffs and do his own delving into that treasure hole. And he was delayed again when he passed the lower pasture to find Strumper's caravan forming for the march on to a fair which promised better returns than one small coastal village.

Murray reined in long enough to exchange greetings with the circus owner. Strumper on his white Arab mount was accompanied by a second rider. Bargee sat sidewise on the broad back of one of the big horses used for trick riding, that mount's twin running free beside, the deaf-and-dumb boy seeming to control both horses through some mysterious, invisible leading rein. As they swung past Murray into the road Bargee looked up.

His intense questioning gaze steadied on the other for a long moment and Murray again had no doubt that, far from being "touched" or "wanting," Bargee's round, unkempt head held a brain as keen and knowing as his own. Just as he could have no doubt, either, about the malice underlying that examination. Chilled and bewildered, he stared blankly back at the boy. Bargee hated him bitterly— why?

The trick rider never looked back. That one hot glance, which was both a threat and a testing, was all that passed between them. Puzzled, Murray lingered as the painted wagons and carts, the

wheeled cages and the trotting horses and ponies
filed out into the road. Behind the circus proper
came a rabble of small carts, some pulled by a
single horse or pony, others by men, the material
of the side shows, the lesser booths, not really a
part of Strumper's, but tagging along to pick up
the crumbs of patronage from the audience his
show attracted. The gypsy woman called impu-
dently to Murray and there was a cackle of laughter from three or four drabs who tramped in her
company. Then all were gone, leaving only trampled sod and trash to mark their camp.

Thoughtfully Murray rode on up to the cliff
head. The sea rolled high combers below and sea
birds screamed and dipped in the bright sweep of
blue overhead. Several luggers, at the moment
prudently deserted by their crew, swayed at one
another in the cove. He did not doubt that all
would vanish in the dark of the moon, whether or
not the army and navy had withdrawn from
Tregarth.

Murray dismounted and went to peer down upon
the scrap of beach, then dodged back. Then he
laughed at that guilty reaction of his own conscience.
Lord Farstarr had nothing to fear from that man
below. But there was no mistaking Hurrell's brown
coat, nor that brindled beast which pattered on
four sure feet behind him.

The Preventive Man was followed by four
redcoats, who, even from this distance, could be
seen to have a dejected air as they prowled through
tide-dampened sand and clattered over weed-slimed
rocks. Hurrell was still doggedly beating the bonds
in search of fugitives.

Murray sauntered over to the standing stone. It was runneled with white bird droppings, and shocks of coarse grass grew about its foot. The "Pocket," so even and deep a hole that it might have been bored to serve the use generations had put it to, was chest high. Murray, drawing off his riding glove, thrust in his hand until his fingers closed upon a twist of paper.

Unrolled, the paper held a grey pebble, sea smoothed, such as might be picked up anywhere on the beach. Save that this pebble also boasted a center hole which turned it into a thick and clumsy ring of stone. Murray smoothed out the paper. In the large hand of an unaccustomed writer he read:

"Our thanks to you. This ring use, should you need a mate to lend a hand. With a tankard maybe."

Murray chuckled. Fastening the stone ring on the chain of his watch fob, he tore the paper into tiny bits and flung them to the breeze which whirled them well out to sea before letting them drift to wave level. He could not foresee any reason why it would be necessary to call upon the free traders of Tregarth for aid, but he believed that Broome's word was a great deal better than many men's bonds, and that he now possessed an entry into certain select circles should he ever desire to use such.

Another inspection of the sea shore informed him that Hurrell and his disconsolate followers were out of sight, probably poking into yet another small cove where their splashing advance would be good enough warning for anyone with reason to avoid such a meeting.

The day held another surprise for Murray when

he returned to Garth Holme. Mail from London again had arrived and among it a letter from Trews with real news. An East Indianman had docked, bringing the first tidings from his father. Murray was on his way upstairs, the letter still clutched in his hand. He wanted to learn more of this from Trews first hand, to talk to that ship's captain, hear every detail! A pull at the bell cord, a spate of orders for Clagget and Knapp, and before the hour was past he was in a chaise on the main highway.

Though he pushed, bribed and berated postilions, it was mid-morning on the next day before they pulled up at Starr House and Murray climbed stiffly to the door. However, he was in Trews' chambers shortly thereafter. The news was not of the best, as far as he was concerned. Fitzhugh Lyon had been located by the Hong merchants, but his affairs there could not be speedily wound up. It would be four months before he could settle his business and embark on the long voyage to England. It might be a full year or more before he would reach London.

In the meantime such powers of attorney as he could legally grant were made over without reserve to Murray; a letter leaving much to his son's judgment was included. Though that did little to lighten Murray's disappointment.

Groggy with fatigue he returned to Starr House in the dusk. The house had been officially closed upon his departure into the country, most of the servants were gone on board wages. But Murray was glad that he had the large house mainly to himself. He ate a solitary dinner—for which a great many apologies were offered—and found it good. And he was just about to take up his candle for bed when the single footman on duty scratched at the Book-Room door.

"Yes?" Murray was impatient.

"If your lordship pleases—it is Captain Whyte—on most urgent business. Is your lordship at home?"

"Whyte?" Murray echoed stupidly. Why at this hour? How had the man known of his return to town? Above all, what was so important that Captain Whyte should make such persistent efforts to see him?

He set his candle down on the desk. This might be a foolish move for him, but his curiosity was aroused. He had to know what business was so urgent.

"Show him in," he said to the waiting footman. Then, for some reason he could not have put name to, his hand went beneath his waistcoat and his fingers closed on the hilt of his knife. He drew it out and balanced the blade on the palm of his hand. In spite of Brooke's disapproval he had no intention of laying the weapon aside. It was one last link with the past. Now, as the door opened, he realized that he could not be found awaiting the Captain steel in hand, and he pushed it half under a newssheet as if it were a letter opener.

"Good evening, Farstarr."

The fellow was assured, too assured. Murray reacted by becoming "his lordship," upon whose good nature some inferior presumed. He arose, but he did not offer his hand to the man who now stepped into the full circle of the candlelight. And he resented the other's assumption that he was not only welcome but that he came as an intimate.

"Good evening, Whyte." He went directly to

the point. "Since this visit to town on my part was quite unexpected, I am at a loss as—"

"To how I knew you were here?" the other caught him up smoothly. "Ah, but I am so often underestimated, Farstarr. That sometimes is the root of future difficulty."

"For you?"

Whyte showed excellent teeth in a pleasant smile. "For me—yes—to some extent. But in the ordinary way it is more fatiguing and distressing to others. I have been under some pains to arrange this meeting. You are a singularly elusive person, Farstarr." Without invitation he seated himself and gave a measuring glance about the shadowed room.

"There has not been any change in poor George's house, I see." His tongue clicked in a little catch of commiseration. "I so very well recall the day those Candlettes were purchased. Poor George did not pretend to a full knowledge of the arts, but he always had the great wisdom to rely upon the advice of those who did."

"Among which you were numbered?" Murray could not resist that.

"I?" Whyte laughed without restraint. "Lord, love you, no! I'm no expert on dabs good or bad—though these were said to be capital stuff when George laid out his blunt on them. No, George would ask me about a pair of carriage tits, or a bit of good blood for flat racing. But not those!" He made the murky paintings a gay half-salute. "Though he relied upon my judgment in many matters."

Murray guessed that Whyte was at last coming to the point. Did the Captain expect to be taken on

again as advisor in some matters to the Lyons of
Starr? The cool effrontery of the man charmed
Murray into listening without comment.

"Yes, George has his little faults," there was a
suggestion of rueful disapproval in that small shake
of the head, the shading of voice. "But then when
one is heir to such an estate as Starr there are
many, many temptations. George did not inherit,
you know, until late in life. The old Earl was close
to ninety when he finally threw in his cards. You
must be aware yourself of the shifts he faced,
Farstarr." Apparently that was only a rhetorical
question, as the Captain, now very much at his
ease, did not pause for an answer. "Poor George,
he was burned to the socket before the end, went it
too fine. I used to tell him: 'George, take the hill
on the curb, my boy, or your wind'll break before
the end of the course.' But he was too high
spirited."

Since the late Earl of Starr, among other disagreeable traits, had been widely noted for his
power to consume a vast amount of hard liquor at
any hour of the day or night, Murray was willing
to concede that "spirits" probably did contribute
to his end.

"A steady goer, George, it was always play and
pay with him. We were most particular friends,
and I find a sad lack in society since he has
gone."

"In truth, a blow for you," Murray found himself murmuring conventionally before he snapped
it off short.

He was willing to admit that the Captain had
charm, possessing as he did passable looks, an air

of fashion so finished that it took a deep and knowing eye to detect the counterfeit, a pleasing voice and general address, and that strain of sincerity he was able to load into his tone upon occasion. Yes, Captain Lionel Whyte had charm, he was no ordinary example of the genius toadeater. His patrons would be selected from among the highest ranks, and those who did allow his company might almost be deceived into believing that they were the honored ones.

"Yes, a sad loss for me. You are entirely in the right, Farstarr." He lapsed into a pensive study, a gentle melancholy in his expression.

Murray did not trouble to suppress a yawn. He wanted his bed and that speedily. It was time to spur the Captain to the point.

"Since it was never my fortune to meet my father's cousin," he broke in upon the other's reverie, "I am afraid that I cannot join in your feeling of loss."

Whyte's gaze focused on him, a look which raked Murray as if the younger man were some bit of blood being paraded to show off its paces at Tattersall's. With that he betrayed himself. Murray's own eyes were half closed through lack of sleep, his face impassive. He hoped that he presented the picture of a gull easy to pluck.

"Ah, yes, your branch of the family is from the colonies."

There was a tentative barb in that, designed to tickle him into response if he were other than he seemed.

"From the United States of America," Murray corrected with weary courtesy. "It has been some

time since we could be spoken of as colonial. I am
not English born, though I am a Lyon.''

"But there are Lyons and Lyons.'' Whyte's
fingers formed a church steeple and he regarded
that erection with fond pride.

Murray blinked sleepily at the candle flame, not
rising to the bait although it had alerted him.
"There is undoubtedly meant to be some meaning
in that statement, Captain. But so far it eludes me.
You can explain?''

"I am merely suggesting, Farstarr, that there
could be heirs discovered nearer to home, if a
proper search were made.'' That came out quickly
as if Whyte could no longer quite control it.

"Mr. Trews assuredly would not have gone all
the way to Maryland after me had that been true. I
believe that he has acted throughout in the most
proper manner.''

"George did not lay bare all his affairs for that
bag wig to pick over,'' Whyte flashed back. "As
you may know he was not on good terms with his
grandfather—from whom he inherited. He always
took some pains to keep secrets from those who
were only too ready to run and wag their tongues
in that direction. George was married.'' He said
that calmly and again favored Murray with his
raking glance.

"If there is the least vestige of truth in that
statement, you should inform Mr. Trews at once.''

The Captain laughed. "Come now, Farstarr,
don't expect me to believe that you have wheels in
your skull! I can prove the marriage right enough,
should it be necessary. I can also produce the fruit
of that marriage: a son and heir. But since poor

George, in a mistaken caprice, married far beneath his rank and family, that son is no ornament to the name of Lyon, nor worthy of the earldom of Starr. Why should the world be turned awry for everyone—especially for those who can better fill that position?''

There it was, laid out neatly. But the truth—was there the smallest basis of truth to that fantastic tale?

"Naturally, in return for your aid in the matter, we shall be inclined to cherish a friend who holds our interests to be so closely allied to his own?''

"I said you were no bumble-wit, Farstarr.''

No, nor country gull into the bargain, Murray added silently. Do you expect me to swallow such a mouthful on nothing but your dubious word alone? He translated that into a politer question.

"Men of the law are, by the nature of their profession, inclined to be suspicious. Upon my first meeting with Trews it was necessary to provide a large number of documents certifying as to *my* identity. Your heir will be asked to show the same, will he not?''

"If matters reach that point, he can ably do so.'' Whyte spoke so confidently that from that moment Murray believed him. There had to be proof, proof of such a nature as would stand hostile examination—for Trews certainly would be hostile to Whyte's claimant.

"But,'' continued the Captain, with his frank and open smile, ''why should it ever come to that? As I have told you, the young man in question would be no fit peer. He was born in dismal surroundings and nurtured in worse.''

Murray permitted himself to show surprise. "Surely the late Lord Starr, even though he found it expedient to keep his marriage a secret, was not so out of pocket that he could not provide his wife and child with decent living quarters?"

Captain Whyte's smile did not fade at this implied criticism of his dear George; if anything it grew a shade more friendly. "Ah, but you must understand that George was under the impression that the young woman he had, in a manner of speaking, been tricked into marrying was dead. Which she was. And that the infant was dead with her, which it wasn't. George was not a family man, those who knew him best could see no purpose advanced by bringing such an encumbrance to his notice."

"However," Murray thrust in, "as his particular friend it was also your duty to keep in touch with the unfortunate infant against a possible future need."

Captain Whyte again built his fingers steeple. "Exactly, Farstarr. I can foresee that we shall deal very comfortably together, you have a mind which complements mine. There was another point which had to be taken under consideration at that time: the legality of the marriage was in definite dispute. That was decided in the favor of the woman when she could no longer profit by it."

"So there was no death-bed righting of wrongs?"

Captain Whyte shook his head. "No, time fought against us. Poor George was taken before he could know that he left one of his own begetting to fill his shoes."

Murray arose and went to the fireplace, taking a

stand with his back to that dark cavern. "I should suggest that you call upon Mr. Trews with these proofs of yours—and the heir."

Whyte laughed. "Please, Farstarr, do not try to come it over me now. What right has a brat from the stews of London in Starr House? Any intelligent man can see the folly of that. This has been a well-kept secret, it can easily remain that. Or, what's better, a completely forgotten one. To succeed to Starr assisted your father out of grievious financial difficulties, brought you into a life you could not have hoped to know otherwise. There is no need to trouble, for I promise you that I alone hold the key."

"Which you wish to sell to us for your own profit."

"Can you cry me nay on that count, Farstarr? But you will find that I am a relatively modest man, no one shall say that my demands will be dictated by greed."

Murray wanted time to think. He would not be pressured into any quick answer. Whyte must have something, his self-confidence was too complete to be backed by fraud. He'd best stall for time. The Captain leaned forward with the familiarity of a householder to snuff a candle and Murray spoke.

"Give me a day."

Whyte nodded affably and arose. "Two if you wish, Farstarr. I'm not an impatient man. I may be reached at my lodgings in Whifton Street. Goodnight." With an urbane bow he went out.

Murray came back to the desk slowly. The sensible move would be to dump this all upon Trews. Only he couldn't shake free of the notion that

Whyte, for all his confidence, was playing a smoky game. Wouldn't it be far more to the Captain's advantage to produce his heir openly and keep him under control—as he might well do—than to try to blackmail the present holder of the title? Blackmail would be the move only if that claim had a flaw. Murray wanted to know more about Lionel Whyte. Suppose he didn't go to Trews just yet. What would happen if he asked to see those all-important proofs, even to meet the heir?

All of Murray's past training argued against running to Trews. Without conscious volition he picked up the knife, juggling it from hand to hand as he walked to the Book-Room door deep in thought.

6

Notes in an Occurrence Book

By morning Murray had a plan of action. Until he knew more about Whyte and his scheme, he was going to handle the matter alone. There *must* be some hole in the other's case or the Captain would not try blackmail. And, if such a hole existed—!

He stood by the window looking out through a drizzle of rain. Now his lips shaped a soundless whistle as he thought he saw an answer to part of the problem. Stukley! At their last meeting the crippled ex-Runner said he took private inquiry cases. Well, this was an inquiry which had to be private, and had to be pursued by someone—or under the direction of someone—who had a greater knowledge of London than Murray possessed.

Murray wrote a note, sent it by a footman, who had been instructed to lay aside his livery while on that errand, to Bow Street. And before noon Lord Farstarr was waiting in the tavern to which Stukley had introduced him, using the bottom of his glass to print a series of wet ring patterns up and down the table.

"A mizzlin' day, guv'nor," Stukley slid into the room almost as if he had desired to creep upon Murray unawares. "Comin' down a soaker now, it is." He shook himself vigorously and sent a small stream spurting from the curled brim of his hat.

"Not bad enough to keep you at home though, Stukley."

"I ain't a sugar cake to melt in a little sky water, m'lud. Not that water's ever comfortin' to a man, inside or out!" He sat down with a sidewise lurch of his stiff leg, and Murray took the hint and ordered a glass of grog for Mr. Stukley.

"Now then, guv'nor. You'll pardon, but I ain't mentionin' no names nor titles from now on, 'cause I takes it that you wants somethin' particular and private."

At Murray's nod, he continued: "Particular *and* private *and* maybe in a hurry. But first I has some news for you, guv'nor. The Barker was mad as fire at you ticklin' him up that way. But he's passed the word around that this is strictly his lay—between you and him. And he's gone off to that hidey-hole what we've never boned yet. So 'til he comes out into the open again, you needn't get a crick in your neck lookin' over your shoulder on dark nights. But I don't think it's the Barker you've come to crack your jawbones over!''

"No, it isn't." Murray had already half forgotten that encounter on the Bath Road, so much had happened since. But he was still hesitating. How much should he, could he, tell Stukley? Why did he feel that he could better share such a confidence with the ex-Runner than with Trews? Was it because that here the relationship would be between employer and employee and with Trews he would be a minor to be ruled by his legal mentor?

"Private and particular." Stukley repeated as if in encouragement. His bright eyes went from the contents of his glass to Murray and back again.

"What do you know about a Captain Lionel Whyte?" There was no reason that the ex-Runner should know anything. But Whyte was slippery and his reputation was such, according to Brooke, that he might just linger in the other's boasted memory for queer 'uns.

Stukley swallowed, drew out a handkerchief and wiped his lips genteelly before he answered.

"Now there's a peevy cull," he remarked. "Not that we've ever been able to put dabs on him, you understand, guv'nor, though he's been under observation." It seemed to Murray that Stukley's ruddy eyes held a new gleam, one quickly hidden by discreetly lowered lids. "There's those movin' 'round free and easy in this town what we can't never pin aught to. They're knowin' birds. Few of 'em ever go up the ladder to bed." He sketched a circle about his throat with a forefinger to suggest just what type of bed awaited them at the top of that ladder. ''Sometimes they has to skid over the water to foreign parts to sit out some mistake like—but they is usually uncommon clever in their doin's and they knows secrets here and there which makes others take care of their skins when it looks like they could be turned up. What sort of a fetch do you think the Captain is up to? Somethin' which sets him a-treadin' on *your* toes, guv'nor?''

''Blackmail, I should say,'' Murray plunged.

''On you, guv'nor?'' Stukley's lips puckered. ''Aye, that'd be a lay as would suit the Captain. He's a pretty loose fish, but he ain't no stand-and-deliver man. He would want it soft and easy—no play as would end up in some dead meat as could be traced to him!''

Stukley had asked no question as to the basis for blackmail, but Murray realized that he would have to tell the ex-Runner the full truth if he would have efficient assistance.

''He came to see me last night; he has been trying to arrange such a meeting for some time but my people turned him away. Now he tells me that the late Earl of Starr, from whom my father inherited, left a legal son, and he is willing to forget that fact—for a consideration.''

''Pretty, very pretty. And you, guv'nor, do you believe this?''

''It has a fifty-fifty chance of being true. The late Lord Starr was secretive concerning his affairs. Trews, our family man of law, told me that at our first meeting. According to Whyte, the Earl married before he inherited, and kept it all a secret because the lady in question was beneath him in birth. Then there was some argument later about the legality of the marriage. She died and Lord Starr thought that the child did also.''

"Only it didn't, and the Captain knew it." Again Stukley sipped and then wiped his lips "Aye, and the Captain is willin' to disremember all this—should it suit his pocket? What do *you* want, guv'nor? That it be disremembered but that the Captain don't make no profit?"

Murray flushed and arose to that with some show of heat.

"If his tale is true, then I want that son, who-ever and whatever he is—and according to Whyte he's not presentable—established in his rights. Neither my father nor I will accept anything which is not lawfully ours. On the other hand, if Whyte is playing a deep game because he thinks I'm shockingly green and a gull he can easily come it over, then I want to bring him up short!''

"Well enough, guv'nor. It's a game I'll be willin' to play, if them's the rules. There's ways we can clap ogles on the Captain's comin's and goin's. But if you could find out a few little hints now as to the past, it would give some tracin' lines, as it were.''

"Whyte says he has proof which will stand examination.''

Stukley's eyebrows rose. "Has he now? Did you say as how you was wishful as to see it, guv'nor?''

"At the time I told him to take it to Trews. He said he could make another deal easier for us all.''

Stukley nodded. "Of course, bein' as he is, the

Captain'd think no cove is goin' to toss away a cornet and bags of roundboys. He'll judge you by hisself. And he thinks you ain't goin' to screech it out to no law man. Well, was I in your stampers now, I'd walk it that way for awhile. You ain't broken with him flat out, has you?''

"No. Just said I wanted to think it over."

The ex-Runner gave a sigh of relief. "That's good. T'other would have put the cat in the cream jug proper. So he has no call to be hipped with you. Supposin' you acts like you has thought it over good and that you ain't goin' to throw away everythin' for some ding-boy as you ain't never perched ogle on. The Captain'd believe that. But you got to play it smoky, guv'nor. Run along him 'til you can get us a lead to work on. Meanwhile I go out and taps a few lines of me own here and there."

Murray took out his purse and laid down a couple of banknotes. "You'll need money." He laughed ruefully. "For all I know I have no right to this, but you've been fairly warned. And I assure you that, whether I'm Farstarr or not, I'll see you don't lose over it."

Stukley regarded the notes. "That's a prime pocketful, guv'nor. I takes only the regular, a guinea a day—and expenses, should I have to go out of town. That's fifteen shillin's. We understands each other. Now, when you has somethin' for me—or contrary-wise when I has somethin' for you—we has to arrange a way of meetin'."

"Look here," Murray broke in. "I posted up from Cornwall yesterday. As far as Trews knows I'm going back today. He'll think I'm at Garth

Holme—they'll believe that I stayed over in London. If I see Whyte, or send him a message today, and then apparently leave town, can't I hole up somewhere until we know more about this matter?''

Stukley rubbed his scarred forehead. ''Now that's an idea, guv'nor! This here very pub has rooms to let above stairs. And I knows the people here. So I pass the word there'll be no loose talk about any new lodger. But,'' he eyed Murray's clothing with a critical eye, ''you are a flash cull right enough in that rig. And a flash cull a-goin' in and out of here regular might be remarked.''

''Trust me that far, Stukley. I have other clothes, far from the first fashion, I assure you.'' He thought of the suits he had brought with him, those hurriedly made by provincial tailors while he was waiting for ship passage. As far as he knew they were still in a trunk stored at Starr House and he could have them out within an hour.

It took more planning to perfect his arrangements for covering his tracks, and that occupied him until the appointment he had made with Whyte for late in the afternoon. The servants were told he was accepting an invitation to visit for a day or two on his way back to Garth Holme. Luckily Knapp was not with him and he was able to pack his own cloak bag, laying out to wear a suit which no London tailor would pass.

Before changing into it he went off to his meeting with Whyte, hiring on the way an anonymous chaise to call at Starr House later that evening. The continued rain was in his favor, giving not only an excuse for wearing a cloak but helping to disguise the identity of the chaise if any servant were curious.

He had time to counterfeit some unease of manner—he need not pretend excitement which he legitimately felt—before Whyte arrived in the private room he had bespoken in the tavern recommended by Stukley.

"You have had time to consider the matter, Farstarr." Whyte was not only at his ease, but so sure of his mastery of the situation that he came directly to the point with none of the fencing in which he had indulged the night previously.

"You spoke of proof," Murray returned. "I wish to see it."

"Naturally. I have anticipated your desire." From the breast of his clawhammer coat, Whyte produced three papers. "These are but fair copies, Farstarr. The originals are too valuable to carry about so openly. But I assure you that they are most safely bestowed with one who knows their worth, but not their contents, and will prove a most zealous guardian. George's marriage lines, such as they are—" he laid down the first as one might show a winning hand at a game of chance, card by card. "And I swear to you, Farstarr, they will stand in any court of this land." He placed the second across the first. "A sworn statement by the attending midwife at the birth of the child. And lastly, a letter from George to the woman he had married, acknowledging both the marriage and the parentry of the child."

"I thought Lord Starr was not aware of the existence of his son?"

"Oh, he knew that there was to be a child. And

his wife demanded such protection for it. There were reasons at the time why he was compelled to accede to that demand. It is not necessary to go into those now. And, to put it bluntly, George happened to be in his cups and so in an amiable mood at that hour. He wrote and she carefully kept it. It was his belief that both mother and child died. And, having come to realize the utter folly of his rash attachment, he accepted that news with a thankful disposition."

Murray read the three papers, noting names and places to be passed on to Stukley. They should furnish such leads as the ex-Runner needed.

"These are indeed convincing." He laid aside the last.

"Convincing *and* true."

"Except," Murray pointed out, "you have yet to prove that the child mentioned in these still lives. Can you bring *him* forward as well?"

Whyte did not appear in the least disconcerted. He must have foreseen such a demand. "Saving that he is not still a child, but perhaps some two years your senior, m'lord—yes, should circumstances demand it, he can make his bow publicly. But, again I must warn you, he is not a relative you would care to own in your circle of society, even indirectly. Born in sordid obscurity, raised in the stews of this city—a territory you cannot conceive of, Farstarr—he is totally removed from the polite, secure world you have always known."

Murray was almost forced to open laughter. How polite and secure had been the Creek country when, as a lad of thirteen, he had been forceably introduced to *its* society by watching one of his traveling companions burn at the torture stake, never knowing at what hour his own body might not be so treated by his capricious captors? If Whyte thought he was summoning a boogy fit to frighten a green provincial into quick submission, he had better seek farther. Only, to allow the Captain to know he remained unimpressed was a false move. Murray must play the innocent gull ripe for plucking. A little reluctance, some stubbornness was permissible, too much would afright the other. He spoke quickly to cover his amusement.

"I must meet the claimant," He watched Whyte narrowly, but again the Captain appeared to accept the justice of that.

"It can be arranged, since you press it, Farstarr. But one instance of such a meeting will suffice, I am sure, to convince you that my suggestion is the most practical. I shall be able to reach you at Starr House?"

Murray had not foreseen this when he had made his plans. He shook his head. "I am pledged to Rogsberry—" he used the first name he could think of. "However, a note sent to Starr House will be forwarded promptly, I prefer to keep this matter quiet."

"Extremely prudent of you, Farstarr. We shall deal admirably together. You shall see your heir as soon as I can summon him."

Murray had to be content with that rather loose promise. He gave orders to the footman at Starr House that any note from the Captain was to be forwarded to the tavern, where it would be called for. Then he went through the business of moving to the room Stukley had found for him. As he

unpacked his cloak bag there he hummed a queer
minor chant to which his whole body had once
thrilled in answer as drums picked up its beat
under an orange August moon.

That painful twisting of the guts which followed
the "Black Drink" of the warriors, a pain no signs
of which a Creek male could display, tore once
more in reminiscence at his middle. While his
feet, in the narrow boots of civilization, moved in
patterns learned from strange teachers. War! Here
was no preparatory scalp dance, no boasting of
deeds on past raids. But it was war, and the sterile
boredom which had greyed his days recently vanished as if it had never been.

"Now that, guv'nor, be a good beginnin'."

Murray accepted Stukley's words of approval
with pleasure. The ex-Runner noted names and
addresses in his well-thumbed "occurrence book"
as Murray described the three papers he had been
shown. "This Whyte, he ain't never been what
you might call a steady goer. Sometimes he's full
to the pocket, spends his mint-sauce like he stamps
it out himself. Then another day he's pockets to
let, sets his man out on the street and pigs it
alone."

"Gambles?" Murray hazarded.

"Maybe," but Stukley sounded dubious. "Only
to my mind the Captain ain't no neck-or-nothing
cove. Unless, in a manner of speakin', it's a sure
thing he's takin' a plunge on. But he's off again,
on again with his servants, that I do know. And
footmen and such have a way of wagglin' their
jaws free, 'specially if they didn't take kindly to
their manner of leavin' service. Under suitable

persuasion they can spread their tongues mighty wide. You see, guv'nor, flash culls like the Captain, they don't rightly know how much of their private business is free spoke of below stairs. If you're wishful to know that, come along o' me tonight. I see,'' he favored his employer with one of his sergeant-major stares, ''you got rid of the Bond Street Beau right enough.''

Murray grinned. In place of the expertly creased and crimped, starched muslin folds, his cravat consisted of a Belcher handkerchief patterned in violent colors, and his rough drab coat was less smart than Stukley's. He thought he might pass as an off-duty groom and made that suggestion to the ex-Runner, but the other was less certain.

''Just keep your bonebox shut, guv'nor. You may look like you knew what the inside of a stable was for, but you don't talk like it. Use your ears 'stead of your tongue.''

''Where are we going?'' Murray curbed his swinging woodsrunner's pace to the other's crippled scuttle.

''To the Broom and Mop. Servants what are out of places, they drops in there. When they is workin' they pays in their tanners regular, when they ain't— well, there's bread and cheese there and a place to doss. Then there's news of places what are lookin' for men. The Broom and Mop, it's flashier'n some. Valets, butlers, upper footmen and such go there. We'll have a word with Raskall. If there's aught to be picked up about the Captain, he'll tell us where to do that pickin'.''

The Broom and Mop had the usual common room, its air at this hour of the evening thick with

smoke and the fumes of gin. Stukley pushed through
the throng to a table at the very back of the ill-lit
space where sat a small man, his white hair raked
back in an old-fashioned tail, his coat bearing
tarnished lace, worn over knee breeches of an
earlier day.

He had a tankard of beer before him and was
engaged, as the two came up, in carefully fishing
out the scraps of toast floating thereupon. Murray
blinked as he took in the table top and its population.
But no one else appeared to find anything extraordinary in the scene. In fact no one watched as the
old man fed the bits of sopping bread to two large,
plump rats, talking to them in a caressing, though
admonishing sing-song:

"My beauties. Aye, a bite for Sampson, a bite
for Sheba." He fed them alternately, waiting for
each to sit up in the prayerful attitude of a begging
dog before he handed over the reward. "And a
smidgen of cheese to come for them as minds their
manners and acts prettily. Aye, my lady, speak for
it now!"

One of the begging rats squeaked earnestly, its
beady eyes fixed upon a dainty held just a fraction
out of its reach. At the third squeak it was rewarded,
while its companion waited politely to be served in
turn. As Stukley and Murray reached the table
both rats slued around to look up at the newcomers.
Murray was almost persuaded that their sharp faces
mirrored annoyance.

"Stukley! It's a good night, lad, when you remember old friends and pop in to have a crack
with 'em!" The man gave a hearty welcome. "Let
me set these little people their feast." From a side

pocket he brought a small packet, tumbling out of a twist of cloth a hard yellow cheese end. This he broke evenly in half, and presented a share to each of his table companions, at the same time waving Murray and Stukley to seats. The rats fell to eating avidly, taking no more interest in the strangers.

"Raskall, this here's Jem Hale," Stukley indicated Murray. "He's up from Devon, been groom for the Lyons. He's been offered a Lunnon place, but he came to me to ask 'bout it, seein' as how his mother and mine were cousins. What do you know 'bout Captain Lionel Whyte?"

The old man sipped his beer. "All you probably know already, Ned. That he ain't no proper master for any young lad as has just come to Lunnon to make his fortune." He gazed sternly at Murray. "You stay clear o' the Cap'n, he's a ramshackle sort o' cove, he is. Seein' as how this young cully is kin to you, Stukley, I'll do some askin' 'round. We'll find a place where he ain't goin' to be diddled none."

"The Captain under a repairing lease again, eh?" Stukley's expressive eyebrows went up.

Raskall shrugged. "Some sort of fetch goin' on there. Dolan was sent packin', and Whyte has only that wapper-eyed cull as he keeps close to him as a brother."

"Dolan'll spill to us over a pint, maybe?"

The old man gave a cackle of laughter. "So there's more to it, Ned, than just a place for the lad here? One of your own particular lays? Dolan, he ain't about tonight. But we'll find him, do you say it so."

The rats, either overcome by the strength of

beer-soaked toast, or the richness of their dining, had gone to sleep on the table. Now Raskall picked up their limp bodies and stowed them away in a bag he produced from under his seat.

"I do say so," Stukley answered that last question. "And I'll take it kind in you, Simon, to bring him soon."

When they were out in the street again, Stukley faced Murray. "I'll be about other business now, guv'nor," he tapped the pocket where he had bestowed the occurrence book. "You can find your way back from here?"

Murray snorted. "I'm not such a flat as you think, Stukley. But I hope you can uncover something."

Stukley leaned on the cudgel which served him as a cane as well as a weapon. "If there's a lead to be got, guv'nor, Ned Stukley'll find it!"

The streets were still alight. Most of the small London shops did not close until ten. Murray was glad of that, since the bad weather had put out most of the street lamps, and where there were no store candles, pools of shadow extended in dark pits. Murray had almost reached his lodging house when that forest-bred sense told him he was not alone.

The sound of feet speeding across cobbles brought him around, but not quick enough. He reeled back against the wall, dazed from a vicious blow, which had not, because of his turn, landed square. But it was enough to keep him dizzy and only half conscious while hands tore at him, dragging open his coat.

Then the assailant was gone. Murray's hands

went to his coat. He had prudently carried no purse, no watch. What had the thief taken? He had nothing worth that search.

He froze, a cold shiver between his shoulder blades. He *had* been carrying something else in a contrived hidden pocket. His knife was gone! And he had been searched as if that alone was the loot the foot-pad wanted.

Slowly, because every step caused a beat of pain in his head, Murray pulled himself up to his room. Some one had followed him—some one had searched him for the knife—who—why? And his dazed thoughts could turn up but one name for that ill-wisher: Whyte!

7

Grave Matters Concerning a Knife

"—a wisty knock on the noodle, cully." The waiter from the tavern below wrapped a wet cloth about Murray's aching skull with what the patient considered entirely too cheerful an attitude. "You is goin' 'round like a whirligig?"

"Just about." Murray braced both elbows on the table and rested his mistreated head on his hands. "Though I'd say a coach and four to better the whirligig," he got out between set teeth.

The other put a small glass down before him.

"Drink that up, lad, and then take to your bed. You'll be right and tight again come mornin'. Playin' at single-sticks with some ding-boy on the prod is enough to make anyone crop-sick."

Murray swallowed the unpleasant concoction obediently and weaved weakly over to the bed under the other's guidance.

"Stukley—" he murmured before he was settled back on the thin pillow and had to promptly shut his eyes against a horrid vision of spinning walls.

"Lor' bless you, lad, we'll see as how Mr. Stukley knows what's upped with you. And them what had popped you one will find as how it ain't wise to give no one of *his* kin a ding on the canister."

Murray lapsed into an uneasy slumber. He awoke with an aching head to face grey dawnlight, and tried to piece out for himself some reason as to why he had been plundered of the knife. The more he went over his hazy memories of the attack, the more certain he was that the thief had wanted nothing but that blade, had known he carried it on him, and nearly where. In itself the weapon had small value. On Loot Alley its sale might bring a shilling or two. And surely it was not worth risking the hangman's noose to collect—unless there was a more definite reason to make it valuable. He could not help connecting it with Whyte. The Captain was the only enemy he had. Unless— Murray remembered the Barker. But though the highwayman might have a good motive to beat him, he had none for appropriating the knife which had spoiled his play on the Bath Road. No, it must be Whyte, but why?

He moped in his room most of the day, picking at the meals the waiter brought him, pestering the man for news of Stukley. But the fellow kept saying that they had not been able to reach the ex-Runner with any message, that for some reason Ned Stukley could not be found in any of the places he made a usual point of visiting.

By nightfall Murray's headache was a dull thump he could almost ignore, and, though there was a fat blue lump over his right ear, he discarded the bandage. Unable to stand confinement in the room any longer, he put on his coat, accepted the loan of the waiter's hat—his own must have been left to mark the scene of battle—and prepared to hunt Stukley on his own.

The uneasiness he had felt upon discovering his knife gone matured into a full-fledged foreboding. Murray could not rid himself of the nagging worry that he had to regain the blade or the future would hold some unpleasant surprise. He pinned his hopes of recovering it on Stukley's knowledge of the underworld, either to get it back or provide him with a reason for its taking.

Bow Street, in the now-dim past, before the great Fielding brothers had reorganized the magistrates' office in the middle seventeen hundreds to be a truly "thief-taking" and not "thief-making" service, had possessed a sinister reputation. A man losing valuables could apply to the magistrate there, pay an agreed-upon fee, and have his goods returned, both the thief and the thief-taker sharing in the profit. Even, it was rumored, having jobs well marked down in advance, to the reward of both. The Fieldings had cleaned up the office, made the Runners an uncorruptible body of law enforcement men, and had set up an admirable system of nationwide crime suppression.

But no one could deny that the Runners—except for the Mounted Watch they were all plain-clothes operatives and a semi-secret company depending largely on their close acquaintance with the outlaw population of London's underworld for their efficiency in office—had their own lines of communication and could supply without hesitation the names of malefactors, using the habits of the criminals as a means of identification when combined with their own encyclopedic memories.

During the Gordon Riots, when the mob had opened the prisons, they had also sacked the magistrates' office in Bow Street, burning irreplaceable records. But they could not destroy the memories of men such as Stukley.

Murray hesitated between visiting Bow Street or making another call on the Broom and Mop, deciding upon the latter, because he could just be recognized at the former. Someone might be able to pick out Lord Farstarr and wonder at his wearing a Belcher handkerchief stock and a disreputable coat—wonder enough to ask questions.

The Common Room of the Broom and Mop was filled with the same stale fug which had fogged it the night before, and Murray's head throbbed as he sucked into his lungs that smog of gin fumes and tobacco smoke. But at his table at the far end of the long room was the antique Raskall, beer mug before him, again doling out tidbits to his rats.

Murray lingered by the door, studying the others in the room. Most of the men wore either the remnants of livery, or tags of castoff finery which were plainly the prerequisites of servants in good houses. But nowhere did he sight Stukley's brown coat. His last hope for locating the ex-Runner remained with Raskall.

Tonight the old man was not alone with his pets. A tall young man, to whose busy head of hair still clung streaks of footman's powder, hunched over the board—keeping a good distance between him and the rats—staring down into a very small tot of gin as if he strove to read his future in its colorless depth. His half-scowl suggested that his humor was not the happiest, and he had something of the attitude of a person constrained to his present seat against his will.

"An hour you said, Mr. Raskall," he was growling as Murray approached. "Well, I've bided your hour, now where's the cove what wants to have a crack with me?"

"Patience, lad, you must learn patience in this weary world," Raskall's thin old voice reproved. "Look to these little ones: they have learned to wait with patience, and they be but dumb brutes and not men with wits in their heads! So they are rewarded, the little dears." He presented each of the rats with bits of toast. "You must learn to curb that restlessness of yours, Dolan, or else you will lose much good in this life."

Dolan snorted, grimaced at the rats, and tossed off what remained in his glass. Murray spoke:

"Have you seen Stukley, Mr. Raskall?" He gave the patriarch of the tavern the deference he guessed that oldster expected. The old man looked up and then smiled a nutcracker welcome, displaying gums bare except for a widely separated yellow fang or two.

"Ah, 'tis Stukley's young lad. No, Ned, he ain't been around tonight. We has been a-waitin' for him. This is Roger Dolan, the lad what he asked to have speech with—who was in the Cap'n's service."

The red-haired giant grunted. He was continuing to stare into his glass with an intensity which suggested that he hoped by the very urgency of his desire to set it brim-full again. Murray took the hint and beckoned a waiter to bring beer for Raskall, gin for Dolan. Using the excuse of suffering from a bad slam on the noggin, he abstained from the festive round.

"So you worked for Captain Whyte, cully?" he asked the ex-footman.

"Whyte!" Dolan spat at the floor before he broke into a highly colored description of the Captain's morals, manners and probable future destination, a destination toward which he would be assisted by a number of eager volunteers, if his late servant was to be believed. Murray listened with admiration and some bewilderment—since quite a few of the terms used were highly technical and hitherto unknown to him, though he was acquainted with the cant of the half-world picked up from Rogsberry's friends, with whom it was a carefully cultivated affectation.

"An' what do *you* want to know about the

Cap'n?'' Dolan finished, a trace of suspicion in his tone.

Murray shrugged. "I was offered a place there. Cousin Ned prigged him as runnin' a queer pitch. He said as how 'fore I took his hirin' shillin' I should talk with one as has worn his livery."

That provoked a second outburst from Dolan which made very plain to all within earshot that only a ninny-hammer completely lacking in the brain-pan would have anything to do with Whyte's erratic household.

"The Cap'n's bad enough, with his smarmy ways. Talks quiet and pounces like a mousin' cat, he does. But that there Jory what he keeps as close to him as a shadow, he's the devil hisself, with a phiz as would scare a maid out o' her skin! Nasty a cull as you wouldn't care to meet up with even in broad daylight—'less you had both your fambles free to give him a leveler. Or else a barkin' iron somewhere handy to hand him his account for keeps! He's been away, in the country, but now he's back. And me, I was shown the door when he turned up. Just as well, he makes my back bone creep in me, with his slimy sneakin' ways—so he does!" Dolan gave an exaggerated shudder illustrative of one's back bone on the creep.

"In the country?" prompted Murray. He had no idea of what might be turned up in this interview. But anything about Whyte or his household should certainly be of use. If he could keep Dolan talking, over a plentiful supply of gin, he could put to good use the time spent waiting for Stukley. It was plain that Haskall had brought Dolan here to meet the ex-Runner.

"Aye, huntin' a circus! 'Twas noised about below stairs. A circus, mind you! For why, I want to know? 'Tis a wonder they didn't clap Jory up in a cage as a misbegotten beast when they set their ogles on him square."

"Did the Captain send him?" Murray asked.

"So 'twas said. And so I can swear to meself!" Dolan twiddled a freshly emptied glass and Murray signaled the waiter again.

"They was havin' a crack together in the parlor, see," Dolan's tongue, oiled by a hearty swig of Blue Ruin, was in business again. "Me, I was bringin' up breakfast. Does hisself well in that department, does the Cap'n—beef, side dishes, he likes knife and fork work—though he ain't got no belly on him out o' it yet. Well, I was bringin' up a platter and I hears Jory givin' him a report like—that was just afore the Cap'n pounces on me with me notice. I didn't go right in, the Cap'n ain't one as takes kindly to interruptions. While I waits there I hears it: Jory, he was sent to find somebody, they don't mention no names. Only this somebody ain't to be found. And the Cap'n is fit to flip when he hears that. He calls Jory some very choice and fittin' names and slams a cup on the floor—smashes it all to flinders. But Jory, he takes it calm enough and says back, real pert-like, that there's other ways o' catchin' fish aside from nettin' 'em. Then the Cap'n quiets down a bit. He tells Jory to keep an eye on the circus so they'll know if you-know-who shows up. Jory, he says as how he weren't breeched yesterday and that's already covered. So the Cap'n simmers out and all is right and tight again. I goes in with the platter and

STAND AND DELIVER 125

he hands me the sack. That was the day afore
yesterday. I'm tellin' you, cully, just keep yourself
out o' that place! The Cap'n's poison, and Jory,
he's sure death. He'll end on the gallows someday.
The pair o' 'em, they'd give the devil hisself a
smart run for a finish purse!''

That was his major bit of news. For though
Murray continued to press him, while Raskall
chirruped to his rats, paying them little attention,
Dolan could only repeat variations of the tale he
had already told. Finally, he lurched to his feet
and left. Murray became aware of the late hour as
Raskall gathered up his now comatose pets, put
them in their bag, and prepared to follow the
footman. He shook his head at Murray.

"Ned won't be comin' now, lad. He's bound to
turn up, but no later than this. Best be off to bed.
Larson will be closin' up soon.'' He indicated the
burly tavern owner who was overseeing the setting
up of window shutters. The majority of the patrons
had withdrawn, leaving one or two to snore in the
corners. And these were being routed out by a man
of muscle whose battered face proclaimed an earlier try for glory in the ring.

Murray was still reluctant to leave. He should
have learned Stukley's address. Now he appealed
for the last time to Raskall.

"You don't know where I can find him?''

The old man was settling his cocked hat with
some care. "Not me, lad. When I seen Ned, I
seen him here. No need to go roamin' up and
down the streets a-callin' him. But Ned'll turn up
right and tight, he always does. 'Least most always.
Though there was that time five o' 'em set on him

in a dark alley. Dreadful banged about Ned was
that time. He walks crooked 'count o' that. Had to
give up bein' a full-time Runner. 'Bout broke his
heart, it did. But then he finds out it's what's in
here,'' Raskall put his thumb to his forehead,
''and not just a cove's legs as matters. Ned's a
peevy one, he'll come to no harm. When he's
ready to see you, lad, he'll be huntin' you up.
Good night, all,'' he called aloud to the room and
shuffled off, clutching the bag of rats to his narrow
chest.

Murray had to be content with that. But he was
restless as he came back to his lodging. No message from Stukley there, but something else. A
note, marked with the prints of several dirty fingers,
was produced by the waiter who hailed him as he
started up the stairs. By the candle in his room he
read the curt message.

''The person you wish to see will be at lodgings—
12 Royal Street—first floor, front chamber—come
at 10 on the 11th.''

That was tomorrow—and he should see Stukley
first. Ten in the morning, or ten at night? Murray
reread the note, but there was no other indication
of the hour. He would go in the morning. Royal
Street. The address meant nothing to anyone as
ignorant of London as he. He put the paper to the
candle flame and saw it black into ashes as he
debated about calling on Trews.

Only that core of stubborn independence, the
result of his past training, held him back from that
step. This was something vastly important to the
Lyons. He must confront Whyte and his candidate

for the earldom of Starr alone, as he knew that his father would choose to do in his place.

Murray did not pass a restful night. In the early morning he put off the disguise of Stukley's young cousin up from the country to dress in the one well-cut suit he had brought with him, its coat of an inconspicuous slate grey. Leaving a message for the ex-Runner, he went to the Bow Street magistrates' office. Discreet inquiries there informed him that no one had sighted Ned Stukley for the past twenty-four hours.

"But that be like Ned," he was assured by one Runner. "Lor', guv'nor, there ain't no better nose hereabouts for smellin' out gallows-meat than his'n. He can take to any lay—play-actin' like—and the cove what lives by it thinks he's found him a proper mate! If he wasn't dot and go with that game trotter of his'n, he'd still be Cap'n of a squad. He was that, you know, 'fore them warper-eyed culls caught him four to one and busted him up. Sir Sampson Wright, he thinks a might o' Ned, throws him jobs when he can." The burly man surveyed Murray shrewdly and then added, "If he be workin' for you on some little thing, guv'nor, don't you take it to mind that you ain't had a crack with him lately. He's doin' his best for you and that ain't sayin' a little!"

Murray had to be satisfied, but he was not content. He speculated concerning a visit to the two taverns he knew Stukley favored. But the hour was growing late and he ended by asking directions to Royal Street—walking there instead of hailing a hackney, striving to work off his nervous impatience with action.

The London known best to those of wealth and fashion was a limited section of the sprawling city, and even most of that was strange to Murray. He had come to Starr House at the end of the ''season,'' a period when most of the families in the narrow circle of the ''ton'' were withdrawing to country estates or to make a tour of the smart watering places and spas. Out of policy he had remained in town for Brooke's tutoring, to learn the ways of those same families, meeting a handful of men of birth who for one reason or another had stayed within visiting distance, striving to wade in the pool of high fashion before he had to dive into its main current.

So his knowledge of the streets through which he passed—falling unconsciously into the distance-eating lope of a woodsrunner—was confined to a few houses and a handful of people, most of whom he knew chiefly by sight. He located Royal Street at last as a small thoroughfare running from one major avenue to another, the sort of address to be favored by one with a restricted purse but a desire for a genteel residence. And, unless the man he had been summoned to meet was only a visitor there, the address did not fit Whyte's claim that he was socially unacceptable.

Number Twelve was two houses from one corner and Murray knocked at the door, puzzled as to whom he should ask for—Lord Starr? He smiled at that. Would it upset Whyte's game if he did? For a moment he was sorely tempted.

A maid stood in the half-open door. Nothing could be more respectable or commonplace than her clean print dress, her round face with its pert, up-turned nose, and the frankness of her appraising stare as she waited for him to state his business.

"I was told a friend of mine is here—the first floor, front room," Murray made the most of the little information he did have.

But it was not to be that easy, for she was shaking her head.

"That gentleman bean't in now, sir."

So. The appointment was for ten at night. But how was he going to wait out the day?

"I'll be back," he said with some vexation as he turned away.

The weather was fair. He was almost tempted to return to Starr House, get a horse from the stable, and ride into the country—perhaps to the Pair of Fives. But his better sense took over and he roamed the streets in aimless exploration. In mid-afternoon a display of hunting knives brought him into a small cutlery shop where he set about selecting a replacement for the one which had been stolen.

In the end he departed with a set of four blades, perfectly matched, each with a small animal head on the pommel—as distinctive in their way as the Moorish one. He had taken the full set because he found it impossible to choose between fox, stag, otter, and bear. And back in his lodging he tried them for throwing balance as he had not cared to do in the shop. They were not the perfect weapon his own had been, but a few practice throws would familiarize him with their idiosyncrasies and he could perfect himself in their use.

Still no word from Stukley. Murray put away the knives, changed into his coarse clothing and went to the Broom and Mop. Raskall was not at his table, nor was Dolan in the room. And he was shy of asking questions of strangers.

Somehow he got through the hours until he could once more set out for Royal Street. He was before the hour, but he could no longer wait as he went up the steps to the front door. To his surprise the door swung inward as he touched the knocker.

Whyte's arrangement to prevent a meeting with the maid? Thankful that he did not have to face her in his present semi-disguise, Murray went into a narrow hall. A single candle stood in a pewter stick on the newel post of a stair, the flame flickering so that Murray closed the door quickly, having no mind to be left in the dark in a strange house.

Three doors gave on the hall. All were closed. Murray was wrapped in a silence which was too thick. He blinked at the candle. It burned with a thin blue flame, unlike the honest yellow glow he was accustomed to. A half-forgotten tale of his childhood bobbed to the surface of his mind. Evil stalks under a roof where the candle burns blue—

With the brooding silence there was something else, something he struggled to put name to. Emptiness! He felt that if he opened any of those doors fronting him he would not see a carpeted floor, a normal number of chairs, a table or two, ticking clocks, innocuous bibelots and pictures, curtained windows and other furnishings—but instead bare walls and stripped rooms would face him.

He dropped his hand upon the inner latch of the street door. Every forest-trained instinct gave this the smell of a trap. A prudent man, a sensible man, would go out of Twelve Royal Street and forget he ever knew that address.

The blue flame of the candle stood straight now, no breath of air stirred it. And the silence had a sound of its own. A prudent man would press down upon that latch, seek the street with its lanterns and city noises.

Murray moved, soft-footed; his boots might have been a panther's broad pads. He wished he had brought one of the new knives with him. This was no house in which a man wished to go unarmed.

He left the candle where it was, a beacon on the newel. When a tread of the stair creaked faintly he paused, searching again with both ears and eyes, and also with a hunter's senses. At that moment he would have taken oath that the house was empty, yet—

In the smaller stretch of upper hall there stood a small candle table, on it was a second beacon. Burning to light a visitor in? Bait to entice the unwary? Again three doors fast shut, but the candle was close to the front one.

Murray no longer hesitated. This might all be play-acting on Whyte's part, a desire to build up an atmosphere which would disconcert his prey, soften a man by working on his nerves. If that was what was intended the Captain would discover that a warrior of the Wind Clan had already passed through a course of training which prepared him to cope with situations far more racking. Murray smiled grimly at the candle, visualizing a scene or two which could be rigged to throw Whyte into a panic—given the right time, place, and actors.

He lifted the latch of the front room door with

care. If Whyte waited him—though he still could
not rid himself of the conviction that the house
was empty—he wanted no advance warning of his
coming to alert him.

Standing well back, Murray sent the door swinging open with a sharp push. More candles, a blaze
of them! But no sound. He stepped within and
stood very still, his breath expelled in a sharp hiss
as he took in the full scene and understood!

There was a table spread for a meal. A bottle
had rolled across the white linen, leaving a garnet-
red trail in its wake. But that was no redder than
the patch on the shirt of the young man who had
been dining there. He had a thin, rat's face, with
pinched features and a mouth which snarled now
as if that lifted lip came with ease of long practice
in ugliness. Murray would not have willingly turned
his back upon him without taking precautions.

But though he regarded Murray now through
sly, half-open eyes, there was no need for precautions. The knife in his breast made that certain.
And Murray knew that knife. He knew it even
before he saw it clearly.

Mastering his repugnance Murray came to the
table. The other had not used his napkin. It lay
folded, its edge stained with wine. Murray picked
it up to shield his fingers as he pulled out the
knife.

The man was not long dead. He must have been
killed with the hope of enmeshing Murray—for
Whyte's profit. But where was Whyte? Why had
he been allowed to enter the house without a witness to cry murder for the betrayal which the other
must have planned?

Murray wiped the knife clean and tossed the napkin to the floor. He did not look again at the victim as he tucked the weapon back in its secret pocket in his waist coat. Whyte's plan must have gone awry. He need only leave this house unseen and—

There was a thunderous knock below, and the door in the street hall burst open. A babble of voices, the opening of those other doors down there, a tramp of heavy feet! There was no way to lock this room. Its two windows faced the street—he could not drop from either. Escape— where— how—?

8

Disappearance of a Lyon

Instinct rather than any logical plan took over to direct Murray's next action, but it was an instinct which had served him well in the past. He went out into the hall, crossed to that other room which he believed to lie at the back of the house.

Luck was with him, for that second door was also unlocked and he whipped inside as the tramp of feet on the stairs warned him of how limited his time was. Light preceded the newcomers, a stronger

light than could spring from the single candle he
had left on the newel.

Keeping his breathing to a minimum, Murray
peered through the crack between door and frame.
The man who stumped first up the stairway, a
lantern in one hand, a pistol in the other, was not
Whyte. Murray's hand stiffened on the latch bar
until the iron bit into his flesh. Then he shut the
door firmly. As he swung around to look for the
window which must be behind him, he licked dry
lips.

Not Whyte—but Stukley! And behind the limp-
ing ex-Runner had come another who still had the
authority of Bow Street as a solid backing, the
very man he had questioned that morning as to
Stukley's whereabouts. Runners in the house—and
a dead man to be found! A man who had been
killed by a knife which a half dozen people in
London, including Stukley, could swear was the
prized possession of Murray Lyon, a knife he was
an expert at using and which was now on his
person!

Rank meant power right enough, he had been
surprised in the past few weeks to realize how
much power a Viscount Farstarr could wield at
times. But peers hung for murder as quickly as
commoners, even if the rope which swung them
off was of silk. It seemed to Murray that all the
evidence now was against him.

Stukley—Murray groped his way across the dark
room to the oblong of faint light to test the catch
on the window— Stukley had come here expecting
trouble, armed, with a Runner. Was it all part of a
trap set by Whyte? Trap or not, Murray had no

intention of giving himself up now. He looked out upon a roof a little below, no drop to extend anyone's agility, providing he could force the window. He eased it open inch by inch.

There was a smothered cry from the hall. They must have seen the body. So spurred, Murray swung out and dropped. He slid down a slanting surface and tumbled into a dark alley. Above and beyond, a church chime told the hours. He counted the strokes half aloud as he crept down the passage: "—nine—ten—"

If he had not been early to that rendevous he would have been found on the scene by Stukley, or walked in upon a reception party who had already seen his knife in the fatal wound. Perhaps he *had* spoiled the plan. Now that he was out and away from Royal Street, the knife with him, there was nothing to connect him at once with the case, except the little that Stukley knew. And if Stukley *could* be a double agent, working for Whyte as well—in spite of all his pious talk against the Captain—then he knew it all anyway.

Murray did not emerge from the mouth of the alley until he had given the street beyond a careful inspection. He had been hunted before, but never in a city. Here he could not take to a cover he knew. His speech, his ignorance, his clothes would all mark him as foreign. But it might be otherwise out in the country.

As he walked he began to plan. Get out of London, at least until he could be sure whose game Stukley was playing, and whether it was the Captain's. If the fellow was in league with Whyte,

Murray had left himself wide open to a leveler for sure.

Get into the country, work his way back to Garth Holme, where Lord Farstarr could come into the picture once more and defy his detractors to prove he had any possible connection with Royal Street. As he thought about the journey back to Cornwall, Murray suddenly recalled Strumper. To hide a thing, put it in the open. That was a bit of old wisdom which still held true. Suppose a man had to hide out for a space, or travel under cover. How better could he do it than in a circus?

Murray returned to his lodgings and picked up the cloak bag he had left there, putting the coins for his accounting on the table. Luck may have deserted him momentarily at Royal Street, but it was working once more in his favor, for the friendly waiter was not about. Before midnight he reached Starr House, where he must discover an unconventional method of entry. If the footman obeyed orders, and Murray had no reason to believe that he did not, the doors were barred.

So he struck around through the stable mews, where a window was forced to allow him into the scullery. There he bumped into a table and bench on the way to the kitchen, where a dying fire showed him a lantern, from which he extracted a stub of candle.

Up the stairs, past his own chamber, more stairs where he had to go stocking-footed, leaving his boots behind, to creep past the dormitory of undermen servants to the box room which held his luggage from overseas. He laid out a blanket weathered—by harsher suns than any England knew—from bright red to rust. The candle gleam glinted on beads and quills as he smoothed fringed buckskin and piled other things on the hunting shirt.

He dared not take the rifle, but he did add a pistol, remembering how his father had given it to him when he had started west on that fatal trip to visit their kinsman, George Hawtrey. It was a minor masterpiece of gunsmithery, made by the same artist who had fashioned the rifle, and Murray had fought a duel to regain possession of it once his status among his Indian captors had changed from prisoner to adopted son. As he made up the pack he was already relishing escape, not only from this house and London, but—for a space—from Lord Farstarr.

The Mounted Patrol beat the roads about the city, he knew that. However, he was also reasonably sure that any Hue and Cry for him could not get into circulation before morning. While getting out of the city on his own two feet seemed a more likely escape than trying to take seat on one of the coaches which were always under regular scrutiny of the Runners' scouts.

Only, leaving London by foot was very different from whirling along in a well-sprung chaise, as Murray discovered. He kept to side lanes wherever he could and, as dawn greyed the sky, he found that the roads had a population that the average well-to-do traveler might never know existed. To him the market women, balancing their baskets of fruit on their heads, or stopping to rest those same baskets on the posts placed for their easement at intervals down the road, were strange. Also he began to fear that they might well be pairs of eyes to pick him out and later inform upon him.

Thirst brought him to one of the public wells. But he had no more than raised the chained dipper to drink when a most curious party drew up in the lane down slope from the spring, and two small figures clambered down from the head wagon, a bucket swinging between them.

Strumper's wagons had been a riot of eye-catching color, so calling public attention to his wares. In its way the lead van below was as startling. But because of macabre restraint, instead of lavish splash.

It was painted a dull and funereal black, and the two horses which drew it were of the same somber hue, without a lighter hair on them. Their harness was well rubbed, the metal parts gleaming. Lettered plainly in white on the side of the box-exterior of the equipage—touched discreetly with enough gilt to draw full attention—was a two-word slogan Murray found so intriguing as to forget the water he had raised to his lips. For there was something so primly proper in the style of lettering, and something so weirdly fantastic in the words, that the contrast was doubly startling.

"Holgar's Horrors!" Murray read aloud.

"Holgar's Horrors, sir! Come and see a true and faithful representation of the life of the gentleman highwayman, Mr. James MacLaine, in three fine scenes; the Death of Jack Sheppard; the piteous execution of King Charles the First, God rest his soul!; the death of the late King of France and his

Queen; and many other wonders. A penny for a peep, sir, only a penny for a peep at all true scenes of horrors out of the past!''

The chant arose from about the level of Murray's belt, and he dropped the dipper, splashing his breeches. The barkers were in miniature, they were also in duplicate. Two round faces were turned up to his, eyes half closed as they sing-songed the advertisement they had learned by rote so far in the past that the words no longer had much meaning for them. Not only were those chubby faces copy-book copies of each other, but the boys' short coats were of a dull black to match the coach from which they had descended, their long trousers of the same shade. They might be juvenile mutes on their way to a funeral.

Having recited their invitation, they pushed briskly past Murray and set about the business for which they had come, the filling of their bucket. Only the nearer glanced over his shoulder to add, in close to a peremptory manner, "Penny a peep, sir!" as if he expected Murray to go straightaway and avail himself of this wonderful opportunity.

Murray reached over their shoulders to take firm grip on the handle of the outsize pail. "Let me carry that for you." He looked at them inquiringly, to be favored by two very profound bows, but no break of answering grin on either small solemn face.

"Marcus Holgar," proclaimed the nearer as if he were adding the title of another illustrious death scene to his list.

"Fabian Holgar," echoed his twin as dolefully.

"And I am Murray Hawtrey," Murray returned, borrowing his kinsman's name in what he hoped would be a good cause.

"Marcus, Fabian!" The call from below was one to be obeyed, and Murray, trying to hold the slopping bucket well away from his person, followed the twins down slope.

He had been so impressed by the first vehicle that he had hardly glanced at the second. But now he came toward it to discover that in its way it was fully as noteworthy. It was much smaller than the hearse of the Holgars, hardly larger than a pony cart, but covered with a rounded hood of canvas. The team which pulled it was equally odd, consisting of an old and bony nag hitched tandem with a small brown donkey that now lifted its head for a prolonged bray.

"Quiet you, Fedora!" Reins slapped on the donkey's back and the old mare gave a sighing wheeze as if completely disgusted by her present employment. A round red arm of considerable girth reached out from beneath the hood and handed a second empty bucket to one of the twins.

"Give the critters a good drink now, Love. They be good critters and *you* be more nimble'n Maria Dapplegar—much more nimble!"

There was a rolling laugh and a moon face, reddened to a degree which suggested close acquaintance with a giant's rougepot, peered out. Curls sausage-thick and somehow unnatural bobbed beside those big cheeks, and a white cap much crimped as to the edge and frilled with lace, but very clean, gave anchorage for a huge straw shepherdess hat.

"Marcus, Fabian!" That summons came from the Holgar wagon and the second twin made a grab for the bucket Murray held. So urged, he walked to the front of the van. The driver's seat was very much occupied, and both of those occupants surveyed Murray with a cool curiosity as frank as his own.

The driver was a girl. Her black frock was plain of cut and high at the throat, ending in a white ruffle just under her small, pointed chin. She wore black gloves on the hands which fingered the reins so expertly; and a black chip bonnet, untrimmed save for a discreet white bow, shaded her face. It was not by any means a pretty face, for it was too thin, the cheekbones plainly marked, a tiny frown line between the dark, well-shaped eyes. Murray took off his hat and made his manners as he would to any young lady in whose drawing room the Viscount Farstarr was welcome.

"At your service, ma'am."

The twin had pried the bucket out of his grasp, and went to water the horses. Miss Holgar displayed none of the giggling mock-shyness of a young miss. Her chin was up a bit, she was not frowning exactly, but neither was she showing any gratification for Murray's small assistance.

"Thank you, sir." Her answer was infinitely remote, pitched to chill the presumptuous.

Her seat companion showed teeth in a noiseless snarl. It was the largest all-black cat Murray had ever seen, and it was very apparent that he found no favor at all in its eyes.

"Cassy!" That call came hollowly from the

body of the van, to be followed by an impatient rap on the boarding behind the driver's seat. "Lucasta, why do we stop?"

"To water Dis and Hel, Pa. It's the Oxhead Spring," she called back.

There was a rattle from the interior and then a door opened in the rear to emit a tall lean man, lank black hair plastered over his domed skull. He was stockless and in his shirt sleeves, those same sleeves rolled up on his arms. But his breeches and boots were of the same black as clad the rest of his clan. And his hatchet face possessed a death's head outline which made him the fitting supervisor for a collection of horrors.

"I must not be interrupted like this," he burst out in a complaint close to the border of peevishness, though his voice was rich and deep as that of a tragedy actor's. "Right in the midst of a new creation, a truly great conception which shall make the name of Holgar famous! Oxhead Spring, indeed!" He glared balefully up the hill as if to wither the spring with an unspoken curse.

Neither his daughter nor the twins paid him the least attention. Murray, taking the empty bucket, went back to refill it, carrying it and the one for Mrs. Dapplegar down hill again.

"Now that's right kind o' you, young sir," Mrs. Dapplegar greeted him. "Give Fedora a suck first, do. She's apt to bray the ear off'n our heads do she not get served first."

She watched him hold the bucket for the donkey with a critical eye. Being able from this angle to view her truly heroic proportions billowing out within the small cart, Murray could understand why she did not attempt to do this for herself. The tiny vehicle could contain very little else than the overflowing curves of its owner.

"You on the tramp, lad?" Her first greeting had had a fraction of uncertainty, but she had been studying both his garb and the bundle he had left beside the hedge. It would appear that he was now to be accepted as an equal.

Well, this was as good a time as any to try his new role. "I'm to join Strumper's." He did not amplify that, for already she was nodding.

"I knowed you warn't no common tramper, not with that pretty speech o' yours. Why, you might almost be gentry! And what do you do with Lucas, ride one of them trick horses of hissen?"

"You know Strumper?" Murray tried to bypass the question.

She laughed heartily, setting all three of her chins a-tremble. "Know Lucas? Lord love a duck, lad, I has been to half the fairs in this country, only to find meself cheek by jowl with Lucas' folks. Good folk they be, too, not like some others I could set name to. Raggle-tails no decent woman would give the time o' day to. No, I be headin' now for the hirin' fair at Fairleigh. Like as not Lucas will be movin' in on that pitch. He has a talent for fairs."

Murray studied the tented cart. There was no sign on its side to advertise the owner's business, no hint of a learned pig or educated hen, or even a choice selection of "horrors." Mrs. Dapplegar rightly guessed at his search for enlightenment.

"No, Maria Dapplegar ain't no lady equestrienne," she rolled the last word drolly in her mouth, drawling it with a fine flourish. "Nor yet any teller of fortunes and such like. I has me own trade, and a good one it is, too, lad. Though I don't think you'll be the guessin' o' it in a month put altogether of Sundays! Give o' Bess a suck of that there water now. Fedora don't need no bath."

The donkey blew noisily and Murray advanced to let the discouraged mare drink in turn.

"What be your name, lad?"

"Murray Hawtrey."

She pursed full lips to repeat it. "Hawtrey— Egyptian, ain't it? Well, you do have some of the look of them about you, with all that black hair and brown skin. And they take natural to the road. But you ain't said as were you a trick rider, nor stilt dancer, nor what."

He was almost tempted to claim the stilts—an intriguing way to make one's living—but was afraid that he might be called upon for a sample of his skill. So he answered with the truth.

"I play a wild man, an Indian from America."

Mrs. Dapplegar received that with a faint hint of disapproval. "It sounds excitin', but it ain't much of an art, now be it?"

"Perhaps you can guess the better of that later." He was a little stung by this dismissal of his pretensions as a performer. There were several tricks he could do, involving his knives, which might surprise Maria Dapplegar and the general public.

"Maria," called Lucasta Holgar, "we're moving on."

"So?" Mrs. Dapplegar shouted back. "Well, drive ahead, gal, when you please." She smiled at Murray. "It's dull work, rattlin' along by meself. Git your gear, lad, and tramp it with me. I'd say climb aboard, but what with all o' me, an' me fixin's, there bean't a mort of room."

Amused, Murray handed up the bucket and picked up his pack, sliding his arms through the rope loops so it settled into place between his shoulders. All he needed now was the weight of the rifle across his forearm and he could believe himself heading back into Indian country once more.

Mr. Holgar had disappeared into his van. The twins scrambled up on the horses, to ride postilion fashion. Lucasta gave a slap of the reins and a cluck to set the team moving, sparing no glance for Murray as he waited to fall in beside the smaller cart.

"Cassy," confided Mrs. Dapplegar in a kind of subdued roar which was apparently her version of a dropped voice, "ain't no common van sort. She's a lady." Murray walked beside the cart at an easy pace and he was glad that the distance between Fedora and the van was widening steadily, hoping that this conversation would not carry to those ahead.

"Been to school, she has. And Holgar's be well known. People keep on the watch for 'em. They gives a pantomime, too—'sides the peeps. 'Babes in the Wood.' It's real sad. The twins, they sing and die together with their little arms about each

other—so pretty, the dears,'' She sighed in tribute
to that touching performance. ''Twins is always
uncommon, and them Holgar twins be a double
draw. They can make a body cry her apron wet,
do they take a mind to it, them not half tryin'
neither!''

She made no effort to urge her queer team to a
better pace, and the Holgar van was soon out of
sight. But she continued to amuse and instruct
Murray with a flow of sprightly information concerning the traveling-show life, what such purvey-
ors of entertainment might expect to encounter on
their regularly established routes about the country,
and about life on the road in general. He was well
content to leave the subject of conversation to her,
picking out bits of lore he thought he could use to
advantage if the need ever arose.

Within the hour he saw his new traveling companion go into action herself. They approached the
pillars guarding the gate of a country-house park
and the mare and Fedora, without urging, turned
in. Murray was drawn by simple curiosity to tag
along.

They left the main curve of the drive for a side
way which brought them to a courtyard faced by
kitchen quarters and a stable, where a groom laughed
at the sight of the team, and a maid, emptying a
bucket of scrub water into the gutter, came running with a cry of welcome.

''Mrs. Dapplegar!''

Maria Dapplegar, beaming good will, hoisted
her bulk out of the cart, an occupation Murray
hastened to assist. While she stood puffing on

the sanded flagstone, wiping her crimson face, their audience grew in a stream of maids from the house.

"Now, lad," she ordered Murray over her shoulder, as if he had been brought there to do her bidding, "fetch me that there basket o' mine. Lasses, lasses," she rounded on the circle of chattering maids. "Aye, Dapplegar's got pretties in plenty—only what has you got to show Maria in turn?"

Two or three of the girls, with rather smug glances at their less fortunate companions, started back into the house. Maria smiled at the disconsolate remainder. "Don't you fret none. There's more ways o' pickin' flowers than jus' cuttin' their stems."

Murray found the wicker basket heavy as he carried it over to put down on the bench she indicated.

"I'll have the box out, too, lad. Right here."

He went back to fetch the box, still wondering about the nature of the Dapplegar business. When he brought the second container he found her setting out on the bench a line of beflowered cups and saucers, some small jugs of quaint patterns, a plate or two of fancy china. And the lid of the box was lifted to display lengths of ribbon and common lace, packets of pins, some pinchbeck brooches set with bits of colored glass.

Surrounded by her stock, Maria Dapplegar proceeded to bargain, and Murray learned of a totally new traffic in the odds and ends of a great house's discards. Tea leaves once used by master and mis-

tress could be sold by the cook. Maids and footmen had call on respectable lengths of good wax
candles—some of which, as Murray saw now,
could only loosely be termed "ends." Maria inspected each offering with a critical and expert
eye. Then two of the maids crowded up. They
were dressed with some pretense to fashion and
they carried over their arms such discarded clothing of their mistresses as they wished to trade.

The transaction of such business took more than
an hour. Murray helped one of the grooms reestab-
lish Mrs. Dapplegar in the car and they departed in
a hail of cordial farewells. Maria went as far as to
slap the reins over the team, getting no burst of
speed, but only a twist of ears from the donkey
and a reproachful whinny from Bess.

"That there sprigged muslin, the pink one," she
mused aloud, "ain't hardly worn 'tall. Knew I
could fetch somethin' good out of young Rose by
showin' her that there pitcher and bowl with the
violets on 'em. She's walkin' out with Harris, as is
head groom, and she wants house pretties for her
settin' up. So she gets her pretties, and I gets the
muslin as can be freshened up a mite and sold
good to a gal as I know in Hartebridge. Everybody
be happy all 'round. Lor' bless us lad, look lively
now—what be this?''

They had just emerged into the main road.
Murray, catching sight of the phaeton bearing down
upon them at a spanking pace, jerked at Fedora.
For once the donkey responded. Maria's convey-
ance was out of the center of the road as the
fashionable equipage whirled by. But the driver
was ill pleased. Murray started at the sting of a

lash tip as it caught his shoulder, cutting the cloth to flesh.

For a moment of sheer amazement he did not realize what had happened. Then, white with a rage he did not try to control, he swung around. But there was no hope of catching up; the swaying, high-wheeled vehicle was already almost out of sight.

9

Showman's Zeal

"Do the Lord have mercy!" Mrs. Dapplegar leaned forward in her seat at a perilous angle, her features expressing dismay with the mobility of an actress. "Now there be a rare one! Fannin' the daylights he does in town, I'll wager a pocketful. Shove a body in the ditch without ever carin' or lookin' back to see if anybody be still a-breathin'! Come on, lad, no use standin' there a-glarin' with your two eyes like you want to set him afire. We's well out of range, even if you could take a pop to him. Get along now, Fedora, Bess, you two ain't got no cause to plant yourselves there like you'd never been shoved aside by some gentry spark out to prove he can handle the leathers bang-up.''

The donkey took a step forward and Bess, with one of her wheezing whinny-sighs, followed. Murray swallowed his rage and kept pace.

"That one'll break his neck someday," observed the woman with a relish. "And there'll be few to pull the long face or go into the sullens over it. Meanwhile, lad, you be castin' you eye about, as I shall be likewise, lookin' for a nice quiet place where we can light down and have a bite or two in comfort, it gettin' near the hour when me stomach rumbles about if I don't have somethin' sustainin' in it.

Murray was agreeable to that. However, before they found their quiet place they came upon a scene of real disaster. The Holgars' black van, which had pulled ahead upon leaving the spring, was in the ditch, only kept from lying flat on its side by the hedgegrowth. Two wheels were canted up into the air quite free of the road, and one was still spinning slowly.

The black horses were tangled in the traces and one, snorting with fright, reared and almost crashed back upon the van, even as Murray threw down his pack and ran forward to render what aid he could.

When the team had been freed from their harness and led to one side by the shaken twins, some traces of tears about their eyes, Mr. Holgar was brought out of the wreckage of the van's interior to sit, shaking with wrath and shock, on the bank,

while Maria bound up a still sluggishly bleeding
scratch on his high forehead. Lucasta, her bonnet
hanging by its strings down her back, a smear of
road dust marking her cheek, but otherwise as
unruffled as she had been on their first meeting,
went with Murray to assess the damage.

One of the wheels in the ditch was broken. The
harness must be repaired. After a single glance
into the interior of the van, Lucasta's chin went up
even higher, her pallor took on a greenish cast,
and her expression was as close to a grim one as
her features could assume. Murray dared not ask
the results of that examination.

A village a half mile on harbored a wheelwright
and the means of mending the harness. But from
their stricken silence concerning the contents of
the van, Murray suspected it might be some time
before Holgar's would be in the same condition it
had been that morning. When he helped them pull
out and sort through the wreckage, he understood.

The peepshow was far more elaborate than any
of its kind he had chanced to inspect. Instead of
one box to be seen for a penny—the very humble
bottom rung of the theatrical world—the Holgar
collection consisted of a whole series of miniature
scenes delicately fashioned with the skill of an
artist, each boasting a specially made background
peopled dramatically with tiny figures so well mod-
eled of wax as to be true works of art. That the
scenes were mainly of a bloodthirsty nature made
the vigor with which they were reproduced the
more realistic.

When the show was on exhibition these were set
out, Murray gathered, on a trestle table, while the

patrons filed down a narrow aisle, after paying their admittance, to see each in turn. And the whole was followed by some pantomime, such as the "Babes in the Wood," acted by the Holgar family in a body.

But now the boxed scenes had been tumbled from their traveling racks. Little wax people were broken, tiny trees snapped, finger-sized furniture broken to bits. The twins, grieving afresh as each new disaster was revealed, mourned openly with the tears their elders could not shed.

Holgar hunched up, his hands to his aching head. He expended a few choice words in the direction of the young fool whose driving had sent them into the ditch to avoid a worse smash. Lucasta wasted no time so futilely. She settled her bonnet back on her disheveled head with a jerk of its strings and said briskly:

"That does no good, Pa. There are as many fools in drivers' seats as there are elsewhere in this world. We'd best see what we can do to get this into order. Time's going and we don't want to miss a showing if we can help it."

They made a camp of sorts in a freshly mown field beside a stream, the villager who owned it giving permission. Mrs. Dapplegar chose to share their pitch and do what she could to help them. Fronted by the catastrophe, the big woman had halted her flow of speech, and, drawing one of the scenic boxes to her, studied it shrewdly.

"Now, Cassy, m'dear," she broke out in honest relief, "it bean't as bad as eyes might make you first think. Look here, gel, this manikin has gone and lost his head sure enough. But 'tis wax. Warm it a little now and pop it back on his neck and he'll be as good as new! We'll get these put to rights in no time 'tall.''

They ate hastily of country fare: brown bread, sage cheese, and onions bought at the neighboring farm. Then the whole party went to work at restoration. Only one or two of the small figures had suffered past repair, and Holgar put those away with the comment that they might possibly be used in future scenes of massacre and murder in their present state of dismemberment. He brought out his molds to melt and recast, and within an hour he was whistling at his work. While the twins bounced back with the equilibrium of small boys whose world had straightened out once more.

Only Lucasta's frown grew no lighter. She sat on the seat cushion of the van, her back as straight as if she had been fastened to that board used by young ladies' schools to correct for posture, the big black cat beside her. Tom cast an eye now and again at a bird, but his attitude was still one of extreme disapproval as his mistress sewed with sharp jerks of the needle, fashioning scraps of clothing for the new manikins. To Murray every impatient pull of that steel sliver exposed her inner turmoil.

"You've managed to salvage a great deal," he ventured. He had just restored the unfortunate Louis the Sixteenth of France to his place on the guillotine in the representation of the recent Revolutionary fury across the channel.

"We were lucky." But her tone did not agree with her words. "More than just doll necks might

have been broken. But what can strolling vagabonds expect?''

"Strolling vagabonds?" Murray was surprised
at her bitterness.

"That's all we are in the sight of the law, you
know. We must always be content with our lot,
and tolerably composed if some young gentleman
with a fancy that he is a whip of note chooses to
run us off the highway. In the general way we
must rejoice that the damage is so little and make
no stir about it. Suppose a chaise with the squire's
family in it had suffered the same turn back there.
What would have happened? But then, all this
cannot signify to you, sir.'' She speared a red
ribbon with needle point.

"Why not? I'm on the tramp too. That same
flash cull laid his stinger to me when he went by
us!" Murray's hand went to his shoulder where
the lash had cut his coat.

Lucasta glanced at that rent and then at him with
a cool measurement he found discomforting.

"You may be on the tramp, sir. But it's all just
a bit of funning on your part, as well you know.
And that Bond Street Beau would have known it
as well, had he chanced to look beyond the cut of
your coat. Are you doing this for a wager?''

Murray laughed. Perhaps in a way he was engaged in a wager, his neck against a frame for
murder. But he could not tell her that story.

"So much of a wager that I am on my way to
join Strumper's circus. And you'll find that my
pockets at the moment are so to let that I couldn't
raise more than a tanner to risk, even on a
certainty.''

Lucasta shrugged, and lost none of her cool aloofness.

"As you say, sir. But I know that you are not of our sort. And you needs must learn your part better, unless you wish to be marked as quite out of the common on the road."

She put the last minute stitch in her work, got to her feet, and went to the fire where she set about the devising of a stew, compounding in the kettle various vegetables, and making it quite clear that she did not welcome idle talk from young men with mysterious pasts, whether they were honest or not.

It was two days before the small cavalcade was ready to move on. Once he had seen them prepared for the road again, Murray cut off across country westward, determined to waste no more time. On the evening of that third day he came across a field to see the gaudy carts he had once waved into pasturage on Garth Holme land.

Passing the traveling carriage of the learned pig, he approached the caravan which was both home and office for Strumper. The showman, his laced coat laid aside, sat in his shirt sleeves, his feet cocked up on a stool, a pipe in his mouth, and several slips of paper in his hand. He was conning these earnestly as might an actor learning his lines.

When Murray attracted his attention by a gentle cough, he gave a start which was no actor's counterfeit. For the young man who fronted him was neither the polished young lord of the manor, nor a rough-coated lad on the tramp, but a son of the House of Wind of the Creek nation in the full dress of the Corn Festival.

Strumper blinked at the bead-and-quill embroidery, at fringed buckskin delicately edged with threaded seashells, at a beaded belt from which swung tomahawk and hunting knife. Above all that barbaric splendor he faced a mask of red and white paint (begged from Holgar's stores) which turned Murray's well-cut features into an unrecognizable and threatening demon's visage.

The errant Lord Farstarr had not been able to produce the necessary long braids of a warrior with their interweaving of fur strips, but a beaded band shone bright against his black hair, and, as he moved, an impressive double-strand necklace of beaver teeth clinked grandly.

Strumper's first astonishment quickened into interest. With narrowed eyes he examined the apparition almost inch by inch. He ended with a question which held none of the deference he had shown to Murray previously, but rather was the demand of an employer delivered to a would-be employee.

"And who in the name of the devil are you, my fine lad?"

"White Hawk." Murray gave his Creek name its English translation. "I from America." He made an expansive gesture to the west, trying to give his words a gutteral accent.

Strumper put down his pipe. "And what be you doin' hereabouts?"

"I show—" Murray kept to his assumed speech. "I do this—" His hand went to his belt. There was a silver flash and the throwing knife stood quivering point-deep in the stool, just beside but not touching the pipe.

Strumper showed no surprise. "A shiv fancier, eh?" was his comment. "All right, m'lad, let's have the rest of your bag of tricks."

Murray threw his knives at a target, ending with sinking his tomahawk beneath them. He split or pricked what marks the circus owner suggested, and was hardly conscious of the gathering crowd of circus people, now off duty, until he needed a living prop for his last trick. Then he turned to the spectators and pointed to the watching Bargee, the only familiar face in that gathering.

"He—" Murray's finger singled out the deaf-mute, "hold this—over there." He pushed into Bargee's hand one of the slips of paper Strumper had put down and motioned him back against a tree.

Bargee stood stubbornly where he was until Strumper talked on his fingers. He shook his head vigorously at whatever message the circus owner relayed. Then Strumper, exasperated, reached to catch the lad by his shirt collar, giving him a shove in the proper direction. A statue of complete distrust, Bargee stood as if frozen by a sudden curl of artic wind. Murray threw. The paper was caught up by the spinning knife and whipped out of the boy's hand.

There was a murmur of applause from the watching performers. Only Bargee, released from his position as assistant target, slouched back scowling. Strumper was all brisk efficiency, talking terms, concluding his bargain with so much amicability that Murray suspected the result had been in the showman's favor, which did not bother Murray at

all. If Strumper believed himself the gainer, so
much the better.

He asked for Bargee for his regular assistant,
only to be informed that the boy was a performer
in his own right and was not free. But Strumper
promised to fill that position from the working
crew. And just before the start of the evening's
act, a young man came up to Murray with word
that Strumper had sent him. Murray had been
practicing with his quartet of hunting knives, and
he believed that he was now familiar enough with
their peculiarities of balance and weight to use
them without mishap. He was so intent upon planning a simple round of tricks that he did not pay
particular attention to his new assistant. Yet there
was something about the fellow which caught at
his memory as a puzzle, and he found himself
looking up now and then to study him.

He was shorter than Murray by several inches,
but he moved lithely, almost with a gypsy's liquid
grace—when he forgot himself. At other times,
chiefly when he believed himself under observation,
he assumed a lumpish lout's shuffle—as much a
mask as the red and white paint dabbing Murray's
own face, in its way just as deceiving. His thick,
too-long hair was matted on his forehead in an
unkempt tangle and hung about his ears in lank
brown strings; plainly he did not wash too often or
too thoroughly. But, Murray noted, his boots,
scuffed and shabby though they were, were of
excellent cut and made to hold his small, high-
arched feet. His face was swarthy, his expression
sullenly dull. The only answers he made to Murray's
instructions were grunts. But when the other began

his act, he discovered that the man was just the foil he could wish for, presenting so excellent a target that he was able to try more elaborate throws than any he had dared with the excitable Bargee, ending his exhibition by breaking a clay pipe the other held in his teeth—to the excitement of the paying customers.

In the dawn the circus was on the move again. Murray found that he rated a mount, as most of the men were required to ride show animals to keep them in line. Before him in the half-light was his assistant of the night before, sitting one of the Arab dancing horses with the grace of a practiced rider. Yet he did not appear in the ring. In fact, Murray had not seen him engaged in any circus business except as his own target.

The goal of Strumper's caravan was now the Hiring Fair at Willingham, a festival which combined, Murray gathered, some of the features of an employer—employee's meeting, with a more ancient assembly for animal dealers. A yeoman could hire a herd and a dairy-maid, and buy a prize ram at the same time, which made it no small attraction for that whole section of countryside. Certainly one where pennies and even shillings could be swept in.

Unfortunately, though the fair was not yet officially open, there was a second circus to vie for the honor of being the prize entertainment. It was past noon when one of the tent men, sent ahead to pay camping fees and the town tax—and to spy out the best available pitch—came pounding back at a post rider's pace. Strumper listened to his excited report as the caravan came to a stop and then swung his arm vigorously to bring in all the men.

"—that be the right o' it, guv'nor! Hales, he comin' in and he's ready to fight us for it. There ain't but that one good pitch."

Strumper's teeth showed in a snarl which matched that of the peevish caged wild cat. "So Hale's goin' to mill it out, is he? Well, we'll show him how cow hearted we are about that, eh, lads?"

There was an answering growl from his men. Two or three of them started back for their carts, and Strumper called:

"Don't be dawdlin' now. We'll take 'em with nob-crunchers and fists, but nothin' more! Keep that to mind. We'll have no cry rope for this affair." He looked straight at Murray as if to impress that particular warning on him. "You, White Hawk, or whatever your name is, don't you be free with any of them stickers of yours, nor that chopper neither. We don't show steel—and that's comin' it strong!"

So they expected to fight for the pitch? And with no weapons more lethal than the cudgels which now appeared about him? Though, judging by the thickness of those same offensive and defensive staves, and the determination of the men carrying them, the mill might become as nasty as if they were using steel.

To be on the safe side, Murray unfastened his belt with its knife and tomahawk, and tossed it into the rear of Strumper's own van, the showman nodding approval at his action. Then, with Strumper in the lead, some dozen men made off at a gallop down the road.

As they shot off the highway into a field and saw the grey tower of a church rising from a screen of a copse, the edge of the town before them, they were also aware of a similar body of horsemen coming in from the north. Their horses were superb, with satin-groomed coats, the look of show animals, but the riders were as motley a company in dress and appearance as those Strumper headed.

There was no attempt at a parley, the troops met in battle shock on the field to accompaniment of such yells and screeches as might have awakened even the dead in the churchyard beyond. Murray was so lost to all but the excitement of the moment that only when his Creek war whoop rang in his own ears did he realize he was screaming too. Nor had he any idea what a fearsome appearance he made as he pulled his mount alongside one of Hale's contingent and, grabbing the man by his collar, half ripped the coat from his back in the process of jerking him off his horse.

It was, as they afterwards agreed, a mill to end all mills. A crown or two was cracked, there was at least one broken arm among the enemy ranks. Bruised and broken ribs, black eyes, and noses dripping gore were too universal to be reckoned.

Murray was on the ground trading blows with an opponent who had some scientific knowledge of how to use his fists, when he staggered from a shrewd thrust of a stick stuck between his legs. A quick roll, learned in such rough-and-tumble wrestling as even this company could not imagine, brought him out of immediate danger. And he had a glimpse of the tripper going to earth under a beautifully timed and delivered punch from the hand of his assistant.

"Thanks!" he panted before lunging forward to grasp his opponent about the knees and bring him down in a fall designed to drive most of the breath out of him. Though the man was game enough to try to keep up the struggle by clawing feebly at Murray's face.

He finished him off with as expert a blow as the one his aide had used, and then sat up, his chest heaving, to look around. The field had been largely cleared. Save for a personal squabble or two still in progress, the Hales men were either sleeping peacefully or withdrawing in defeat. It was plain that Strumper and his able cohorts could claim this pitch as their own.

Murray rubbed his hands across his sweating face and then stared in dismay at the mess of color streaking his fingers. He had forgotten his war paint which he had so carefully renewed that very morning. Now he pulled a tuft of grass and scrubbed away at his forehead and cheeks, continuing the process as the young man who had saved him from being tripped came up leading both their mounts.

"A prime turn-up—puts me in mind of a little hum down Bristol way." The sullenness seemed to have been shaken out of the other by the late struggle and he surveyed the battle field with the critical eye of a military tactician. "Them Hales has had it proper. They'll go on the mop 'fore they comes at us again in such a pelt. You take a bad ding on the brain-box, cully?" he ended with a shadow of concern.

"Thanks to you, no. They were cutting me down to a finish when you put that other one out of the mix."

"You displays good, cully." The young man looped the reins of both horses over his arm and ran his hands through his hair, raking it back from his face. Where his palm scraped his forehead the result was almost the same as the mishap to Murray's paint—a streak of the swarthiness was now lighter. And through the tatters of his torn shirt sleeve Murray caught the hint of a raw red scar, hardly healed on his right forearm. Then the sun struck full across his features and Murray's vague memory came into sharp focus.

This was the pushing youngster from the Pair of Fives, the one who had caught his attention at the cockpit. Puzzled, he stared straight at the other—to see those eyes narrow, the mouth become a line. Recognition was apparently mutual, but he thought that the other had not noted him at all at the cockpit. Cockpit—Bath Road later—a fresh half-healed wound on the right arm—

While those clicked into a pattern to astound Murray the young man wheeled and swung into the saddle. As his right hand groped for something which should be hanging at the bow and was not, the tatters were pulled aside and that tell-tale wound was well in sight. Murray shoved the last bit of the jig—saw into place triumphantly:

"The Barker!"

The highwayman favored him with a mirthless grin. Now the stolid country lad was gone, Murray faced a very clever and very dangerous man, in his way as clever and as dangerous as either Captain

Whyte or Ned Stukley. All three of them shared one quality: they ranged themselves fearlessly against the organization—Ned against the underworld, Whyte and the Barker against the law.

Mechanically Murray continued to rub the grass across his face until he realized what he was doing and threw it from him. It was he and not the Barker who spoke first.

"What are you going to do?"

The other laughed. "I should be the one askin' that! You flash coves know everythin'. What are *you* a-doin' here, m'lord?"

Murray thought he knew the right answer to that. "I'm not hunting you, if that's what you fear."

The Barker shrugged. "I ain't feared o' anythin', m'lord. And I don't have to listen to a lot of bamboozlin' talk. You're not trampin' it to play at single-stick with Hales' men—though you does that well," he was scrupulously fair to the enemy. "This is a queer pitch and no mistake. Only I'll get meself out of it, never fear. The man ain't been born nor breeched yet as can give the Barker the shoulder slap! And that includes you, m'lord!"

He grinned again, but this time in honest light-hearted humor. Then he cantered lightly away, disappearing into the road before Murray could reach his own horse.

10

The Barker Rides Once Too Often

Apparently the Barker rode out of Strumper's employ when he spurred away from the field. Murray, his face paint restored, the worst of his bruises treated, could find no trace of him later, and heard only the most evasive answers to any questions concerning him. Whether the show people were well aware of the highwayman's identity and were covering his trail, or whether they honestly knew no more of him than they knew of

Murray, the latter could not decide. And he had no way of forcing the issue.

His Indian clothing an attraction to the juvenile population of the town, Murray had ventured into its streets in his search for the Barker. But the press of those coming to the opening of the fair was enough to conceal three or four Barkers as adroit at disguise as this one.

The town crier, his coat of scarlet turned back with blue, his cocked hat set straight above his leathery face, headed a procession for which the throng made way. Behind him, on a rather moth-eaten cushion of garnet velvet, was borne a glove stiff with gilt. The parade rounded the market cross, ending before the principal inn. Then the glove was fastened to the pole set up there, the crier took breath enough to fill his lungs to the last inch and boomed forth:

"Oyez! Oyez! Oyez! The glove is up! The glove is up!

The fair is open! God save the King!"

A grinning inn servant, holding a fire shovel well before him, ran out and scattered its contents in the road, to be scrambled for by the children. There were some cries of pain and much sucking of blistered finger tips, but every one of the hot pennies found owners amid the cheers and encouragement of the elders. Murray, his shoulders back against a wall, watched as enthralled as any plow boy in from the fields.

He remained where he was to let by the crowd escorting the garlanded town bull, being cheered through the streets before its fights with dogs which would be a main attraction for the afternoon. While the hawkers of ballads, the tellers of fortunes, the sellers of cakes and gingerbread were making the air ring with the cries of their wares.

On one of the lanes leading away from the market place the hiring lines were forming. Milkmaids with tufts of cow hair fastened to their Sunday bonnets, wagoners with their descriptive whipcord badges, and all the rest of the indoor and outdoor servants seeking new masters for the coming year—eagerly waiting their hiring "silver" into the bargain, the latter largesse to be spent on the delights of the fair—fidgeted impatiently, hoping for the business to be soon over so their day's pleasuring might begin.

Murray, having catalogued the services represented there by their trade markings, wondered in amusement what would happen if he set himself in one of those lines, his knife on display to mark his skill at hunting and trapping. But in a country where poachers suffered the severest penalties in the power of the local magistrates, that might not be such a clever idea.

Strumper's tents and booths went up rapidly on the pitch he and his men had won. There was already a thin trickle of early comers about the caged animals. One of the hands led the camel back and forth on display, the creature moving at its usual majestic, arrogant pace, grunting ill temperedly and chewing at its cud with noisome juiciness. It was a prime attraction, and a small procession formed about and behind it—at a safe distance—to comment freely on its physical peculiarities.

Murray rounded a booth into the backwater where

the performers were bringing out their own trunks and boxes, putting up a few canvas screens behind which they could don the worn finery from those same boxes, to be transformed from vagabonds of the road to the elfin people of the rings.

Since his own costume and equipment were on his back, Murray was free for the moment. He had kept aloof from the others, mainly for fear of being unmasked, trying to hold to his role of savage from overseas to whom language was an additional barrier. Now he joined none of the chattering groups but wandered about until his attention was captured by the sight of Bargee leading into the open the male 'roo. The animal on the leash was almost as tall as its keeper, but it appeared tame and amiable enough, hopping sedately along as if it relished its freedom from the confines of the cage. Bargee was dressed for his appearance in the ring, spangled orange-yellow tights and shirt making him a vivid contrast to the dun fur of his charge. They were an odd but harmless-appearing pair out for a comfortable stroll and Murray was almost tempted to join them.

But the peace of that scene ended. From under one of the vans darted a small white dog. Yapping loudly, he sped straight at the 'roo. Remembering Strumper's story of what had happened on a similar occasion, Murray sprang forward.

The 'roo reared in its man-like stance, facing the dog, its hand-paws dangling over the lighter fur of its belly. It was watching the dog intently, though as yet it had made no hostile move. Its doe-head turned so that its eyes were always on the smaller beast. While the yapper, perhaps intoxicated by its own clamor, circled in a series of rings, drawing ever closer to the 'roo.

To Murray's astonishment Bargee was making no attempt to drive off the dog. He stood watching the scene with the detachment of a spectator at a well-rehearsed show—though he still held the leash. Perhaps, through that strap, he had better control over the 'roo than it seemed to the observer.

However, Murray thought it better to take no chances. He tore loose a strip of canvas from the nearest improvised change room and threw it over the dog. The pup, entangled in the thick fabric, rolled over snapping until Murray was able to scoop up and hold the wildly struggling little body under his arm.

The 'roo still kept its pose of a boxer waiting for time to be called. Beyond the beast's shoulder was Bargee's handsome face with those questioning eyes which seemed to serve double duty for the other senses he lacked. Only the eyes were far from questioning now. It was with a shock that Murray read what lay in their depth—too late.

For the boy's grip on the leash slackened. While the pup in Murray's hold chose that same moment to voice a fanfare of frenzied barks, struggling so convulsively for freedom that Murray had to almost squeeze the breath out of it to retain his charge.

Perhaps the barks aroused the 'roo to attack. It moved with a speed which Murray would not have believed, had he not seen it in action. He stumbled back and the dog wriggled free. There was a whirl of movement, a shriek of pain from the pup, and Murray, who had tripped and was on the ground, saw death loom over him as a hindfoot with the drive of a maul thudded almost across him. Only the fact that that blow did not land cleanly saved his life—or at least prevented serious injury. But he lay gasping and helpless, trying for strength to roll away from a second blow.

Someone was shouting as that brown, clawed foot was raised again. But it didn't fall on him, for the 'roo was jerked away, with a speed and force to send it sprawling. Murray, fighting for breath, levered himself up with his hands to see Strumper and one of his grooms hauling on the leash to pull the 'roo away from his victim. While Bargee, his face contorted, capered about them, trying to snatch that restraining strap from them and get the 'roo into his own control once more.

Only a limp mass of white hair, now horribly blotted with oozing red, marked the remains of the pup. Murray fought sharp nausea. He might have lain so had the 'roo not been dragged away.

A second groom hurried up with a crop and Strumper used it freely to reduce the frenzied beast to submission. Murray watched, both hands nursing his aching middle, while they got the 'roo under control and herded back to its cage. Bargee, mouthing weird cries which had no resemblance to human speech, beat with his fists on the door of that cage when it had been locked, and then turned to spring at Murray as if he had caught the contagion of the 'roo's rage and was going to finish off what the animal had started.

Strumper put out a foot, sending the boy sprawling on his face. Then he applied the lash of the crop in vigorous retribution to Bargee's heaving

back. At first Murray watched that punishment
with satisfaction. He was still wheezing, and the
shuddering fear of a nasty death shook him. But
when Strumper still swung with all the force of his
strength a moment or two later Murray got to his
feet and tottered over, to catch at the up-raised arm
of the circus owner.

"—had enough—" he got out with difficulty.

Strumper, a queer white line about his mouth
under his weather tan, shook his head in denial of
that. But he did not bring the crop down again. He
stirred the now quiet Bargee with his boot.

"He had his orders, right and tight, not to let
the beast out in any town. Dogs send it wild, as
well he knows. And you might be lyin' like that
there." He pointed to the dead pup. "Understand
that? Rider or no rider, for this he hits the road!
I'll have no more of him about here."

He stamped off and the others followed him.
Murray half collapsed, half sat on the steps of the
nearest van. But Bargee remained where he was,
face down on the trampled ground. His bright
tights were smudged with dust and green with
grass stains. While the vigor of the beating had
torn his shirt in one place to show a raw red weal.
Murray hesitated for a long moment. When the
boy made no move he began to be vaguely worried.

There was no doubt in his mind that Bargee had
deliberately loosed the 'roo on him in that moment
when, because he held the dog, the beast would
identify him as an enemy. Also he was certain that
he would have suffered the pup's fate with Bargee's
willing cooperation. But why? What had he ever

done which had awakened such a desire for murder,
or a particularly nasty kind, in the afflicted boy?
He must discover the answer to that.

Wincing, he got to his feet and reached for the
dipper resting in a van water bucket. With some of
the liquid sloshing over its rim as he limped over,
Murray came to Bargee and, kneeling, caught the
boy by the shoulder, avoiding as well as he could
touching the marks left by Strumper's crop.

Like a puppet who had no control over its own
limbs, Bargee allowed Murray to turn him over
and raise his head with supporting arm and knee.
Those alive eyes were closed, the strained face had
a death-mask rigidity—as if Bargee had pulled far
inside himself, a hurt and frightened animal cower-
ing within a burrow which was the only safety it
knew.

Murray forced the edge of the dipper against the
pinched lips, dribbled in water until he saw the
muscles of the throat move in an answering swallow.
Uncertain as to how he could break past the barrier
which cut Bargee off from his fellows, he continued to sit there, the rough dark head on his knee,
watching for any sign that Bargee was aware of
him.

The eyes opened, regarded Murray with a sullen
impassivity which might deceive the onlooker into
believing that the boy was indeed ''wanting.'' Murray made no move. He had forgotten that barbaric
mask of paint which cloaked his own features.

He sighed when the boy gave no sign of
recognition—neither fear nor hatred. It was probably useless to think that he could question Bargee,

could discover the reason for the boy's manifest hatred of him.

For it *was* real hatred, he had had no doubt of that since the episode with the 'roo. He proffered the water again.

Bargee's hand came up swiftly, striking the handle of the dipper and upsetting its contents over both of them. Unwinking he stared back at Murray, lacking the open rage he had shown during the attack, but with unfailing hostility. Then he twisted, as the pup had earlier wriggled in Murray's clutch, winning free. On his feet with the grace of a tumbler, he smoothed his bedraggled costume as if Murray had ceased to exist and all that mattered now were the stains which disfigured the bright clothing.

The boy could neither have heard or understood Strumper's abrupt dismissal. He must believe that life was to proceed for him as usual, that he had a performance in the ring before him. Yes, he was heading to the picket line where the horses waited, as serene as if the last hour had been wiped out of memory. Murray went after him.

Bargee halted beside one of the wide-backed horses used for acrobatic riding, smoothing its well-curried coat with quick flicks of his nervous hands. The horse lowered its large head and nudged him playfully in welcome.

The boy leaped to the big animal's back, having loosed its picket. At a rolling gait, geared to match a drum beat beside the ring, it moved out, its fellow trotting in perfect time beside it. Bargee stood up, balancing easily on his living platform. His muscles tensed, he flipped a turn to the second

horse and then back again. Then he sat astride as
both horses headed toward the ring. If Bargee had
been exiled from Strumper's it was plain he did
not know it, and nothing short of physical force
was going to keep him from making his usual
appearance.

Murray retrieved his belt with knife and hatchet
and got the hunting knives in preparation for his
own act. One of the grooms had been drafted into
taking the Barker's place as his living target and
was decidedly unhappy about it. Though Murray
impressed upon him that all that was required of
the assistant was a statue-like stance.

The fellow's nervousness was communicated to
Murray, still stiff and shaken from his encounter
with the 'roo, and Murray was almost minded after
a few warm-up throws to beg off showing this one
time. But Strumper was plainly in a black temper
and made himself so unapproachable that he did
not try that plea. The rumor of the dog's death and
the 'roo's part in it had spread through the town,
and there was some talk of forcing the circus
owner to take desperate measures with that rare
and expensive animal should the creature get free
of its cage a second time.

Murray made his entrance with his customary
war whoop, calculated to draw the attention of
every one who did not suffer Bargee's disability.
Then he went into his act with spinning knives and
whirling hatchet, winning the usual amount of startled exclamations as the steel hit into the board
screen behind his shrinking target. The latter jumped
down thankfully after the last throw, patches of
damp plainly visible on his brightly colored shirt.

Certainly his attitude, Murray thought, was not a tribute to the knife thrower's skill.

The Barker's unconcerned coolness in the same position had made him the perfect assistant, inspiring Murray to tricks he dared not try with the groom. Yet the Barker had felt the bite of his knife thrown in earnest and not in play. Considering that, Murray's respect for the highwayman grew. Somehow in his mind he classed the Barker with Max Broome. Both operated outside the law, but with such a coating of respectability of their own self-confidence, that they almost took in the law-abiding to believe that they were in the right.

Knives in hand, Murray started back to the section of the dressing booths, mulling this idea over. However, he forgot it all when he saw Strumper in close conversation with a man there was no mistaking. He dodged about the nearest van, the one bearing the tiger's cage.

His respect for the Runners leaped up, not a step, but a whole flight of stairs. For he had seen that thick-set man, now standing with his feet a little apart and planted firmly as if he were prepared to withstand some determined assault, twice before. Once at Bow Street and again in the hall of the Royal Street house in company with Stukley. How had they tracked him here so unerringly and so quickly?

He had best follow the Barker's example and cut away while he could. But not dressed so. He glanced down at his fringed shirt and leggings, his beaded moccasins. With the last acts still in progress in the ring, the dressing booths would be semi-deserted; he darted for their shelter. He found his bundle, ducked into an empty cranny between two screens and hurriedly rid himself of the barbaric trappings of a Creek warrior, to assume the clothing he had worn out of London. He slipped his knife into the secret pocket of his waistcoat, and tucked the pistol into the waistband of his breeches, ending by scrubbing his face free of paint. A quick survey in a scrap of mirror told him that while he no longer resembled a savage of the American forests, neither did he look like Viscount Farstarr. Surely he could mingle with the crowd in town, get away with some homeward-bound band of merrymakers before the Runner spotted him.

Murray had rolled his buckskin suit and other belongings into a tight pack covered with the blanket, and now he eyed this doubtfully. An unencumbered man would not be noted, but one bearing a pack might be remarked.

On the other hand, he had no wish to lose his gear. If he had a single friend here with whom he could leave it. . . . But it had been his policy of caution to keep aloof, lest he be unmasked. Strumper was the only one he knew. Dared he cache his bundle in the owner's van?

Murray heard that faintest of sounds. His right hand was at his waistcoat, fingers within plucking distance of his knife. He hummed unconcernedly between his teeth, but his body tensed, like a mountain cat ready for the spring. That spring must carry him against the shadow waiting just beyond the screen.

A sweep of his left arm send the flimsy barrier

flying, and it slapped full against the lurker, bringing a startled exclamation out of the man who pawed at it in surprise. Murray tore it away from between them. He was half crouched, his fingers gripping the hilt of his weapon. But the other made no hostile move.

"Neat a trick as I ever seed," he commented admiringly. "And how are you, m'lud? You keeps your peepers open wide, but there ain't no reason to show *me* that shiv of yours. It's been about a bit too much as 'tis."

"Stukley!"

"Just so, guv'nor." The ex-Runner was grinning. "Ned Stukley is me name. And a pretty little diddle you has tried on for size!"

"How did you find me?" Murray kept a wary eye on the other's vaunted cudgel. As slippery a fighter as Stukley was rumored to be, Murray was still confident that he could win if the encounter went without recourse to arms.

Stukley laughed. "Lor', guv'nor now I *could* say as how we was a-trackin' you with our noses flat on the ground like we was hounds. But we warn't a-lookin' after you 'tall. Though we did come down here on your business. Tell me, m'lud, did you ever visit a house on Royal Street?"

The ex-Runner lost his air of good humor as he shot that question. He was suddenly a schoolteacher determined to have an answer out of a recalcitrant student—or he could be an even grimmer inquisitor, with a hint of hot irons and such trifles in the background.

"And if I did?" challenged Murray. His hands

balled into fists. He could jump Stukley from the
left, set the ex-Runner off balance, and bowl him
down without hurting him much, then be away
before the other could raise any proper alarm.

"You upset as pretty a plan for the trappin' of a
gull as I ever set these here ogles of mine flat on."
Stukley leaned back at ease against the high wheel
of a van. He had all the signs of one about to
discuss the matter at length. "I take it, guv'nor,
that you went there at night, and when you left
again you took somethin' away with you. That
shiv of yours, maybe? Why else should we find a
hole in a corpse and the knife missin'?"

"It wasn't used by me," Murray was stung into
that admission, and then furiously angry at himself
for the slip.

Stukley nodded. "So it would seem."

The ex-Runner's ready agreement with his plea
of innocence again threw Murray off stride.
"How—?" he began almost stupidly.

"I takes it you had no reason to go carvin' up
that there young sprout. He bean't any long-lost
cousin of yours!"

Murray began to relax. "You know that for a
fact?"

"For a fact as I can swear to truthfully in any
court of the land, should you wish that same done,
guv'nor. That there sprout was a cull on the dub-
lay—clever with his fambles. But priggin' out of
some flash ken was all he knew. I knowed him
well of old."

"Whyte said the heir was not respectable," Murray reminded him.

"Maybe he ain't. But neither is he—was he Bart Long. I've knowed Bart since he was a draggled brat sleepin' in the glass-house ashes o' nights and priggin' wipers for a bit of bread. And I knowed his dam and his pa 'fore him. His pa was turned off by Jack Ketch proper for usin' a club a mite too free. He had an argument with a pal, and the pal never come out of the sleep he put him into. No, Bart Long warn't no Lyon. But Whyte, he's lost track of the right man and got Bart to play the part for a while. Only Bart got big ideas and was plannin' to cry rope on Whyte, thinkin' you might make him more in the pocket for spillin' the truth. He sends me a message from Royal Street sayin' as how he was ready to wag tongue. I gets there—and you know what I finds.

"Maybe the Captain, he got a peevy idea of how to settle Bart and put you in a queer pitch, too. He leaves Bart a-sittin' there. And he used a shiv 'cause you is knowed to favor one. Findin' that missin' made me guess as how maybe you found your own particular shiv a stickin' in Bart so that the most wrapper-eyed cull couldn't miss it."

Murray, trying to keep abreast of that flood, nodded dumbly and Stukley grinned again.

"Only his timin' went wrong. You musta come too early. You gets the shiv and is over the hills 'fore he can arrange to have you found in the pitch. Or maybe he saw me and Alf comin' and thinks we'll do the discovery business for him. Anyway Bart's dead, you is gone, and so is the Captain. But he leaves some trails behind him and one of 'em leads here, to Strumper's. You've been makin' yourself handy around here, guv'nor. Now tell me if you has seen a brisk young cull—smaller a bit nor you—got brown hair with a touch of red to it, regular fox brush— rides good, but has the sort of face you don't remember too well.''

"You're after the Barker!"

"The Barker!" It was Stukley's turn to display open-mouthed amazement. "I ain't trackin' down no bridle-cull, m'lud. What has the Barker got to do with it?''

Briefly Murray explained, and Stukley shook his head wonderingly.

"Now this *be* a nasty turn-up, m'lud. We has good reason to believe as how this here cove I has described be your Lyon cousin. But if he is the Barker too,'' again that shake of the head, "we are in a mess. Seems like we find your kin just in time to send him up the ladder to bed! It ain't good, it ain't good 'tall!''

"You're sure they're the same?''

Stukley had lost all his good humor and answered with an impatient flare. "No, I ain't! We've got to lay dabs on him and ask some questions 'fore we can be sure. Even then maybe we've got to scrabble about a bit for proof as will stand in court. But we can't hunt him for this when he's got his neck in the rope for a squeezing on 'nother account. This'll take a bit of thinkin' over on the heavy side, m'lud.''

Only they were to have no time to consider the problem. For when Stukley's friend, the Runner, joined them a moment later he was full of news.

"Ned, we has us a 'ficial job on our hands

now," he announced. "They has took up the Barker right here in town. Information was laid and they has him right and tight in the inn strong room. We has been asked to ride him back to Lunnon on the night stage! The Barker, Ned. This be our lucky day, ain't it?"

But neither Stukley nor Murray could join in his pleasure at such good fortune.

11

A Camel, Two Kangaroos and a Lyon

In spite of the number of counter-attractions at
the fair, there was a crowd about the door of the
Eel and Pye as Stukley, Murray and the Runner
came up the street. Murray had accompanied the
other two without really knowing why. He had a
vague plan for taking the stage back to London, of
rousing Trews with the story, to see what the
Lyons' man of law could do to bring some sense
out of the present muddle. If only the Barker had
not been captured!

Then he realized the possible trend of his own thoughts and flushed. Certainly the young highway-man had not been taken just to annoy Murray Lyon and cause trouble for the Earl of Starr. There was only one future ahead of him now—death on the gallows—and that would come soon. If Murray kept his mouth shut, if Trews were not brought into it, their problem would be solved once and for all. But that was one point where his mind was fully made up.

He had seen this unknown kinsman only briefly. But in that very limited association the Barker had not made upon him the same type of impression as Whyte had left. He could not believe that the man who had so joyfully mixed in the mill for the meadow pitch, fighting with a boy's delight in victory, could have joined with the Captain in a blackmail scheme. Thus Murray determined that the weight and influence of the Starr name would be engaged on the Barker's behalf. He was deciding upon this when Stukley spoke:

"You is takin' a hand on his side, m'lud?"

"Whatever we can do, must be done!"

Stukley shook his head. "He's well known in his trade, m'lud. There'll be a round dozen ready to swear his neck into the noose, now we have him safe by the heels. This is one row he can't mill his way out of—neither with his pop nor his fambles. Do you want as how I should ask him those questions now, m'lud?"

"No. Let Trews see him in London. But what we can do for him, we must!

"Right enough. That's wise in you, m'lud. No

use givin' him aught he can use against you, does he have a mind to.''

The Strong Room of the Eeel and Pye was a cubby without windows, a stuffy closet of sorts. A single door, well barred on the outside, was thrown open for Stukley and his companions to crowd into the tiny cell.

A beefy man with the leather apron of a smith still fastened about his considerable girth stood over a stool, and on the stool was the Barker, a Barker both changed and damaged since Murray had seen him last.

The grime of his groom disguise had been washed away, taking with it much of his swarthiness and the grease which had made lank dull strings of his hair. Perhaps a few of the bruises and rips were relics of the battle for the circus pitch. But blood was oozing from a fresh-cut lip and the swelling rising about one eye had not been there that morning. When they had taken the Barker he had not surrendered meekly to capture.

His arms were pulled behind his back, his wrists shackled together with crude irons. He sat with his eyes closed, his face drawn but very youthful under the lines of strain.

The smith was not his only guard. A man wearing the coat of a parish officer was dabbing at a cut lip of his own and glowering at the captive.

"—proper young devil!" he was commenting bitterly as they entered. " 'Saulting an officer in the pursuit o' his lawful dooty!" He put a finger in his mouth to test the stability of a front tooth. "Like to knock all me front biters out! Needs

lessonin' and here's them what will give it to
you!'' He looked to the Runner in hearty welcome.

''Watch 'im like you had eyes in your back as
well as your face,'' he warned. ''He's as slippery
as n'eel and twice as nasty!''

The Runner inspected the clumsy wrist irons
with professional interest. ''We knows how to
handle such ding-boys. Lucky he didn't loose off
his pop. He's one as hits the mark when he does.''

''He tried to. Would have shot the man as laid
the information on him,'' commented the parish
officer. ''Only his iron misfired. Well, gents, I
leaves him to you. This be no sort o' day when
one o' my callin' can sit to his ease watchin' one
prisoner, even if he be a bridle-cull what's been
hunted from here to Lunnon and back again. Come
away, Matt, and let the officer take 'im in charge
and be welcome to 'im.''

The smith and the parish officer left, and Stukley
promptly clapped the door behind them, to the
displeasure of those who had pushed their way into
the narrow corridor to view the notorious Barker
run to earth at last.

''Well, cully, you has got yourself neck to the
hammer, ain't you?'' the Runner observed in a
close to friendly tone. He had the air of one gam-
bler who has won from another, with no hard
feelings on either side.

The Barker did not reply. But he opened his
eyes and looked straight at Murray.

''Sent him to blow the whistle on me, didn't
you?'' he spat.

''If you means as how he laid information,''
Stukley caught that up quickly, ''you is straight

wrong, Barker. You has been on Hue and Cry, and that there wagoner what peached to the constable keeps his ogles to the wide when he's on the tramp. He saw you a-drinkin' your ale in the open like you was an honest man and tells it in the proper place.''

The Barker tried to shrug and found the gesture impossible, the way his hands were secured. "When do we go?" he asked tonelessly.

"With the night mail," the Runner informed him.

"Do you go with us?" Stukley asked Murray.

"As soon as I can collect my gear, I'll be back." But when he made to leave the Barker spoke directly to him once more.

"You're goin' back to Strumper's?" He spat blood from his cut lip and then added: "Strumper didn't know my lay. I tell you all that now, and I'll take oath to it too!"

"Granted," Stukley returned. "But there was one with him what did."

The Barker was spurred by that reminder. "You'll not lay your dabs on the boy! He's wantin'! He doesn't know naught."

"Save to give you shelter when you needed it," Stukley agreed.

"Look, m'lord," the Barker appealed over the ex-Runner's head to Murray. "You a flash cull what knows how to talk to them as can help the lad. You're a lord, ain't you? Bargee didn't know my lay. He don't rightly know right from wrong the way the law sees it. He thinks he must do as I want 'cause—"

" 'Cause," Stukley cut in in an oddly detached

tone," you kept him from starvin' when he was
turned adrift for bein' a want-wit. Had the fever
didn't he, when he was just a little brat, and then
his ears went bad and he was queer, so he was
kicked out."

Murray wondered where Stukley had dredged
up all this information. But the Barker was retort-
ing with some heat:

"He ain't dinged in the noggin queer, if that's
what you mean! Bargee don't lack wits—though
he can put on that he does when he has a mind to
play it so. He's earned his keep and more with
Strumper's. Leave him be now. I'll swear he don't
know about the lay and that he warn't hidin' me
against the law!"

"Granted," said Stukley for the second time.
"We ain't goin' haul him off along of you, Barker."

But the Barker wanted more than just that
assurance. He made a second appeal to Murray.

"Talk to Strumper for him, m'lord. You can do
it. See as how Bargee gets kept on there."

Murray thought it best not to say that as far as
he knew Bargee had already been discharged.

"Strumper, he can talk to him with the fingers.
He'll tell him I've got away. Then Bargee'll just
believe that it is as always and he'll never know.
He gets wild-like where he's crossed, and he might
do hisself a mischief were he to know the truth."

"All right," Murray promised, "I'll do what I
can."

It was getting on to dusk as he walked back to
the bottom land where Strumper's vans rested. The
flares before the booths made ruddy patches of
light and there were clots of villagers before most

of them. Murray looked around for Bargee or Strumper. He was a little afraid that the circus owner might have already sent the boy away, though Bargee's ring act had gone undisturbed earlier. Neither was in sight. By his own van Murray at last ran Strumper to earth. The circus owner met him with some coolness.

"You has had your fun, m'lord, and now comes to tell me as how it has all been a hum? I must say, you has the makin' of a showman."

Murray offered his hand. "It was more than just a trick on my part, Strumper. I'll give you the whole story some day. But—where's Bargee?"

Strumper looked a little self-conscious. "He's gettin' ready to ride, m'lord, if he knows what's good for him!"

"Does he know that the Barker has been taken?"

Strumper had fresh cause for complaint and voiced it. "The Barker, is it? Maybe he is that, I ain't one to gainsay Bow Street. But we knowed him as Jack Kevin, a horse dealer. And that's *only* how we knowed him, we'll take our Bible oaths on that! Master hand with horses he be. That bit of blood of hissen is prime stuff. And he picks prime stuff, too. Brings me a beauty now and then. Bargee came along o' him three-four years back. They was both younguns, Jack without a hair to that peaked chin of hissen and the t'other just a runny-nosed brat. He says as how the brat's a proper hand with animals, shows off his ridin' and says as how he'd rather the boy was ridin' here than slammin' 'round the country where his lacks might get him into trouble. So I takes him on. And, mind you, 'spite the boy's temper and his

flare-ups, he ain't been so bad up to now. It's like
he's taken a special spite to you, m'lord, that's
why he loosed the 'roo. If he's turned mean,
though, I don't want him. Too likely he'll try the
same trick again, and we might not be so well out
of it next time. But I can't turn him loose to tramp
the road—him bein' wantin' as he is.''

Strumper turned his pipe around in his fingers
and studied the discolored bowl as if he could read
some solution to the problem cupped within it.

"But does he know about the Barker?" persisted Murray.

Strumper's uneasiness became open. "I think he
does. There's a sort of finger talk he can understand,
only he won't answer to it now. 'Bout an hour ago
he came runnin' in—wild—wouldn't even look at
me. I got him locked up in the van until time for
him to take the horses in. When he comes out of
the ring Handley'll see him straight back here.''

"Will you keep him, then, until I can make
some safe provision for him?" Murray came directly to the point.

When Strumper looked dubious, he added a
strengthener. "You won't be out of the pocket any
by it.''

" 'Tain't that," the other disclaimed. "But he
hates you, m'lord.''

"Don't let him know that I have any interest in
him. I hope to find a home for him on one of the
Starr estates." If it turned out that the Barker *was*
Starr, all the better.

"Well, I'll do me best, m'lord.''

How good that best might have been they were

never to know, for at that point the groom Handley came running, gasping out his news:

"The 'roos, guv'nor, they be gone! Empty cage—"

Strumper sprinted, racing in and out among the vans and booths, dodging among the fair-goers. Murray, his imagination picturing for him what might happen with the beasts loose in such a gathering, forgot all about taking the mail coach, even about the Barker. He was certain as he joined in the chase that behind the freeing of the animals lay some malicious mischief of Bargee's planning.

The cage was empty, its barred door swinging free, only trampled straw inside. Strumper ran his hand along the edge in search of something he could not find. When he whirled about, the light from a booth flare brought his expression into plain sight, and it was grim indeed.

"The leashes—they're gone! He's taken them!"

"Bargee?"

"That imp of the devil! Let me get my hands on him and he'll get such a hidin' as he'll remember for the rest of his life. Keep him here?" Strumper was white with rage now. "After this, I wouldn't keep him as long as it would take me to strip his skin off his bones! We get him and then—after we gives him the lesson he's asked for and won't forget in a hurry—you can have the pieces and welcome!"

That threat rang as if Strumper meant every word of it. The circus owner was past the point where he was willing to make any allowances. If Bargee wasn't going to get a crippling beating, someone other than Strumper or his rightfully angry men had better find him first.

Why had the boy freed the animals? They would be dangerous in a crowd, maybe even unmanageable. It would be fatal if one of the village dogs came upon them, while their presence loose should attract attention at once. The fact that no confusion had been yet noted in the crowd suggested that Bargee had not gone toward the village.

Which left three-quarters of the landscape to be searched. Strumper had apparently been struck with the same idea. For he summoned as many of the grooms and handymen as he could gather, and had brought out the extra horses, mounting his hunters with instruction to fan out from the camp site. A good enough plan as long as they did not fall afoul of any manor house with walled parks, or a game preserve.

Murray joined the searching party without invitation, though Strumper did not deny him use of the mare he picked at random. He rode slowly through the edge of the crowd, noting no uproar, no sign of Bargee's passing. Then he had gained the end of the pasture and rounded the hedge to the highway. It was close to full dark and the flares of the fair were a spot of light fading behind him. On the harder surface of the road the hoofbeats sounded so loudly that, as a matter of precaution, Murray sent the mare unto the grass boundaries before he realized that such caution was not necessary with the quarry he hunted tonight. Then, from behind, he heard the clamor of a coach horn and knew that he had outstayed his time; the night mail must be pulling away from the Eel and Pye.

A narrow lane ran to his right, and he turned into it to let the coach pass. But he had not foreseen Bargee's reckless determination to achieve his own ends.

The coach began to pick up speed, once out of the village, with an open and deserted road before it. It was still, luckily, bowling along at a medium pace when it passed Murray's lane. A fact for which those inside it might give thanks for the rest of their days.

There were no roof passengers, only the guard and the driver aloft. Somewhere within would be the Barker between his two guards, his wrists ironed, no hope now of beating the law. Or so Murray thought as the lumbering vehicle passed the mouth of the lane.

There came a wild shout, the blast of the guard's musket, to be close followed by screams and cries of alarm. Murray kicked the mare in the ribs and galloped out—to see the coach waver into the ditch, the horses gone wild, rearing and screaming aloud in their terror as a black shape leaped in great bounds in front of the maddened leaders and another figure scrabbled at the coach door. The explosion of a pistol cut the night with fire and sound, and more figures erupted from the coach, scrambling down the curve of its side, now turned to the sky. There was the swirl of a fight before one broke free, running back toward Murray, a hopping shape in pursuit.

Another queerly shaped blot lurched ponderously across the road, and Murray's own mount caught the contagion of frenzy, rearing with a neigh and pawing the air as its rider fought for control. He coughed at a whiff of rank odor. Not content with using the 'roos to upset the stage horses, Bargee had somehow brought the camel in addition, knowing how its presence would frighten all the other beasts.

The newcomer strode majestically along, while Murray's mare backed into the ditch and hedge, nearly brushing him off in the process. However, the 'roo kept on down the smooth surface of the road, a black mark against the lighter ribbons of gravel and stone. Then it, too, made a wide circle to avoid the camel. The figure it had appeared to chase had melted into the darker shadow of the ditch, perhaps going to earth there in panic.

With the camel safely past, Murray had the sweating mare subdued, and was about to ride to assist those at the coach when a voice spoke out of the dark slightly behind him and a hand jerked at his coat, attempting to bring him out of the saddle.

"I'll trouble you for the loan of the nag."

Blindly Murray struck down at the source of that voice. The sentence ended in a grunt as his fist met flesh. Not too far away another horse blew nervously. Against a scrap of sky Murray saw a rider picking a careful way along behind the hedge as if in search of someone. His last assailant must have sensed help in that direction, for he slid from Murray's side and thrust through the mass of leaves and brush to gain the field.

There was a scrambling and then a horse, now bearing double yet able to make good time under that burden, cantered across the field away from the road, picking up speed as it went. Bargee and the Barker?

By the time Murray was able to win through into that same field they were out of sight. He headed in the direction he had seen them take. A hoarse shout or two came from the stranded coach, but Murray paid no attention to that. The snap of a pistol shot, however, was something else. When he was struck forward by a blow across his short ribs which numbed his whole left side, he realized that they were shooting at *him*!

Before he could recover from the surprise of that, or let them know their mistake, the mare had carried him down slope and, he hoped, out of range. There was a dark line before him, another hedge or fence. Too late he knew his own foolhardiness and tried to check his mount.

Excited, perhaps still fearing the camel, thrown into a greater panic by the shouting and the shot, the mare he bestrode had her bit in her teeth and was running wild. Murray had only a moment to settle himself for the leap he prayed she would try. Luckily Strumper's horses could be expected to essay jumping, but to take that obstruction in the dark, without knowing whether level land or another ditch marked the landing point, was insane folly.

She sailed over without breaking stride, as pretty as a hunter trained for broken-country running. The effort tamed her somewhat and her pace slackened a little as she fled across the stubbled field on the far side. Murray swallowed. He dared not lessen his grip on the reins to explore the damage beneath his left arm. The first numbness of the wound was wearing off, giving notice of trouble with darting flashes of pain around his middle and up into his shoulder. Trickles of something thicker than sweat was creeping down his body beneath his clothing. However, he couldn't have been hit vitally or he wouldn't be able to stay in the saddle and keep his wits about him.

Luckily the hedges appeared to be now all behind them for a space. They were out in a rolling country, dotted here and there with thickets but free of artificial barriers. The mare could run her legs off, and the sooner she tired and he could bring her around, the better. Intent upon trying slowly and cautiously to influence his mount, Murray was not aware at first of the other horse a goodly distance ahead. Nor did he see one of the two riders slip from its back to stand waiting for him.

For Murray had just made the frightening discovery that he was not in such good case as he had first thought. He knew that the mare was flagging, but when he attempted to tighten rein and bring her to a halt, he could not exert any pressure at all. The ground, shadow crossed, was rippling as if waves of the sea rather than a stand of grass surrounded them.

A whistle, low but carrying as a bird's trill, registered only dimly with Murray. He was possessed by one determination now, not to fall from the mare—and lie alone in this stretch of wasteland. Now he dropped the reins entirely, to clutch with all his remaining strength at the saddle horn as the mare swerved and put on speed once more in answer to that whistle.

Hands on him! Instinctively Murray struggled. But he was thrown to the ground with a force which tore a smothered cry out of him as the shooting pain in his side struck at his head, fogging his eyes and brain. He heard dimly an exclamation as he tried to pull away from a grasp which added to his torment.

Then came the thud of hooves heading away and he was alone. How long he lay there, he could not have told. At last he stretched out his right arm, grabbed a handful of wiry grass, and pulled and levered himself to a sitting position.

The moon was up, a wide white circle in the sky. His hand went to the sodden patch on his coat, pressing it tight against his side as if that pressure would stop the pain. He doubted if he could get to his feet, and nowhere in the sweep of countryside about could he see any light which might mark a farm or cottage promising help.

Bleakly, well aware he was still losing blood, too much of it, Murray tried to plan. Only his spinning head was too light to hold any thought except in a very misty fashion. His native stubbornness kept him from dropping back to the ground and losing all interest in his plight.

He was still fighting in his own dogged way when the horse came back. Not only the horse but a rider. The man who dismounted beside Murray and pulled him to his feet was only a foggy shape. But he was boosted up on the bare back of a mount. Then an arm was thrown about him as the rider settled behind him and they moved on in a swinging canter Murray found familiar but could not identify. He did not know where they were going, and was now past caring.

12

Path of a "Gentleman's" Mare

There was light, if only of a flickering, unstable kind. Murray found himself lying on what his groping hand told him must be a pile of dried bracken and grass. His coat, waistcoat and shirt were gone, and there was a damp chill in this place. He shivered and then cringed, as hands came into the circle of light and gave him sharp jolts of pain, dealing with his wound with a rough efficiency.

Hands—those hands were oddly decorated at the

wrist with wide bracelets of iron, bracelets anchored in place with bindings of rags.

"What—who—?" He got out the whisper, able now to see that the feeble light came from two candle ends embedded in a puddle of their own grease on a board, held close for illumination by a second pair of hands.

A last strip of bandage was drawn tightly about him. Then he was able to discover in the far reaches of those candles the Barker's features, now expressing intent concentration as he completed his surgery. The Barker!

Puzzled, trying to fit together bits and patches of memory, Murray lay quiet.

"Where?" he got out the last of his questions. Instead of any answer, a cup was held to his lips, his head raised. He swallowed, to cough, then gasp at the pain that caused, as fiery stuff bit the tissues of his throat and lit a fire in his chilled middle. That was brandy!

"He'll do, for the present." The Barker sat back on his heels, now hardly more than an outline in the general gloom. The hands bearing the board with the candles swooped away. Murray's gaze, drawn after that source of light, saw a portion of bricked wall. He guessed that he was under cover, but where and how he could not tell.

Perhaps it was the brandy, but he found it too great an effort to keep his eyes open. So he slipped from his awareness of bricks, bracken and his own paining body into a deeper and soothing darkness.

It was still dark when he awoke once more— dark with a black absence of light which troubled his nerves, made him push out with his hands to make sure that his first panicky half-fear could not be right—that he had not been buried alive while asleep. There was space about him, a good range of space. His searching fingers struck something, to send it rolling with the clink of metal against stone, a clink echoed in an oddly hollow way from the air above.

"Who's there?" he called, able to muster better than a whisper in the way of a voice now.

There was no answer. He lay very still, hardly daring to breathe, listening for the slightest sound which would tell him he was not alone in this dark place. Murray began to fear that he had been left to shift for himself here. But where was *here*?

Setting his teeth against the pain, against the swirling vertigo which made his head swim, Murray pulled himself up, and sat, steadying himself with his braced arms buried wrist deep in the dried stuff of his bed, wanting to get out of here, find his way into the open.

He was nerving himself to trying a crawl when a faint sound made him tense: the beat of a boot heel on stone, echoed in the same hollow manner as the clink of the rolling thing had been. Then followed a glow, yellow, approaching until he could once more see the bricks of the walls, the edge of a doorway which was linteled and sided with stone slabs. The light struck up to a roof, also of stone, but smoothed by tool work.

A cellar, a crypt, Murray tried to put a name to his present quarters. Was he a prisoner in some dungeon? The light spread farther along the wall, picked out the grimed cavern of a fireplace faced with stone. Then it came into full view as a lantern.

All he could see of the one who carried it was a pair of booted feet and buckskin-breeched legs.

The circle of light flooded Murray as the lantern was placed on a block of stone. There was an exclamation and he who had carried it advanced to be revealed as the Barker.

In his shirt sleeves, those bracelets of his irons still about his wrists, he looked young and in a way more defenseless than Murray had ever seen him. Now he came quickly to kneel beside the other, putting his patient back upon the bracken with a force which could not be withstood, examining the bands of torn linen shirting bound over the wound. When he had done he looked up with a hint of a smile.

"For a lad as has been floppin' about like a whirligig, you is very tail up and chesty now, ain't you? But don't try to come it too strong. You trots before you races, cully."

He searched about the floor until he found the battered pewter mug which Murray had inadvertently set rolling, and filled it from a leather harvester's bottle. Slipping his arm, with a deftness which mildly surprised the other, under Murray's head, he gave him a drink of water.

"I'd take it kindly," the latter said after a good swallow, "if you'd tell me just where we are."

The Barker laughed. "In as tight a hidey-hole as any bridle-cull could wish to find on a month o' Sundays!" He stood up, his boots apart, his fists resting on his hips as he looked about him in mimic of pride and ownership.

"Back in the old days," he explained, "some flash cull, maybe even an earl," he shot a mischievous flash of smile at Murray, "made hisself this good place to lie up in. Maybe he was goin' to hide out from the king's men. Or maybe he did it for a priest. But it was forgot for years—'til it was found again, by them as has good reason to look for a place where they needn't fear nabbers."

"But why bring me here?" Murray pressed the point he found the greatest puzzle: "Why take on the burden of a wounded man when you should travel light?"

The Barker avoided his gaze. He crossed to the fireplace and kicked some half-charred sticks there into a heap before he squatted down to light them.

"I couldn't have cried rope on you, you know, even if you had left me," Murray persisted. That was the only explanation he had been able to find for his present situation. "I hadn't the slightest idea of where you had gone, or even of the direction in which you were heading."

"We has plans for you, never fear," observed the other without turning. "You'll get us out when the time comes."

"So I'm a hostage," Murray mused. Well, that was logical. He still thought that there was more behind it. However, for the moment he'd better play the game the way the Barker had dealt it. This space of time together would give him an excellent chance to learn more of the man reputed to be the rightful Earl of Starr—a man who just might be in Whyte's confidence.

However, it appeared that the Barker was disinclined at present to continue the conversation. He brought out a small kettle, swung it by a chain

over the fire, and gave an absent-minded stir now
and then to the warming contents.

"You have provisions?"

"Oh, we has our ways. Bargee can find a path
through any wood 'fore a keeper can sniff out his
trail."

"There are man traps to guard against poachers—
at least I've heard of such."

The Barker shrugged. "There's a mort of things
to trip a man up sweet and get these on him." He
pulled at one of the iron hoops about his wrists.
"But he ain't goin' to starve a-waitin' for a coney
to jump up between his legs, neither. You takes
your chances—nobody is goin' save our pence but
us."

He was right in his estimate of Bargee's poach-
ing skill. For, when the boy came in not too long
afterwards, he had two plump rabbits slung about
his neck by a cord lashing their hind feet together,
and carried a limp partridge in one hand and some
snares in the other.

"Cast your ogles over that now," the Barker
bade Murray. "He's a proper hand with a snare,
ain't he?"

Bargee's greeting to Murray was a cold stare.
But he grinned companionably at the fire tender
before he seated himself cross-legged on the bricked
floor and skillfully went about the process of clean-
ing the game. The rabbits were spitted to be roasted
over the fire, the partridge quartered and popped
into the pot in record time. A savory odor tickled
Murray's nose, letting him know very plainly that,
in spite of his aches and pains, his dizzy head and

flabby muscles, he was still strongly interested in the business of eating.

However, his period as an invalid, so auspiciously begun, did not proceed so favorably. There was a bout of fever, a time when he wandered back to a forest lodge where he tried not to cower at the terrible screams which came from beyond as a man he had known died hard—died such a death as only painted fiends could devise. Then again he faced up to the assembled warriors of the clan, drank the Black Drink of ceremony and felt it tear him asunder, not daring to give any outward sign of his torment, so that he might take his place among them as a man. Last of all, he climbed a stairway in a dark and deserted house, pushed open a door, and faced a murdered man wearing his knife in his breast as a dreadful decoration.

Murray's second awaking in the brick room did not come in the dark but in the full glow of lantern light. For a long moment he had to struggle to understand what that light was, in some way connecting it with no body—save his own. He raised his hand to shield his weak eyes against that gleam, finding it something of a task to force bone and muscle to obey his will.

Someone came to him as quickly as if he had called. He knew that face, though the expression on it, the lines about eyes and mouth were new. Only he could not put name at first to the man whose hand rested lightly for a space on his forehead, who peered so intently into his eyes as if seeking for something to be found there.

"Barker!" Murray got that out with a little flash of triumph. His nurse was the Barker and he was in the hidey-hole of the highwayman and not in a forest lodge or that room in Royal Street.

"You're right, cully." The other smiled wearily. "And you ain't goin' to be cold meat yet a while—so it looks. You gentry coves has got the stuff. Sick as a horse you has been—but you ain't hopped the twig!"

Murray laughed weakly at that assurance. But the other was beginning to waver in his sight and Murray closed his eyes, sensing that though he was sleepy, he no longer had to fear a return to the land of nightmare.

However, it was still going to be a long pull before he could be on his feet again, or hope to win free of the muddle that his own recklessness and a too-well-aimed bullet had brought him into. He noted, as time passed, a time which could not be regulated by lantern light into minutes, hours, day or night, that the Barker kept close and Bargee continued to supply food and drink. The highwayman was rid of his bracelets at long last, and Murray, noting that, asked a question:

"Perhaps I should be all obligation. Is it my state of health which keeps you here?"

The Barker's right eyebrow went up in that sign of quizzical humor Murray had come to watch for.

"Not entirely, cully. I have some dislike of fallin' a-foul of your friends. They have been runnin' 'bout the country like hounds on the trace."

"Stukley?"

"The small wrapper-legged one what is devilish keen between the ears? Aye, Stukley. He appears not ready to give up 'til he sees me stretchnecked."

It was not just a matter of bringing a highway-man to justice, Murray believed. Stukley wanted to prove that he was right, that Barker was the card Whyte had tried to play in his game of winning rich pickings from Starr.

"I've been trying to plan a little," Murray began slowly. "How far are we from a village called Tregarth, or from the Cornish border?"

"Tregarth?" The Barker repeated as if the name was totally strange. "Dunno. But we ain't far from the border, why?"

Murray shifted on his bed and frowned when his side answered that move with a warning twinge. Would he be strong enough to carry out the plan he had made in those spells between sleeping and waking?

"I own Garth Holme, the manor there. Or," he corrected himself, remembering what might prove to be a pretty legal tangle in the near future, "it is a Starr holding. If we could reach there we would have a breathing space in comfort."

The Barker stared at him. "I keep forgettin' you're Lord Farstarr," he said absently. "Garth Holme might do for you, but the Barker and Bargee had better find another lay-up. We ain't flash enough to suit."

Murray reared up on an elbow and discovered that the rarefied air did not this time make him so dizzy.

"Who are you?" he asked. " 'The Barker' is all right for a fancy name to suit your lay. But you didn't answer to that from your cradle—or did you cut your teeth on the barrel of a well-sighted pop?"

"Devil of a pusher, ain't you?" inquired the other. "No, I warn't the Barker when I was a brat. I don't rightly know who I am," he admitted frankly. "Put out to nurse early, as maybe you gentry coves would say it." His eyes were bleak. "Only I warn't no gentry brat, and the nurse warn't rightly no nurse." He spread out his narrow hand with its long supple fingers, and then those fingers twisted around and around the opposite wrist as Murray had seen them on that first meeting by the cockpit in the Bunch of Fives. "Learned how to use these. Went on the priggin' lay early and was beat if I didn't bring back a good haul. When I was bigger I cut for it. Got taken up by a mutton-headed old cove as thought I had a good face. He wanted to make a groom out o' me, taught me my letters, too. He was fair daft about men gettin' up in the world was they given the proper chance. Was goin' to prove with me as how it could be done. Only he took lung sick and died. Then I was on the road 'fore the parish could deal with me. But I made out fine." He eyed Murray with a challenge in both eye and lift of chin. "There's none on the bridle lay as can match the Barker, 'cause I use me wits. Supposin' as how I made a good haul. Do I blow it where any informer can put the nab on me? No, I goes out to a seaport town and says as how I is a sailor home with prize money. So I lives high without no awkward questions asked. I can pass for flash when I wants to. And I'll do it again!" He convinced Murray that he could and would.

"Until Bow Street blows the horn on you for

good. Look here, you haven't yet told me your name.''

The Barker shrugged. ''I ain't got a proper one as I know of. The cove what took me in called me 'Kevin.' I don't know why. Must have meant somethin' to him, like as not. When I took to the road I put a Jack to the front of it—Jack Kevin, if you want.''

Murray shook his head. ''Kevin Lyon,'' he repeated slowly. ''Try that for a neater fit.''

The Barker sat very still. ''Why?'' he asked flatly, but Murray believed that his thoughts were racing behind his suddenly expressionless face.

''Because it might fit very well. Did you ever know a Captain Lionel Whyte?''

The Barker's lips drew back in something which bore no kinship to a smile. He was on his feet with a cat's lithe grace, and came across the small chamber to stand over Murray, his ruddy eyes holding to the invalid's, an emotion Murray could not assess hot in their depths.

''Aye, I know the Captain,'' his tone was soft, almost caressing, but it was not kindly. Murray, a little shaken, thought he had blundered badly. Was the Barker, had the Barker, been in on the Captain's game from the first?

''What does Whyte want now?'' Again that silky menace.

Murray shut his lips. He had gone too far, but the Barker would have no more from him.

''I said, what does Whyte want?'' From beneath his shirt the other produced a weapon Murray recognized as his own prized pistol.

With his attention on the arm, Murray returned as lightly as he could: "That throws a little to the left, friend. Make allowances for that when you fire."

"This is no flam." The Barker's voice was as businesslike as the way he held that weapon. "I told Whyte what I would do if he came sniffin' on my trail again, and I'll do it as quickly to any agent of his. I'll have no part of one of his dirty mills. I've told him so to his teeth, and he needn't think nobody else is goin' to get around me for him! So you was there to set the nabbles on me if Jory didn't carry through!"

Murray was completely bewildered. "Jory?"

The Barker's pistol hand was very steady. "Aye, Jory. Dressed up like a wagoner come to guzzle a pint—see me—and then split to the Runners. Only I knowed him, too. Wish I could have made sure of him 'fore they pulled me away. But I can of you."

Murray met that boring stare levelly. "I assure you that I have no acquaintance with any Jory. As for Captain Whyte, he is doing his best to scorch me properly. Rid yourself of the notion that I am running Whyte's errand, I beg you. Nothing could be farther from the mark. So far he has attempted to blackmail me, embroiled me in a murder, and the Lord only know what he plans for my future. I can readily believe it will contain anything from arson to treason!"

But that pistol did not move, he was still able to look down its muzzle. The Barker had preserved his freedom as long as he had because he was uncommonly alert and suspicious. But at least he seemed willing to allow Murray to enlarge upon his story.

"Why?"

Murray shrugged and then snapped out a brace of forceful words as that movement of the shoulders reminded him of his present damaged state.

"It's a long tale, and I've only bits and patches of it myself. To put you in the way of what I know—what Stukley has been able to scratch up—it starts with my father's cousin, the late Earl of Starr, a bad lot who never kept to the line." Murray swung into the story Whyte had told, of the missing heir to Starr, and ended with what Stukley had discovered.

Sometime during that account the pistol vanished into hiding once again and the Barker sat down on the stool. When Murray had brought the tale up to date, the Barker made no comment, only sat there, rubbing his wrist in his usual fashion, as if he would rub away some cold touch left by the irons.

"I must be dicked in the nob," he observed at last, "or else you're still talkin' out of a fever. This is a fetch as might be dreamed up by some cove as was guzzlin' a belly full of Blue Ruin. I'd tell you so—if I hadn't met the Captain and knowed some of his little games. But you ain't believin' all this? The Captain's a loose fish, slippery as they come. He'd never tell a straight story."

"Unless he could profit by it!" Murray corrected. "Look at it this way, Kevin. My branch of the family was in dun territory when this fell into our hands. It pulled us out of the river tick for sure. That was noised about and the Captain heard it. Would he believe that we'd throw away Starr for an unknown heir when he could, for a consideration, promise us that heir'd never make his appearance? He plans to settle in and pluck us clean at his leisure. Because he is sure we won't kick up any fuss and lose our soft pitch. In our place *he* wouldn't. In the meantime he would cheerfully do you a mischief, since you won't work with him. Doesn't it read that way to you?''

The Barker nodded. ''In a manner of speakin' you has the right there—though he didn't mouth me no such yarn as he told you. Only said that if I played a hand as he called it, he'd see I warn't cut of the pocket by it. But I has knowed the Captain since I was a nipper, and I ain't never heard as how them what does his biddin' ever gets anythin' by it, save maybe a present of a bit of lead or length of rope. He has diddled men I know out of their breath as well as their proper pickin's. So I warn't havin' none of his schemes. But if all this is true and not some slum-guzzle—'' He frowned at the fire before he continued, ''how'm I any better? A bridle-cull hangs when he is took, be he an earl or a nameless nobody!''

''You've never killed anyone, have you?''

The Barker answered that with a trace of scorn. ''That's a fub's game! If you shoots a horse, or threatens to pop one, they'll pull up fast enough. I've been on the lay for two years now, and ain't never even winged a cove. Between takes I lay low—like I said—playin' the sailor throwin' his Jimmy Goblins about. There warn't never no questions asked. When I'm pockets to let again, why, then," he made a gesture of drawing and pointing a pistol, "stand and deliver, cully!"

"If we can get to Garth Holme and lay low there, I'm sure we can discover some way to push for a pardon for you."

The Barker was instantly alert. "See here, I ain't no green gull up from the country. Why do you want to get me a pardon? You'll have it snug—all right and tight—if you let Stukley and that pal of his nabble me."

"I'm not of Whyte's breed! Neither is my father. Rid yourself of the notion that we'll hold Starr if it isn't rightfully ours. But we must get the lawyers on the business and that speedily."

The Barker seemed moved by that. "And if we get to this here Garth Holme we can have us a breather for a bit?"

"I'm reasonably sure of that. And it's somewhat more comfortable than our present quarters. Also I'd like to be able to check on the Captain before he involves us all so deeply we can't get free."

"I knows those as can tip us the wink on him. When you can get on your feet we'll make for this manor of yours."

Murray took that as a promise. But it was still some time until the night when, leaning on the Barker's arm, preceded by Bargee, who very openly distrusted Murray and was opposed to the move, he made his way down a narrow passage and was pushed through a mass of cloaking brush into a lane so overgrown it was plain that no one had passed that way regularly for a long time.

Wild and open country lay beyond. But the Barker swore that they were not too far from the coast and that if they could get a horse—a task assigned to Bargee—they could be within a short distance of Garth Holme by morning.

Weather ruined that plan. For there was a fog gathering, turning the dusk of early evening into a cottony world. The wisest move would have been to return to their burrow, but Murray, now that he was in the open, urged that they make the try.

Bargee slipped away. His task of finding a mount, or mounts, was not too difficult. For they had noted earlier that horses from a nearby farm were turned out to graze for the night. But, as the wisps of fog twined about them until the bushes had the aspect of crouching figures, Murray began to see how foolhardy he had been to insist upon this. He had come to the point of openly voicing his contrition when a horse plodded across their path.

The Barker sprang forward to catch at the nag's halter, only to stand with a profane and baffled cry as the mare went placidly on her way, followed by a sedate line of ponies, each laden with a small keg fastened to a single-girth band. The Barker made a snatch at the next in line and his astonishment came in one word:

"Greased!"

Murray recalled one of the Tregarth legends.

"Come away!" He stumbled along to pull at the other's arm. Ponies shaven and greased to prevent capture meant only one thing: the "gentlemen" were running a cargo inland, under the guidance of one of their trained lead mares. But, though that

line was moving apparently without escort, that
did not mean there were no guards about.

And his apprehension was based on fact. Dark
figures emerged from the fog and closed in upon
them with a purpose the more sinister because of
the very silence of that advance.

13

A Visit to One's Ancestors

There was no chance for any resistance, not even a token show. The Barker went down under a silent rush, and Murray, before he lost his first surprise, collapsed in turn as a blow from behind sent him staggering forward into a blank more complete than the darkness of dusk and fog.

Once he returned to a semi-conscious state to feel pain stabbing up his racked side. His body was being transported along jerkily, the thick smell of horse sweat added to his rising nausea. As far as he could judge, he hung across one of the ponies. Then the nag stumbled, sending such a pang through him that he fainted again.

Dark, black dark, so tangible in its solidty that one could almost feel or taste it. A dark which closed about Murray with the same sense of entombment as he had known upon his first awakening in the hiding place of the Barker. For a dazed second or two he thought himself back there.

He tried to sit up and discovered that his wrists were lashed behind him, that a gag ran chokingly between his jaw, holding his mouth in a dry, inescapable trap. Also he was certain that he was once more imprisoned under ground. Not in the sea caves the smugglers usually chose, for there was no sound of surf, nor the faintest current of wind. This place had an airless quality he had not noticed at the Barker's retreat, even more like a tomb.

Murray attempted to move his feet. They, too, were looped together at the ankles and he could find nothing solid to brace them against. His efforts sent him rolling, and he shuddered with the pain of his healing wound as he came up against something softer than the stone surface under him, something which yielded a little to the impact of his body.

The fingers of his bound hands encountered cloth, pinched the softness of flesh under that covering. Since the other moved under his exploration but did not speak, Murray judged he had rolled against some other captive in the same straits as himself. The Barker?

Murray lay quiet. He was finding it difficult to

breathe. Not only did the gag tend to strangle him, but what air he could pull into his lungs in shallow gasps had such a lifeless quality that it might have been shut in this prison for ages. He forced himself to fight a rising panic, to lie there drawing as deep breaths as he could, willing his body to relax, his imagination to stop painting an insidious picture of being enclosed in a box with the lid moving slowly down to crush him.

He tried to grip the arm of his fellow captive. The other moved under his fumbling touch. With a wriggle which almost sent Murray rolling again, he nudged against Murray's back. Fingers dug into his wrists, jerked at the bonds there.

Murray chewed on his gag. Each sharp tug sent a stab through his side. If a seaman had knotted those cords, as he thought was very possible, no blind picking in the world would loosen them. But he endured that pulling, forcing himself to be ready to take advantage of any loosening which might occur.

There was no reckoning of time in the dark. The efforts of the other's fingers grew weaker, long and longer pauses came between the jerks. At length the fumbling ceased altogether. Murray could hear a snorting, as if his fellow unfortunate was now fighting for breath. It *was* getting harder to breathe! The air, stale to begin with, must be becoming exhausted. Its stench of mold, of a place forever closed to the cleansing sun was sickening, stupefying. He was drifting away. . . .

Light probed his half-closed eyes, in its way as great a pain as the sudden brutal thud in his ribs which moved his helpless body over to fetch up against a hard surface. Murray blinked his smarting eyes. Facing him now was a slab of stone bearing the carved outline of a shield. And on that shield a heraldic lion rampant and a half-circle of stars. A Lyon with Starrs—his own crest! But where in the world—?

Stupidly he strove to fit that stone carving into some logical explanation. Then a hand reached down, laced fingers in his collar, and brought him up to a sitting position, plumping him roughly back against that shield-marked slab for support.

There were three lanterns lighting a stone floor, stone walls, a cell with a low ceiling. Carvings about the two pillars which supported that same ceiling. Among them the Lyon arms were repeated at intervals. Niches in the walls, some sealed, those having the shield set on them, others open and empty.

Murray tensed. He knew now where he must be. If it had not been for that gag he would have cried his discovery aloud. Though he had never visited this place, he had indeed returned to Tregarth, if not to Garth Holme. This could only be the crypt in which generations of earlier Lyons—before the family had learned to choose the wining side regularly in dynastic wars and so rose to the ownership of Starr and its attendant earldom—lay under the church which their first ancestor on this side of the channel had raised as a thank-offering for the gift of a rich fief. No wonder he had had the sensation of being buried!

He was so amazed by his discovery that he did not at first recognize the men now lining up some small kegs, and smaller packages. However, as he

saw one familiar face after another, his anger began to top both surprise and bodily discomfort.
How dared they use this crypt as one of their
stations for smuggled goods! Surely the vicar could
not know. . . .

It would seem the permission of the vicar was
not needed; they had another conspirator. That
man by the stairs was Holgrave, the sexton. Murray stared at him in angry accusation. Perhaps the
force of that glare drew the sexton's attention to
him. The lower part of Murray's face was half
masked by his gag. But he wasn't so completely
disguised that Holgrave did not study him uneasily
with a growing expression of alarm.

"Lord love us!" the sexton sputtered, his exclamation freezing his companions in mid-act for the
moment. "It's the young Lord Farstarr!"

He pushed aside one of the smugglers and hurried over to Murray, bending to tug at the latter's
bonds. "We didn't know, m'lord!" he shrilled.
"The lads thought as how you was Searchers comin'
out of the fog at 'em and tryin' to lay hands on the
ponies. Oh, m'lord, we didn't know who you
was!"

The others gathered around the prisoner. Murray's
hand and ankles were speedily freed, the gag loos-
ened until he was able to tear it out of his chafed
mouth. He tried to relieve his feelings with a few
choice and well-selected remarks and discovered
he could not summon up more than a faint rook's
caw.

"Brandy!"

"Give him a drink o' Cousin Jack now."

"What he needs is—"

There was a chorus of advice. One of the men
hurried to broach a keg. Liquid seeped and the
heady smell of spirits was added to the general
murk of the crypt's dead air. Perhaps they were
used to drawing test samples of their wares, for a
mug was produced, filled and brought to Murray.
He choked on the fiery stuff, but it moistened his
abused tongue and gave him strength.

His erstwhile captors saw no reason to waste the
contents of the keg. And, since the supply of mugs
was in want, cupped hands, or in one or two cases
a shoe, served the drinkers as well. The Barker
was loosed and Murray passed the reviving mug
on to him. Round eyed, the highwayman watched
the scene in silent wonderment, content to let Murray take command. Then Murray, his tongue able
once more, fully exasperated, launched into a spirited description of the manner, morals, and probable future of those assembled before him—not
quite in the language a vicar would choose, but as
hard on the sinners involved. He had a memory for
vigorous terms drawn from two continents and
languages, and, though 'son of mud turtle' might
not be as great an insult here as it was among his
adopted people, when delivered in the Creek tongue
it carried quite a sulfurous impact. His audience
heard him out, first sheepishly and then with re-
spectful admiration.

"Ain't repeatin' hisself at all," muttered one
listener. "Powerful range of language. Be as good
as an Indiaman's mate, ain't he?"

Only Holgrave tried to interfere.

"M'lord, please, m'lord, let us get you out of

here! It ain't a fittin' place for you, m'lord." He assisted Murray to his feet.

Upright, Murray had to clutch at the sexton for support as the pavement wavered like sea water under his boots; he might be on a luggar deck in a channel blow.

"You're hurt, m'lord!"

"And it's not your fault I'm not dead!" snapped the other. "Yes, get us out of here. How is it with you, Kevin?"

The Barker flashed him a grin. "Well enough, now that I ain't jaw bound. Puts me in mind of Stukley's transport, so it does. New sort of fetch for me. Do we jog now?"

"We do!"

But when Murray started for the stair leading out of the crypt Holgrave caught at his sleeve.

"Please, m'lord. 'Tis best to go quiet like. They ain't twigged this place yet, but they're still sniffin'. That Hurrell, he ain't one to give up before Judgment Day, it seems."

"So Hurrell's still here?"

"Him *and* the redcoats, m'lord. They says as how they ain't a-goin' to leave."

"Then who had the mad idea of running in a cargo right under their noses? You're asking to be nabbed, you fools!"

"We had those as was a-waitin' for the stuff," one of the men chimed in. "When the Cap'n gives his word, he keeps it." There was pride in the reminder. "No redcoat, no, nor that devil Hurrell neither, is goin' to spike up a run of the Cap'n's! We has got our little ways of askin' that, sure and certain!"

"Such as kidnapping innocent strangers?"

The other was plainly disturbed. "But it was the fog, you see, m'lord. And you came up sudden-like to the ponies. We thought as how the Searchers had been hidin' to mark us. So we gathered you in."

"Thinking to take us a-sea and rid yourselves of us there?" Murray, remembering Furth's tales, mercilessly pushed the point. "Well, we're not Preventive Men. And you needn't expect us to trumpet up an army to look for you. I'm for the manor with my friend. That's all."

"We ain't sayin' as how you shouldn't leave, m'lord!" Holgrave appeared shocked. "We just want as how your leavin' shouldn't be remarked by them as has nothin' better to do than nose about. Let me show you, m'lord."

Perhaps it was the dose of brandy which had landed in an almost empty stomach, perhaps it was his rough passage to the crypt, but Murray was beginning to feel quite ill. He had no intention of being lugged up to the door of Garth Holme by members of the present company—a proceeding which would certainly cause talk and raise questions throughout Tregarth. Until the affairs of the Barker were settled, they wanted to attract as little attention as possible.

"All right, but get to it, men!"

As Murray started up the stairs the Barker slipped a supporting hand under his arm, an aid he was grateful for. He was even more appreciative of that unobtrusive help as they emerged into the dark interior of the church, moving past the box of the manor pew to a side door which gave upon the churchyard.

There was no fog here, but it was into the early morning, with a thin drizzle of rain—much too chill for the season—wetting them to the skin as they moved slowly between the clipped yews to the lych gate and so to the lane. Holgrave would have gone on with them, but Murray sent him back. He stood with one hand on the gatepost as the sexton reluctantly retired, wondering if he could crawl the width of the lane, narrow as it was. There were only one or two lights showing in the village. Perhaps they should head for the inn.

"Now where?" The Barker tightened his grip on Murray.

"Garth Holme!" He clung to that just as he clung to the mossed stone under his shaking hand. The massive bed in Garth Holme's Justice Room filled his mind as a beautiful dream. He wanted nothing more than to be engulfed in it.

Longing alone was not going to get him there. He had to make the effort of walking, or rather tottering. There was that short way leading over the wall stair and through the garden; he seriously doubted if he could go around by the lodge and the drive. Along this lane, across one field—he worked it out in his mind slowly. Then Murray loosed his hold on the gatepost and lurched forward, with the feeling that if he allowed himself to pause again he would never make it.

The Barker was with him, in fact Murray was practically draped across the shoulder of the shorter man, who supported him with his wiry strength. Somehow they made the wall, Murray took the

steps on his hands and knees. Then they were in
the mass of rose bush and hedges, striking toward
the black blot of the manor house. Murray kept
going until his boots scuffed on the flagstones of
the terrace. The Barker steered him to a column
topped by an ornamental urn and he clung desper-
ately to that anchorage while the other tried the
door.

"Locked!"

That was only to be expected under the circumstances, but to Murray this last check between him
and the Justice Room was disheartening. How they
could rouse Clagget or Knapp—where the servants
slept, in the pile before them, was beyond his
knowledge.

This setback did not appear to present any problem to the Barker, whose areas of illegitimate
knowledge were as wide as they were practical.
He moved to the nearest window, made a careful
inspection of the panes, and went to work. Then
the sash came up under his urging. With one leg
hoisted across the sill he looked back to Murray.

"Hold on, cully. I'll be around to the door."

He was gone, leaving Murray alone in the rain,
which turned his clothing into a sodden weight on
his aching body, its clammy touch adding to the
chill, which shook him with convulsive shudders.
There was a rattle of bolt to be heard above the
sighing of the wind and the door was open. Murray abandoned his support and tried to launch out
in that direction, but he would have fallen full
length if the Barker had not moved fast to catch
him.

Somehow they got under cover, in the long

parlor. There was the short corridor which gave on
the breakfast room, then the hall, and the stair to
the Justice Room. The route was clear in Murray's
mind but he could not explain it to his companion.

The Barker steered him to a chair and he fell
into it dazed. This time he *was* through, and he
knew it. With a sigh he slid from the chair to the
floor at the Barker's shabby boots.

That final struggle had indeed almost finished
Murray and put an end to the American line of the
Lyon clan. When he came into clear focus with his
world again it was to lie weakly in the great cavern
of the Justice Room bed, eat as might a small child
from a bowl held by Mrs. Clagget, whom he had
no will left to combat. He received the attentions
of the local apothecary—whose skill Mrs. Clagget
held in the lowest contempt, trusting more in her
own secret herb concoctions as restoratives and
fever fighters. And he heard the housekeeper and
Knapp dispute over details of his nursing with no
care as to who would be the victor.

Murray gathered dreamily that he had had a
sharp bout of lung fever, from which the expecta-
tion of his recovery had been far from sanguine.
How many days had dropped out of his life he had
no idea before one morning when, waking with an
unusually clear head and a new interest in his
surroundings, he noted the curtains of the bed had
been pulled well open, and, at the casement window,
a bar of sun struck in to enliven dark oak and
faded tapestry, disclosing in addition a young man
at his ease.

The sun turned that brown head ruddy, accented
the curves of a well-cut mouth, outlined the deter-

mined chin. That certain restlessness Murray remembered, that hair-trigger alertness, as if danger was to be expected from any corner of the horizon, no longer tensed the slight body. Kevin had a book propped open on the window ledge, but he was not reading. Rather he was gazing out as if what lay beyond the walls of Garth Holme was soothing.

"I take it I've been hung in the hedge a trifle." Murray was vaguely surprised at the loud tone of his own voice and how it seemed to disturb the drowsy content of the room.

The Barker turned and got to his feet with some of his old-time speed. His book, disregarded, hit the floor with a thump as he crossed the sun-barred floor to the dais of the big bed, inspecting its occupant narrowly, growing relief mirrored on his face.

"You're havey-cavey now," he observed judiciously.

"Oh, in the pink." Murray did not stir on his pillows; that activity at the moment seemed too fatiguing. "How long have I been out?"

"Close to a fortnight. You managed to hand us all a fine fright, cully."

"Us? Who are us?"

"Those precious Claggets. Lord, you'd think you were their son the way they wrap you in wool and fuss over you! Knapp, Furth, half the village. It's been put about that the 'Traders' near murdered the young master by throwin' him in that crypt, and they ain't so popular hereabout since!"

Murray waved that bit of news aside and plunged

into what he deemed more important matters. "Has Stukley shown—Trews?"

Those here the ones he had to face with a clear head and more strength of body than he could muster at that moment. He hoped that neither had come to Garth Holme. Kevin was shaking his head reassuringly.

"No one from the outside, save the apothecary. Poor devil, he was half frightened to death by Mrs. Clagget. She's a woman of iron, ain't she?"

There was another point on which Murray needed information. The Barker might have been reading his mind at that moment, for he came directly to the point.

"Me—they think I'm a cove what has had dealin's with you over horses. You was held up by a highwayman, see," a shadow grin touched Kevin's mouth and his red-brown eyes danced, "and I comes upon you laid out and gaspin' like a fish. You lays up at my place, where I does a bit o' breedin' and trainin', nice bit o' land in the downs. Got all that, cully? Well, then, when we starts for here we is lost in the fog and them smugglers mixes in. That's the tale I has been spreadin' around. They seem to take it right and tight."

"Neat enough." Murray admired the logic of the story. There were holes in it for one who knew more of the facts, but to those of the household it should hold together for awhile. But to have been out of things for a fortnight! He frowned and moved restlessly on his pillows. That was too long a period of inaction for now. He had a feeling that the quicker some move was made on the Barker's behalf, the better. Stukley was not going to have

Kevin handed over to him, Murray was sure on that point, very sure. All the influence the House of Lyon could muster would be expended toward getting the Barker a full pardon for the past.

"I can't understand why Stukley hasn't turned up." He had been half expecting to find the ex-Runner at Garth Holme before him, trusting in Stukley's guess they would head in that direction.

"You thought he might be here?" again the reading of his thoughts.

"I believed that he might guess I would head for here when I did not follow him to London."

Then he understood how that might sound to the other. Kevin was again rubbing the wrist where the irons had chafed his pistol hand.

"We have to have Stukley," Murray said slowly. "He's been tracing the links between you and Whyte. He, beyond anyone, I think, can prove you are a Lyon. We need that proof."

"We could get more out of Whyte." Kevin seated himself on the edge of the bed near one of the foot posters.

Murray answered that with a nod. "Yes, there are a great many questions the dear Captain could answer, were we able to persuade him into it."

Kevin stopped rubbing his wrist, now he flexed his fingers, and the trigger one twitched. "I disremember when I did aught I would enjoy more than doin' that persuadin'. But the Cap'n ain't green. He's milled his way out of plenty of narrow goes. You still believe this tale he's tweaked you with—that I'm a cousin of yours?"

Murray did not reply but gestured to Kevin to be quiet. The embroidered hangings of the bed were pulled across the foot and he could not see the door from where he lay. But he knew that some-one stood there.

"Come in!" he called.

Some of Murray's tension was communicated to Kevin. His hand went into the breast of his coat. But he did not stir from his perch as they heard the uneven footfalls on the floor. Nor did the Barker breathe the faster as Edward Stukley came into view.

"Lord Farstarr," he greeted, "*and* Mr. Kevin Lyon!"

"Doin' the civil to the sick, Mr. Stukley?" Kevin inquired with a lazy drawl which did not in the least deceive either of his hearers.

"That and bringin' a post bag of new such as you young devils should be glad to have poured out." He favored them both with a nutcracker grin.

"I've one remembrance from you that has played the devil with me already," Murray commented with a certain waspishness. "You shoot altogether too straight for a dark night, Stukley."

"Nay m'lud, that was one of Alf's pops as got you. Were it mine you'd be pushin' up graveyard dirt now, not a-lyin' here all snug and tight, at-tended by your lovin' young cousin."

"Then it *is* true!" Kevin interrupted.

"True, maybe, only we've got to do some provin' of it here and there. First thing, we've got to put fist on the Captain."

Kevin straightened. "I can do that!"

Stukley surveyed him sourly. "Can you now? Well, maybe we'll be askin' of you to do just that."

14

Hue and Cry

"Just a minute," Murray broke in, "we are not so comfortably circumstanced, and this signifies talking about. Stukley, there is no such person as the Barker at Garth Holme, nor was he ever here. That I now harbor a kinsman of mine is all that need concern anyone. That is final!"

His chin was up in challenge as his gaze centered on Stukley's scarred and stubborn face. If the ex-Runner was still bound tightly in the service of the law, then their ways had better part here and now. In the short space of silence following, Murray began a feverish plan for sending Kevin out of the country until his postion could be cleared. Broome's lugger might ferry him across the channel until this tangle was resolved. However, it appeared that all that would not be necessary, for Stukley showed no surprise.

"So that's the way it shapes up, m'lud? Well, if you take the high hand," one of his eyelids moved in a slow wink, "what's a cove like me got to say in the matter? Any bridle-cull what was roostin' here could make a bolt for it 'fore a Runner could come down from town—if I seed such a cully hangin' about, which I don't. Me, I ain't no more an officer with the right of layin' a famble on a cove's shoulder and tellin' him to come 'long now."

"You were quick enough to help take a man in at Willingham," Murray did not trust so easy a victory.

"That was 'fore we found out as there was a devilish deep game goin' on and that the law has been set up to do someone's nasty work for 'em. Tell me," he swung to Kevin, "that there wagoner, he warn't no real tramper, was he?"

"He was Whyte's man Jory," Kevin had relaxed once more, his hands laced about one knee as he lounged at the foot of the bed.

Stukley nodded briskly. "Flyin' high, ain't they? The Captain, he musta took a dislike to your face."

Kevin laughed. "More like to my manners. If he could give me a bit of the home-brewed, without dirtyin' his own fambles, mind you, he'd move in fast. Him and me, we don't pull together, and that's the truth of it.''

"But we need Whyte?'' Murray demanded with some impatience.

Stukley leaned back in his chair, his hands folded piously over his waistcoat, and Murray had a fleeting memory of the elegant Captain making steeples with his white fingers in the candle lit Book Room of Starr House. Stukley and the Captain were both, in their separate ways, very dangerous men.

"There's them as would like to see the Captain right enough,'' Stukley agreed. "Only Whyte, he's a lively man, quick off the mark, as the sayin' goes. Item: We has one young cove (one that was no loss) with a knife hole in him. That hole was made by a shiv as we has knowledge of and what don't belong to the Captain—nay, it belongs to one who might have had good reason to use it on that there corpse, believin' at the time that his victim was someone as was his enemy. The Captain would be the first to point that out—were we to ask it—a-shakin' his head over it mournful all the while.

"Item two: We has a story out of the Captain's own mouth about a missin' heir what he can support (or so he says, and I'll believe that he speaks the truth for once in his life) if you don't ease his pocket to forget the same.''

"The which I have no intention of doing!'' Murray snapped.

"Item three: we now has amongst us a young man what the Captain believes is that heir, is so sure of the fact that he tries to get him removed out of the game 'fore it really begins—that young man bein' you.'' He pointed to Kevin, who neither admitted nor denied that identification.

"Item four: now when he has a lot of questions to answer, Whyte, he takes to cover and vanishes away. Though I has turned Lunnon up and about and shaken it good to get him out these past seven days or more. We can dig and pick and maybe come up with what he knows, takin' it in bits and patches and puttin' it together. But that'll cost us a mite of time. And time's what we hasn't much of. You may say, m'lud, as how you has a kinsman livin' here with you. But supposin' that there cousin or such, as you name him, goes out for a mite of a walk or a ride when you ain't along to put the right name to him. Then comes up some bully boy as wants to make a name with the beaks and—he's piked! Maybe you can get him out of Newgate or wherever they stow him, but maybe you can't. Any way around you have trouble and tongues clackin' all nasty—with maybe questions of shivs and such comin' out the whiles. Whyte sent Jory to pull in this cousin of your'n before. What's to prevent him doin' the same again!''

"So—what *do* we do?'' Murray wanted to know.

"We hunts down the Captain,'' Stukley replied simply, ''as I has said before. We finds him 'fore he gets beyond reachin'.''

"How?''

Stukley jerked a thumb at the window. "Over the water.''

"But we're at war. He'd have the devil of a time shipping out across channel.''

"Aye?'' Stukley smiled grimly. ''If he was re-

ally drove to it he could let the press pick him
up—it would take a deal to pry him back out of
the navy. But I'm thinkin' he ain't that desperate.
The Captain, he likes to lie soft, he ain't goin' to
find no goosedown mattress on a gun deck in a
frigate. Nay, there's easier ways to slip away. You
has 'em right here in Tregarth, m'lud, what will
set a man across water with no questions asked,
long as he lays the right number of roundboys in
their hands. Just like they brings in a man now and
then what has had a price laid on him by those
overseas. We at Bow Street knows about that.
There's farms in the backlands not too far from the
coast what have strangers living' under their roofs
very quiet, strangers what warn't never born nor
breeched on this here island. Aye, were he minded
to it, the Captain could get hisself away all slick
and clean. Only I ain't thinkin' as how he has
moved in that direction yet.''

"Why not?"

" 'Cause the Captain, he ain't one to believe as
how the game's ended 'fore it got a good start, and
him left holdin' all the low cards. He'll be thinkin'
that you Lyons will be in a tweak to keep it under
the table, as it were, that you're afraid of his
wagglin' his jaw too free. He maybe thinks as how
if he were found you might see him quieted proper
and quick—but not by law ways. He thinks you'll
be 'fraid of the law as he is, and for good reason.
That's what'll be windin' 'bout in his head now.''

Kevin nodded agreement to that. "You has him
to rights, Mr. Stukley. He fancies hisself too much
to cut line and go if he believes there's even half a
chance left of winnin'. But I have those in Lunnon

what will talk freer to me than to any man who ever carried the stave.''

''I won't say nay to that. Only does you go up to Lunnon a-huntin' for such and gets the clap on the shoulder from the Runners—who'll likely be told where they can take you up—then how are we ahead?''

''There must be something we can do!'' Murray shifted on the pillows again. It was an interesting enough discussion, but he could see nothing of value coming out of it.

''It's a waitin' game.'' But there was a note of dissatisfaction in Stukley's voice as well. It was plain that underneath he was as impatient as Murray.

''There's one thing we might do,'' Murray suggested. ''Through Trews, can't we start suing for a pardon for the Barker? Then we wouldn't have to fear betrayal on that score.''

Stukley's head was cocked to one side. ''Do we have a lost heir and proof he is that, then we can fight for a pardon. Do we have no proof, we has a real mill on our hands.''

''So we just sit and wait? For what?'' Murray demanded.

''For the Captain to move,'' returned Stukley promptly. ''Look at him now, m'lud. He must know as how you has dropped out of sight. He is not sure whether you knows how he set up that pretty case against you, using your shiv and all. He knows as how the Barker was nabbed and got away again. But he don't know as how you and the Barker has got together. I don't see as how he could learn that. If he can get the Barker out of the way, he thinks as how he has you—right like this!" Stukley held up his right fist and closed it slowly as if he were crushing some small, weak thing. "So he'll get tired of playin' it peevy, he'll want to stir about and find you, find the Barker. To do that he'll move so we can lay ogles on him. We has a watch on Jory and we keeps that tight. If he goes to the Captain, if he gets a message from Whyte, we'll know it right off. We has a man in Lunnon with his ogles clapped tight on where the Captain takes his run when he's to home. We has a cat planted by every mousehole as we knows of. Sooner or later we has *him*!" He brought that clenched fist down on his knee with some force.

"I don't like waiting."

Stukley gave Murray his lopsided grin. "Neither does the Captain, m'lud, you can lay a pony on that. And into the bargain, with you clapped between sheets and not yet steady on your pins, it's better to wait it out so you'll be hale enough to take a hand when you *are* needed. And you," he turned to Kevin, "keep close."

But the other looked obstinate. "There's somethin' I've got to do."

Murray had a flash of understanding. "Bargee! He's not been found?"

"Not yet." Kevin's face was sober. "He wasn't taken by the smugglers. And he hasn't tracked me down as he would have done if he'd seen how we was laid by the heels that night."

"Bargee? That's the lad what's deef and dumb?"

"Deef," Kevin corrected him, "but not dumb— though he can't talk proper, not hearing aught to answer and so learn the rightful words. He can play stupid, but I don't want him nabbled by some parish officer.''

Stukley nodded with some degree of violence. ''Right enough! Pass the word around in the village. They has their ways of tellin' and learnin' what goes on in the country, bein' interested in the 'free trade' as most of 'em are.''

''Only Bargee ain't goin' to come along of one as he don't know,'' Kevin explained. ''He's apt to fall afoul of any as tries to bring him here unknowin'. So best I ride about and do some askin' on my own.''

''That is as rabbit brained a speech as I ever heard.'' Stukley's scorn was vast. ''Ain't I just been dinnin' into your ears as how you might be prigged doin' that very thing? You plays an undergame and plays it peevy when you sits down to roll the bones with that Captain. We'll lay a net for your ding boy, then you can go all quiet and lead him by the nose ring. But 'less you wants to cry rope on yourself and all of us, you don't go trottin' around on your own!''

Kevin appeared unconvinced, but Murray backed the ex-Runner.

''We can search the country through Furth, and through the 'gentlemen.' They owe us something for that kidnapping. Surely there isn't much going on hereabouts that they haven't had wind of.''

So they decided, if reluctantly on Kevin's part. There was another meeting for discussion—which got little farther, since any plans they might make depended upon the moves of the Captain. It was finally agreed that Murray should write a letter of introduction for Stukley to give to Trews, and that

the ex-Runner lay the matter of the missing heir
and Captain Whyte's story before the lawyer—
though the part dealing with the Barker's activities
was only to be touched upon very lightly. Those
remaining at Garth Holme were to do nothing
more until they had news from London.

Stukley left early the next morning. Kevin was
restless, insisting several times in the course of a
too long day that he could have added impetus to
the search had he only been turned loose to pick
up his own information in the slums of St. Giles
and lower Westminister. In fact, so detailed became his descriptions of what he might be able to
do, that Murray was slowly persuaded to his way
of thinking, fascinated as he was with these graphic
accounts of a totally new London, one he had seen
only the fringe of during his meeting with Stukley.

There were cities within cities. My Lord Farstarr
might know one, then there was that of the "cits,"
the city merchants, and a third and fourth in which
Kevin had fought for his existence, all as strange
to one another as if planted upon separate continents.

A little stung by Kevin's assumption of superior-
ity in being able to take care of himself in such
surroundings, Murray launched into a few of the
more daunting events of his own past, countering a
vivid account of a hanging in which the principal
actor was a close acquaintance, with the activities
of a victorious Creek war party, until the other
blinked at him, for the moment silenced.

"You was shoutin' things like that when the
fever had you," Kevin commented. "But I thought
it was dreams. So that's why you painted your
face at Strumper's. These Indians of yours, they

do it to fright the enemy when they go to war. Well,'' he considered the point, ''happens they got them an idea there. You couldn't pull paint off a phiz to see what's under, like you can a scarf. A man could point a pop at his next neighbor and no one the wiser!''

''I wouldn't encourage it,'' Murray hastened to give warning. He knew that Kevin remained sceptical of the story that he was the Earl of Starr, and it would require almost as much proof to convince him as it would to satisfy Trews. If Kevin took it into his head to cut free of them now and live by the road again, there was little Murray could do to stop him, save turning him over to the law, which he would never do.

If he were out of bed and about, he could be a better restraining influence. They might search for Bargee together. To do what he might to counteract Kevin's restlessness Murray summoned Furth and Clagget and set in motion the hunt for Bargee. In addition he had a chilling interview with Holgrave which was very much to the point.

Though the lord of the manor had no intention of aiding the Preventive Officers against the people of Tregarth, he did want the ''Traders'' to understand that the crypt formally dedicated to the burial of Lyons was to be returned to that purpose only, that it was to be sealed at once and never used again as one of the way stations of inland runs. It was a command Holgrave might receive unhappily, but one he had to obey.

Within two days Murray had found his feet to the extent of moving from bed to chair by the window. It was going into early fall now, but the weather was warm and mild and there was a wealth of well-tended bloom in the garden. The sight of the outdoors, the touch of breeze through a discreetly open casement, made him long to be out. He guessed how much more the necessary constraint must chafe Kevin. From his window Murray watched that young man wandering around on the paths below, studying the grotesque shapes of the yew elephants, sitting on the bench by the pond. However, so far Kevin had held to orders and had not gone beyond the park wall.

By the end of the week Murray was able to walk those paths himself. However, his impatience with the very slow move of events was fast reaching the boiling point. There had been no messages from Stukley nor Trews, no word at all from London. Nor had anyone heard from Bargee. He was not in the least surprised to have Kevin announce over Mrs. Clagget's excellent dinner that he had had enough of this inactivity and intended to ride out on his own the next morning.

"M'lord," Clagget's craggy countenance had taken on a grimmer cast. "They do say in the village as how the Searchers be out on the headlands. Hurrell and that hell hound of his'n is a-castin' this way and that. He's mortal angry over them takin' away the solders."

For it had been abruptly decided that soldiers were needed more for the war than for the hunting down of smugglers. The lesser nuisance on the "free trade" would have to wait upon the leisure of the military. While the press gang, on a second visit to Tregarth, had had no luck either. Murray had not heard of Broome since the night he had

helped the lugger Captain in the inn free-for-all,
but he passed along through Holgrave a message
that Lord Farstarr had a burning interest in anyone
seeking a secret passage aboard, and he hoped
Broome would keep that in mind.

It appeared that Clagget's information concerning the present activities of the Preventive Officer
were merely introductory remarks to something of
great importance.

"That one always turns up where he ain't
wanted!"

Murray crumbed a bit of cake. "What has Hurrell
got to do with Garth Holme?"

"There are them, m'lord, as would like to have
speech with your lordship was Hurrell to make
hisself scarce. And this day he is summoned to
report to his betters."

Kevin stirred, Murray threw his napkin on the
table.

"If you was to feel up to a bit of a ride now,
m'lord, up the way of the Searcher, maybe—"

"An idea. Coming, Kevin?"

The other was already on his way to the door.
"Try to leave me behind!"

They trotted along at a sober pace through the
village, coming to the ship's figurehead which
served as an inn sign. Murray grinned at his memory of his last visit there. At least there would be
no tangling with the press gang today.

Seth Ford hailed them from the door and his pot
boy hurried out with two tankards of a steaming
brew, handing them up to the riders. Murray sniffed
appreciatively at the spicy smell.

"You've an empty house today, Ford?"

" 'Tis early yet, m'lord. Was you thinkin' of ridin' up a little, say to the headlands?"

"That's about it, Ford."

" 'Tis good to see you out and about again, m'lord. It's a pleasant day for ridin'." He collected the tankards and they rode on at the same quiet trot, past the lane along which Strumper's circus had found its way to Tregarth, with the rock of the Searcher and his "Pocket" their goal ahead.

Kevin pulled rein as they turned into the sweep of scrub land collaring the cliff. He turned to Murray with a slight smile.

"If I was a cautious cove now," he observed, "I'd have my barker ready to me fist. This country looks a mite too bare."

Murray had that same premonition. Yes, in the sunlight the hill was bare of all save themselves. Yet he could not rid himself of the feeling that just the opposite was true. That awareness acted as an irritant. He was suddenly very tired of all mysteries, of hints and secrets. If any one had a message for Lord Farstarr, let him walk up to the front door of Garth Holme and deliver it properly!

He had already tightened rein to bring his mount about, when his horse pricked ears. There was the shrill, ear-splitting whistle of a small boy giving all his force to a warning signal—and the snarl of a dog.

The slope up to the cliff verge erupted with life as a slight, thin figure broke from the shadowed side of the craggy "Searcher," stood for a bewildered moment staring at them. A black dog leaped from under a bush, but the fugitive gave a convulsive bound and gained a precious second or two.

The dog overleaped, skidded on the turf, fighting
to turn. It did not give tongue as might a hound of
the chase, but ran mute, which in some way underlined its grim purpose.

Then Hurrell arose out of the ground almost
directly before Murray, his face a mask of fury.
He was as silent and ominous as the hound, as he
brought out a pistol. Three other men, muskets in
hand, broke from cover. But none of them attempted to fire at the flying figure. Either they did
not trust their aim, or they feared hitting the hound.

Kevin shouted, though the fugitive could not
hear that cry, and urged his mount up slope. Murray cried a warning to Hurrell, only to know, by
the look on the Preventive Officer's face, that
nothing would make the other recall the dog. With
teeth bared in a snarl not unlike that of his hound,
the other was aiming with the pistol at Kevin,
whose back presented an excellent target. Murray
leaned from the saddle and brought the butt of his
riding crop, weighted with iron for the smashing
of gate locks during hunting season, across the
man's arm.

Hurrell howled, as if giving tongue to the cry
the hound withheld. The pistol thudded to the turf
from numbed fingers. But he stooped and snatched
it up awkwardly with his left hand and tried to
snap it at Murray. When it missed fire through his
clumsiness, he flung it wildly, striking Murray's
horse and sending the mount into a tantrum Murray had difficulty controlling.

At that moment Satan at last bayed, a single,
deep-throated roar. That sound was echoed by a
shout of protest from Kevin. For the hound had

closed with his quarry who had been forced back on a narrow tongue of cliff running into the sea. The great beast leaped for the throat of the slim figure and they both lost footing, spiraling out and over.

Murray closed his eyes for an instant. He could vision only too well what was below—rock teeth wet by the pounding combers. He had no desire to see what must lay among them now. But he forced himself to ride up to where Kevin, white faced, had flung himself from the saddle and gone running out to the last tip of land.

Murray's horse picked its way with caution, refusing to be hurried by its rider, as if it suspected the firmness of the ground under hoof. Murray dropped from the saddle and went on afoot.

Under the light of the sun the water washed golden. But the scrap of beach below was mercifully bare. So sure had he been of sighting horror that Murray could not believe that at first. Then he studied the rock. Nothing. The sea must have swallowed both man and dog.

"Bargee!" It was a shout of hope, of would-be encouragement from Kevin. Murray pawed at his shoulder, drawing him back from the lip of the drop.

Seconds later he saw it, too, a black shape breasting the waves in toward shore, fighting feebly against the power of the breakers. It humped through the surf. A man crawling on hands and knees?

That had been too much to hope for. The shape raised a flat, canine head and gave voice to a mournful, belling howl which was echoed weirdly from all the crannies and pits in the cliff's face.

15

City Within City

Words were sing-songing from Kevin's mouth, an unintelligible babble. His face was green-white beneath its brown weathering. He stood for a moment or two staring down at the howling dog, as if measuring the distance which lay between him and a just vengeance. Then he turned and ran for his horse. Leaping into the saddle, he pounded along the edge of the cliff seeking a way to the beach.

Murray, not only sick from what he had witnessed, but now thoroughly alarmed by what he read in

Kevin's expression—or rather lack of expression—
set his mount after the other, taking no heed of the
shouts of the revenue men.

A boy scuttled across the scrub pasturage as
they pounded along the gradually sinking line of
cliff. Murray recognized Tom Broome. At his hail
the child only hunched his shoulders, as if fearing
to have a lash laid across them, and sped on.

Kevin wheeled his mount sharply to the right,
leaping the animal recklessly from rock and clay to
sand awash by the sea. Then he headed back
almost without pause toward the point where the
hound and Bargee had gone over. A broken leg for
the horse and perhaps a broken neck for Kevin
were the foremost fears in Murray's mind, but he
sent his own horse along the same track, the big
mount snorting its displeasure as water dashed
high from under its hooves, spraying its rider almost to the waist.

Through it all sounded the shouting from the
cliff head, echoed now by a distant din from the
village where Tom Broome must have alerted the
people. A fishing boat was edging in to land,
drawn by the activity along the shore. Murray
welcomed it. Perhaps those in it could watch
for. . . . He swallowed, fighting down the churn-
ing in his middle.

It must have taken only a moment or two for
Kevin to reach the miniature cove where Satan had
swum ashore. But he had not dismounted, instead
he struggled with his horse. For the huge hound,
with the sagacity of an animal trained to make
himself a dangerous weapon in one man's service,
had backed to the far end of a half-moon of sand

and water-washed rock and stood, his lips lifted in an ugly snarl of stark menace.

Kevin's mount, reading that aright, refused to go nearer. Murray, his only weapon the loaded butt of his crop, called frantically to Kevin to stay where he was.

Only the other could not be reasoned with. He jumped from his horse, in his hand the pistol he had depended upon through so many years of danger. The mount, freed from his control, splashed back toward Murray.

Kevin steadied the pistol, aimed at the crouching dog. Satan had been well schooled. Even as the man's trigger finger tightened, he sprang, flecks of white foam showing on his blunt muzzle. The shot rang out, re-echoed from the cliff. Kevin dodged, but not before teeth closed on his sleeve, ripping away stout cloth as one might rip apart a sheet of paper.

Murray's horse was not happy, but it went forward under his rider's urging. The dog whipped about to face this new enemy, giving Kevin a precious moment in which to reverse the heavy pistol as a club. Then Satan made his choice and leaped at the man on foot, marking him as the more easily handled of his two enemies.

Kevin struck to kill, fending the beast away from his throat with the blow. But that had not landed cleanly and, though the dog gave a sharp yelp of pain, he was far from knocked out. Murray spurred in and struck down again and again with his crop. It was a dirty, nasty business, but there was no other way to finish it and save Kevin. The horse he bestrode, aroused to a fury, provided the end, rearing until Murray had to give his full attention to keeping his seat, and coming down to smash the injured hound into the sand with the full weight of its murderous fore hooves.

Murray fought a spasm of retching, refusing to look down. Instead he went to Kevin. The latter had pushed back against the cliff wall to allow the horse full room. His right sleeve was in tatters, the shirt beneath torn as well, and his stock had been pulled loose and mouthed, showing how near Satan had come to bringing him down. His face was still expressionless—his eyes cold and hard—and he held the clubbed pistol ready. Then he glanced once at the thing mashed into the sand and straightened with a sigh of relief.

"Devil."

Murray could agree with that estimation of the hound. Satan, because of his training, was a worse weapon to turn upon any man than the most accurate firearm. The utter savagery of the hound's pursuit of Bargee along the cliff, and the way the dog had faced up to them both, fighting with a wolfish ferocity overlaid with the cunning born of patient instruction. Hurrell had indeed loosed a devil within Tregarth when he had brought his beast in on patrol. They were only lucky that they had no more tragedies to reckon up to a horrible total.

"Ahhhh—" that was a formless howl, resembling Satan's when the hound had emerged from the sea.

Murray glanced back along the shore. Hurrell was pelting toward them at a run by the verge of the waves, taking no heed to his going, so that once he fell face down. But he scrambled up, to limp on, pistol in his left hand. When he caught sight of what the horse had left trampled, he came to a skidding stop, his face twisted. Then his head swung from one to the other of the young men before him, as if he were a bull about to charge.

Perhaps because Kevin was afoot, or because of his disordered clothing, showing Satan's master that he had been the hound's prey, Hurrell made his choice. Only that short pause before the Preventive Man charged gave the other time to prepare, and he raised his clubbed pistol in defense.

Murray, fearing to see murder done, grabbed at Hurrell as the man passed him—too late. Hurrell's blow was fended by Kevin, but the numbing jolt of one weapon meeting the other must have shaken the younger man, for his pistol flew from hand, leaving him unarmed. He threw himself forward and buried his head against Hurrell's chest, carrying the Searcher off balance and over into the sand. Hurrell's hand arose, the pistol gripped by its long barrel, ready to swing butt down. Murray was afoot now, his crop poised. But a sudden frantic squirm from Kevin rolled Hurrell out of striking distance for the moment.

Murray reversed the crop, swinging its leather flap to give a stinging stroke across Hurrell's flailing legs. Then he dared attempt no more in the fury of their struggle.

Someone sped by him shouting. He was dimly aware of several men carrying a dragging wet thing among them. It was thrown over the fighters, tangling them both into submission. Kevin's set face, criss-crossed by a length of fishing net, was

turned up to Murray. From the well-trussed Hurrell
burst a black litany of obscenity.

"Good catch, mates!" That was Penhern, mate
of the Lottery, who supervised the oddest netting
that that coast had probably ever seen. "Mister
Hurrell," he accented the "Mister" with a bite in
his voice, "if you needs you some coolin' off, that
you is gettin'!"

Hurrell was deftly rolled away from his opponent,
though Kevin was inadvertently dragged about in
the process, until he lay in the path of the incom-
ing waves and sputtered as the sea water curled
over him.

"Don't drown him!" Murray was afraid of the
temper of the Tregarth men, fearing their fury
would bring them to the brink of doing murder.
They had long hated Hurrell, and what had happened today was setting a match to well-dried
timber. It would be only too easy to go too far
with their rough idea of justice, leaving a corpse to
be accounted for to the authorities, with swift
official retribution wreaked in return upon the whole
village. "Get him out!"

Kevin, freed of the net by solicitous hands, sat
up, nursing his wrist. He did not support Murray's
demand and from his utter lack of interest in the
matter one could well deduce that he wanted to see
the men of Tregarth proceed. But Murray seized
the shoulder of the nearest net man, pulling him
back with what strength he could muster.

"Get him out, you fools! You don't want to
face a charge of murder!"

"Hop to it, lads." It was Penhern who gave
him the necessary backing. "His lordship has the

right of it. Cool the cove off, right smartly, but we don't want to make a hangin' ploy of this.''

So Hurrell, still wrapped in the net, was dragged ashore once more. The moment he was out of the pound of the waves he fought against the ropes which held him with all the ferocity and vigor of a stranded shark.

As might a shark, he showed his teeth as he spit out threats to embrace the future of all who stood there, allowing him to fight his way out of the entanglement as best he could.

Save for preventing murder Murray had no defense for the Preventive Man. He waited until Hurrell was again on his feet and then uttered his own ultimatum.

''Get off this land! Because of your devilish dog a poor afflicted lad has been driven to his death. Be sure your superiors will have a full accounting from me on this day's ill work. And I think if you will look about you, you will know that you shall not sleep safe of night any more, should you linger hereabouts!''

''I'm in the King's service—you attack me at your peril!'' Hurrell's fury was sinking inwards, to become something colder, far more deadly. He no longer had Satan as his instrument to terrorize, but he would nourish hatred against those who had destroyed the hound.

''I don't care who or what you are, Hurrell. But be out of Tregarth and off my land before moonrise, if you value your neck. Look about you, man, and see that flight alone may save your wretched life.''

Hurrell's hot eyes, which had been glaring at Murray, now did flicker briefly from face to face

around the circle of grim men who ringed him in
on that scrap of beach. He could take no comfort
from the presence of three of his fellows who were
halfheartedly lingering a little beyond.

Armed though they were, they gave no indication that they were prepared to back their leader
and challenge the Tregarth men. What Hurrell read
in the villagers' faces convinced him that Murray
was speaking the whole truth.

He flung off the last strand of net, gave it a
vicious kick, and without another word or a single
backward look, pushed through the crowd and
started in the opposite direction from the village,
along the shore, his men rather sheepishly trailing
behind him.

One of the fishermen spat after them. ''Happen
they don't put on more sail soon, the tide'll grind'em
on the rocks proper.''

''Let it be the sea as does it and not us,''
Penhern answered. ''King can't hang waves if
they is one Searcher less by sunrise.''

Murray went to Kevin and drew aside the tatters
of coat and shirt sleeve. ''Did his teeth break
flesh?'' he asked. But to his relief the quick examination showed no bleeding gash in the skin of the
other's arm.

Kevin moved out of his grasp and went across
to pick up the pistol he had dropped, inspecting it
before he stowed it away. ''I'm well enough!''

''Good riddance,'' remarked one of the men as
he kicked sand over the trampled body of the
hound. ''Now maybe honest men can move freely
o' nights without no teeth meetin' in their throats—

or the thought of that happenin'!'' And that was Satan's only burial and epitaph.

A villager brought up Kevin's horse and he mounted, still-faced and quiet. He was staring over the heaving surface of the sea, as if hoping against all odds to see a swimmer riding in upon the waves. The sun was into late afternoon as they picked their way along the edge of the strand toward the village.

They found a crowd awaiting them there. Three-quarters of Tregarth was milling about, with the wildest rumors tossed from one man to the next, embroidered, retold at the top of everyone's lungs in a babblement of confusion. But there was one knot of men and women, gathered on the wharf, which attracted Murray's attention.

Something dramatic enough to pull them away from the exciting events along the cliff must be in progress there. Murray rode down to see what it could be. After one glance over the heads of the group at what lay in their midst, he shouted for Kevin.

It did not seem possible that all that water could soak out of the sodden rags covering that limp young body. Max Broome knelt over the unconscious boy, pressing in regular rhythm on the lower ribs, forcing more frothy liquid from the wedged mouth by his efforts.

Kevin took one glance, dismounted, and thrust himself through the crowd, to go on his knees beside Broome. They worked on in turns until, long minutes later, they believed Bargee would live. He was carried to the carriage summoned from the manor, and taken to Garth Holme, in-

stalled in a bed there under Mrs. Clagget's fierce
guardianship. Hot bricks were stowed about his
starved, shivering body, with the promise of a
thorough soaking in brandy should he show any
signs of lung fever. A remedy to which Mrs.
Clagget partially ascribed Murray's own recovery.

Murray was back in the Justice Room, propped
against pillows, so tired that he believed he could
not keep his eyes open a second longer. However
when someone knocked at the door he summoned
up the strength to call.

"Come in."

Kevin, his torn coat and stock discarded, but
still with a flutter of rags to serve him for one shirt
sleeve, moved soft-footed to the side of the huge
bed.

"Bargee?" Murray feared that the boy might
have taken a turn for the worse.

Kevin grinned. "Mrs. Clagget is a mare with a
colt—she sent me out of his room for bein' a
'clumsy-hand ninny-pate,' " he quoted. Then he
sighed. "Thanks to your smugglin' Captain, he's
safe enough. But it was only luck that that dory-
man cast close to the rocks where he got a handhold.
To my knowledge he's no swimmer. Nay, Bargee's
right enough. There's somethin' else."

Murray half drowsed and wished his visitor would
come to the point. He was drugged with fatigue,
buried in a rising fog of sleep. Kevin's voice
reached him so faintly he might share Bargee's
affliction.

"—tomorrow—" Murray caught only that one
word, but Kevin was done and looking to him as if
he expected some pertinent answer. What was the

other going to do tomorrow? Murray made great
effort, pushed higher on his pillows, and tried to
put on at least the outward semblance of alertness.
But he had to ask:

"What's for tomorrow?"

"I'll ride for town," Kevin said calmly. "Bargee
is safe now, that is what has kept me here. But
we've heard naught from Stukley, and I'm not
minded to sit here idle and have my life arranged
for me. There are them in town as will tip me the
word they wouldn't give to Stukley or any of his
breed."

"And what if someone such as Jory points you
out to the Runners?" Murray seized upon the first
counter-argument his fuzzy brain could produce.

Kevin laughed. "I've diddled the lawmen for
years. I warn't lookin' for Jory in Wallingham,
now I'm ready for his tricks."

"Jory is still free. What's to prevent him trying
again?"

"In Wallingham I was out of my rangin' ground.
Jory'd find it hard to do me a mischief in the
quarters where I'm goin'. He'd be beetle headed to
try it, as he'd well know. But I ain't goin' to sit
here flat and just wait!"

"Full of bounce, aren't you?" Murray snapped.
"Well, I can't very well clap you up in the dungeon to keep you under this roof."

"You can trust me to hold the line without
settin' no irons on me."

"No, I can't," Murray retorted. "I'll lay it on
you, though, not to go haring off without a goodbye in the morning."

Kevin went to the window. "By the looks of

them clouds to the east, it's set to come down a soaker. Maybe it'll clear again 'fore morning. I'm not so quick off the mark as to go rampin' off as if I was makin' a bolt for it.'' He came back to the bed and favored Murray with the most open and friendly smile the other had ever seen on that thin, fined-down face. ''Thanks are paltry, ain't they? That was a killin' matter, down by the cliff, if you hadn't taken a hand and got me out.''

''And I'd not be here, if you hadn't brought me, either,'' Murray pointed out swiftly in return.

Kevin shrugged. ''Six o' one, dozen 'tother. We make a good pair. Goodnight, m'lord.''

''The name's Murray! And you'll be ill advised if I don't see you at breakfast in the morning,'' he warned. Kevin, laughing softly, shut the door behind him.

Tired though he was, Murray did not immediately slide into sleep when the other had gone. He was certain that nothing short of physical constraint would keep Kevin at Garth Holme now that his anxiety over Bargee was eased. Unless the boy showed some sign of grave illness in the morning, the Barker would be on his way to London. Murray, whose impatience at the slow course of events equaled that of Kevin's, began a few plans of his own.

So when Kevin came to the Justice Room shortly after dawn the next morning to say goodbye, he found the great bed empty. And he was more than a little disconcerted to be hailed from the breakfast room, entering to face a Murray dressed for traveling, making a good meal under the highly disapproving eye of Clagget. Luckily, Mrs. Clagget

was so occupied with her new charge that Murray
was out of her mind at that moment.

Murray nodded to Kevin and said with a firmness which he hoped would squash all further
remonstrances: "We'll post, Clagget. And Mr.
Kevin rides with me so there's no room for Knapp.
He can come later if I stay in town. I'm in no
mood to pick hedge roses along the way, so see
they put the greys in for the first stage."

"You can't! You're not up to such a scramble."
Kevin's eyes met Murray's and his protest was
stilled. Murray pointed to a waiting platter of cold
beef.

"Best stuff yourself, we'll make few stops."
His calm assumption of authority so carried the
day that neither of them argued more.

The heavy rain of the night before slowed the
chaise for the first few miles. Then, once the mud
holes were well behind, they struck a smart pace
which ate up distance. Murray wedged himself
into a corner with the pillows a vainly protesting
Knapp had insisted upon banking there, and proceeded to nap, the swinging of the chaise being
soothing. He roused when they stopped at a toll
gate or to change horses, accepting wine and bis-
cuits at inn halts. Kevin had sat impatiently pushed
forward in his seat at first, but as the day wore on
he, too, relaxed, though there was little conversation between them.

Murray was in two minds about entering the city
late at night. When he mentioned the possibility of
baiting on the road Kevin looked so mutinous that
he did not enlarge upon it. So they were bouncing
through the dark when the chaise pulled up so

suddenly that Murray was flung quite out of his pillow nest, while Kevin stayed in his seat only by gripping the edge of the window.

Then the door was jerked open, nearly pulling Kevin with it. By the light of a small lantern a pistol, looking quite the size of a cannon, was thrust into view. Kevin stared at that as if stupefied, and then he leaned forward and spat out a sentence in a cant so thick that it was untranslatable, as far as his companion was concerned.

He was answered by a startled exclamation from the masked man holding the weapon. Then came a quick apology.

"Your pardon, gents. No call to be hipped, gents!"

The door was slammed shut. But Kevin had it open again in a second and jumped to the ground, apparently in pursuit of this brother-in-arms. Murray remained where he was, laughing so hard that his damaged ribs ached. When Kevin returned he asked:

"I take it that was a competitor?"

Kevin nodded and there was an odd note of righteous indignation in his voice as he said: "Flyin' high, that one is—*him*, a bridle-cull! Lord, he ain't good for more'n slummin' a ken and priggin' the silver feeders off the table when they is lyin' out in plain sight! *Him* on the bridle lay!" He snorted indignantly. "Well, he won't be keepin' to it long. He's so addle pated some Red Breast will have him in Newgate 'fore the month's out. Too big for his boots—and them stolen ones—by far!"

"I suppose you warned him of the dire results

of incompetence.'' Murray pressed both hands to his sore side and tried to bite down his laughter.

"Aye, I told him. He was scorched, but he won't listen none. Howsoever, he told *me* somethin' more into the pocket." Kevin's professional scorn gave way to satisfaction. "I knows now where I can lay hands on a certain cove as I want to have some chatter with."

In spite of Murray's questions he refused to say any more on the subject, rather lapsed into silence during which he undoubtedly was making plans he intended to put into action as soon as the streets of London closed about them.

However, Murray was firm when they reached Starr House. He refused to consider any move that night, insisting that the very late hour of their arrival made that impossible. On the other hand, he agreed to Kevin's stipulation that, for the present, they would keep their arrival in London a secret and not try to get in touch with Stukley. With such an exchange of concessions they went to bed.

Luckily Kevin was not made of iron and needed sleep. So again Murray, having rested in the chaise, was the first awake. Determined not to allow Kevin to slip through his fingers, vanish into that other city where he might never be found again, he softly opened the other's bedroom door and looked in, to know a vast relief when he saw the bed still occupied.

"What's to do!" Kevin whipped up, his hand going beneath the pillow.

Murray raised his eyebrows. "I assure you," he drawled, "I am not slumming this ken to prig the feeders off the table."

Kevin rubbed his eyes and chuckled. "Cockrow is it? So you thought I might cut and run for it?"

"Not at all. I merely wish to make sure of the fact that I shall be included in any plans you are hatching. I have a fancy to see your side of London."

Kevin favored him with a long, slow, measuring stare which arose from the slippers on his feet, up the rich brocaded dressing gown, to his still uncombed head. "You'll be somethin' out of the ordinary there," he warned.

Murray grinned. "Oh, I'll have your expert advice concerning the right trappings. But I'm going."

Kevin did not match his show of good humor. Instead he was scowling. "You won't find it up to your mark."

"I'm not made of sugar—as you should know—the less for a little wetting here and there."

The other shrugged. "Oh, aye, you've faced up to them forest men. But I've seen a few coves in my time as would set your Indians fair foamin' at the mouth. We'll see, cully, we'll see."

16

Two Lyons Overtake One Jackal

The rackety barking of dogs, several of them giving tongue together, came from behind the rotting boards of a fence. Breaking through that hoarse chorus was a shriller yapping, together with the sound of men's voices. Kevin put his hand to a door of warped planks and motioned Murray on.

It was mid-afternoon and there was sunshine overhead. But, in this sink through which they had been plodding for the past hour or so, that sunlight appeared to afford neither warmth nor any great degree of light. The pitted walls about them might well date back to the London Whittington had known; the stinking, refuse-dammed kennels provided a stench which was the end product of centuries of rottenness and filth.

They had looked in upon gin dens, upon thieves' lodging houses, and in each Kevin had picked up some hint of the trail he was following. An exchange of a word or two in a steaming cook house, the unpleasant odors of which did not apparently daunt any of its crowding customers, had at last brought them here.

The wall door gave them entrance into a yard where a variety of small houses bobbled together from bits of old and broken boards were intended to shelter at least seven dogs, each of which was stoutly tied to its lodging place. None of them was of Satan's massive breed, but all raised a lip in warning as Kevin picked a way down the dead center of the cobbled yard, well out of their lunging reach.

"Bosker's," he indicated the establishment with his thumb. "He shouts brick dust for a lay, and breeds them—bull and pit dogs."

Certainly the degree of temper the beasts displayed might well suggest that the wise would put their money on them in the future, Murray decided, edging around one particularly saturnine canine.

But they had not come to inspect Bosker's quarters, interesting as those might be. The persistent yapping of another dog came from beyond and with it the shouted encouragement of men. A dog fight in progress? Kevin was at a second yard door. Here he was met by a keeper who, in the

unintelligible cant of the district, demanded some
entrance fee. Nor did he allow them beyond that
sagging portal until Kevin parted with the necessary coppers.

Here was a second and slightly larger yard. For
a second or two Murray was vividly reminded of
the cock pit where he and Kevin had had their first
meeting. Though here were no benches for the
spectators, there was a pit sunk in the center of the
place, and that was the focus of the crowd's interest.
His height gave him some advantage and he pushed
forward a step or so to see what was going on.

In the pit was a small, dirty, white terrier, its
ribs plainly marked under its grimy coat. It was
watching with wary alertness a large rat which had
just been dropped from a box trap into the arena.

The rat was large, vicious, and in much better
condition than its enemy. In fact its plumpness
added to Murray's instant adversion. It showed its
teeth at the dog and then flashed about the perpen-
dicular walls of the enclosure, seeking a way out.
The terrier remained where it was, content to let
the rat exhaust its energy in such futile spurts,
keeping well away from that darting head, as the
bared teeth snapped in fear and rage.

At last the grey-brown creature crouched in a
corner, its sides heaving, its beads of eyes almost
glazed with the fatigue of its efforts at escape. The
terrier danced toward it, teasing it into another
spring, another racing about. Then, having judged
the right time to the second, the dog went in,
catching the rat by the neck and snapping its spine
with the practiced twist of a veteran of countless
such battles. The dog's master allowed it to worry

the dead rat for a space and then another trap was brought forward, another fat and frenzied victim loosed.

Kevin paid no attention to the show. Now Murray, his curiosity satisfied, turned away to see the other by the far side of the pit talking to a young man whose clothes were better ordered than those of the men about him, who had a look of sharp intelligence, and who was listening carefully to what Kevin had to say. At last he nodded and edged back through the crowd with Kevin, both of them coming around to where Murray now stood by the gate. The newcomer favored Murray with a slow, appraising stare. The latter's clothes, contrived with Kevin's aid to suit his prowling in this district, were still above neighborhood standards and he looked far too clean. But he had hoped to pass, with Kevin's introduction and backing, as a "flash" cove, the operator of small swindles. And he kept his mouth shut, allowing Kevin the lead, trying to look as much at his ease as he possibly could.

At least, as Kevin had thankfully observed when they had started out, he had no touch of Bow Street. Whatever business might be presumed to attract him to St. Giles and the fearful back alleys there, he would not be reckoned a "nark" ready to turn up some man for the reward. Now, when Kevin's acquaintance looked him over—as some hound might inspect a juicy side of beef hung well out of reach—he was glad he had the other to vouch for him.

"Who's the flash cull?"

"Somone as has a score with him Jory runs

for." Kevin's speech was more slurred than that
he used with Murray, heavily larded with cant.

It seemed that explanation was perfectly acceptable as far as the newcomer was concerned.

"Jory!" He spat eloquently and noisily on the
packed earth of the yard, and with no more questions he went out, back through Bosker's kennel
yard into the noisome lane.

"Got some grease for fists?" he demanded of
Kevin, once they had closed Bosker's wall door
behind them.

Kevin nodded. "When was the Barker ever a
wide boy, Jackdaw? Them what talks will be the
better of it. But I ain't sayin' how, or how much.
Only—you knows the Barker."

Jackdaw nodded briefly. It was apparent that the
Barker had a reputation of some standing in this
community, and he was no wide boy to be easily
done in the eye. He'd pay on results only. Which
was exactly what his informants would expect.

"I take no book oaths," Jackdaw warned them.
"What I hears I tells, but whether it be truth or
not," he shrugged. "If you want to lay the nab on
Jory now—" He launched into a very pungent and
graphic description of the man in question, "why
there's them in plenty to give you the clack on that
run. Come on."

Jackdaw's method of hunting for Jory was an
odd one. They followed his guidance into a court a
little less malodorous than some of the surrounding
territory. The houses which leaned toward one
another across the worn pavement were narrow of
window, black of wall, an excellent background,
if produced in miniature, for some of Holgar's

scenes of horror. Even in the open light of day they were sinister, by night they would provide a setting for nightmares. Murray held stern rein on his imagination as he looked about him.

The one Jackdaw chose to enter offered a mild surprise. Ancient odors did indeed still haunt a long room. But there was a cheerful fire well built up on a wide hearth. A table down the center of the chamber with benches on either side was the core of action for as mixed an assemblage as Murray had ever seen gathered together. A slattern, coarsely handsome of face, nursed on her knee a baby sucking at a cloth pacifier, while she gulped down noisy mouthfuls from a pipkin.

Adjacent to her a neat woman, threadbare as to skirts but with patches and mends making her clothes entire, was checking the contents of a little basket of notions such as could be sold from door to door. Then a lad in worn moleskins and a shiny coat of a generation earlier was eating a potato in its skin with the concentration of one to whom a whole hot potato was a rare event. There were men, too, some in the worn clothes of the humbler trades, others beggars. But the table was reasonably clean, there was order in the room, with the man who presided over the table apparently responsible for it.

He glanced around at their entrance, making no move to rise to meet them. By his broken nose and split ear he might once have tried his luck in the ring. In spite of its battering it was not a brutal face, and there was an air of quiet authority about him which in an odd way suggested Stukley. Though Murray was certain that this grey warrior had never visited Bow Street, unless in custody of one of its officers.

The manager of the lodging asked no questions as Jackdaw strode down the length of the room with as little interest in its inhabitants as if they were invisible. He mounted a stair at the far end, Kevin and Murray on his heels. The muggy heat from the fire in the closed room, the steam from the cooking, the thick scent of unwashed bodies, made a fug which they climbed out of into a wide room above, spread with pallets, a few ragged curtains thrown over cord lines here and there to afford the merest suggestion of privacy.

Their boots awoke a hollow sound from the moldering floorboards as they came to the end of the second room. The Jackdaw produced a massive key from somewhere about his person and turned it gratingly in the door lock. Tugging the warped boards open he gestured for them to step in.

Again Murray was surprised. The lodging house had been better than the courtyard outside would lead the uninitiated to believe. And this small room was infinitely better than the lodging house. It was lighted by a gable in which the window had been rubbed to a measure of cleanliness so that the westering sun struck through. The floor had been swept and the covers of the old poster bed were smoothed. That bed, two stools, an old iron-bound chest, a wall cupboard and a table completed the furnishings. In a window hung a cage in which a black bird hopped and peered very knowingly at them, giving several squawks which their host accepted as a greeting as he went to put a tiny bunch of green stuff between the cage bars. Whereupon the bird fell to picking at it avidly.

"Make yourselves easy!" Their host invited them with a wave at the stools. He went to the cupboard which he unlocked to bring out a jug. The stopper came out of this with a pop which set the bird to croaking excitedly.

"We've a matter of time to think about," Kevin raised a half-protest.

Jackdaw flashed good teeth in a wide grin. In this room he had put off some of his suspicious distrust of the world. "You ain't goin' to make Jory pop out of his hole by wishin' it," he returned reasonably. "We sits us down and wets our whistles. If you casts your ogles 'cross the street there, you'll see Jory on the outgo—if and when he makes a dash for it. But if you're thinkin' of pryin' him out of that shell, you'll do it alone. I ain't wishful for to get my gullet slit! Old Harrow, he keeps this lodgin' free of the rough ones. Where Jory's gone to ground, that's a different sort of roof altogether!"

Murray moved behind Kevin at the window. The house across the court was, in its way, no more dilapidated than the one in which they now sheltered. But all its grimed windows presented black eyes to the outer world, and there was such a sealed look about it that it might have been locked up for the rats, deserted by human beings for centuries.

"So Jory's got company?" Kevin asked.

"There's rats in plenty in there, no matter how empty it looks. He ain't got no coves what loves him, but you stir around in that place and you stirs up the devil! There's them what lays up there that don't want none overlookin' them. Along about night time they goes out. Then we'll be able to tail him.''

Time passed slowly. Jackdaw let his pet out of its cage, dressed it in a small set of a vicar's white bands, bidding it perform. It cawed a sermon from one of the foot posts of the bed, then marched briskly to fight Boney, and died for its country with a solemnity which set Murray and Kevin to laughing, pleasing the big young man with their praises of its cleverness.

Suddenly Kevin, who had moved his stool to establish a guardpost at the window, tensed.

''Jory?''

When he nodded in answer to the Jackdaw's query, the other was on his feet at once. The bird was put back in its cage, and they left hurriedly, passing again through the common room of the lodging without any notice from its burly keeper.

It might almost be that the inhabitants of the buildings about that forgotten court sniffed trouble from afar. For the paved way leading out into the street was deserted as the three came out upon its cobbles. Ahead was a single man, like the Jackdaw dressed more neatly than those they had seen in the common room. He walked at a brisk pace, not as if he feared any pursuit, but rather with the air of one on a definite errand.

Kevin sped forward, the Jackdaw drawing equal with him, Murray a little behind. So they closed in upon the man, each of the two to the fore taking one of his arms in what looked like the casual grip of a friend.

"Jory!" Kevin smiled as he greeted their startled captive. "Now this here is prime! I've been castin' about for you, Jory."

The man tried to stop, he made one quickly checked motion to free himself from their hold. But as he glanced back over his shoulder and saw Murray looming up to cut off any retreat in that direction, he must have realized at once the folly of any struggle against such odds.

"I ain't—" he began in a high tone and then stopped short as if he had bitten his own tongue into silence.

"Don't get on the high ropes now, Jory," Kevin advised him. "We is all friends here. We just wants a few words with you, nice and calm, while you is feeling' stout. Just a few words in a quiet place as we know."

Between them they herded the unfortunate Jory down a short passage, going through a gateway into another yard crowded with piles of decaying and pulpy wood, where one side gave on a small river wharf. Murray had completely lost his way in the twists and turns of the afternoon's journeying and had no idea that they could be so close to the Thames.

As they passed through the gate Jory dragged his heels, but the Jackdaw's hand sent him ahead with a shove which might almost have passed for good-natured encouragement. Once inside, the captive viewed the place with the darting glances of a rat cornered in a pit to meet not one but three ready terriers.

Kevin surveyed the same territory with open approval. "A good private place, cully," he com-

plimented the Jackdaw. "I'd lay a roundboy as
how a man could loose off a barker in here and not
have it heard by any as would have cause to come
interferin'." By some magic a pistol appeared in
his own hand. While he did not aim it, his very
ease in handling the weapon was a threat.

"Now," he swung to Murray, "this here cove
fancies a shiv hisself. Does a bit of shiv work to
order now and then."

Murray took the hint, willing to play along so
far with their game. The fact that Jory was in no
way an attractive person made it easier. The fellow's
face was not fantastically ugly, nor scarred, but his
pale, unsteady eyes, his wet, pendulous lower lip
indicated a character far from wholesome.

The American produced the throwing knife he
had retrieved from Bargee. Instantly Jory's attention fastened on it. Murray tossed the blade into
the air and caught it again. He was sure he had
seen Jory flinch. Even if he had, the man had a
rat's courage to draw on as he fronted the three of
them.

"What kind of a game be you tryin' to play,
Barker?"

"No game at all, Jory. Why should we try to
play games with a peevy cove like you? Diddled
me right you did—bein' that honest wagoner tellin'
where was a bridle-cull. Did you get your forty
pounds for cryin' rope so loud? Want I should say
thanks for that, Jory?"

Again Murray caught that slight shadow of change
in the other's expression. Had he been expecting
some charge other than that of betraying Kevin?

"Blew the gaff on the Barker." Jackdaw shook

his head solemnly. "Was all your wits leakin' out of your noodle, Jory boy?"

Kevin grinned. "Oh, it warn't Jory as thought that up, was it, Jory? You was speakin' words as some one else gave you, like a play-actor. He must be beholden to you, cully, for speakin' up so brave and free to turn me up. Didn't he think I'd ever prig him? I knew he was smoky the first time I ever clapped ogles on his bacon face. That's why we ain't attendin' to you here and now, Jory." He twirled the pistol so that its barrel pointed significantly at the sluggish current of the river. The pantomime was clear, but Jory was not so easily broken.

"Stubble it!" He bade his captors. "You ain't dealin' with no flat. I keeps me bone-box shut."

"Do you now?" encouraged the Jackdaw. "You is a proper hero, Jory. We'll pass it along to all the lads as how you only did your prime duty when you put the Runners on the Barker for a quick snabble—and the forty pounds comin' to you, of course!"

There was a long moment of silence. The Jackdaw's tone had been one of hearty friendship with no discernible trace of threat. But Jory shrank a little into himself, pulling at his pendulous lower lip with thumb and forefinger as if confronted by a problem he did not know how to solve.

" 'Course," the Jackdaw went on smoothly, "the lads, sometimes they don't take kindly to the notion that there's them what'll turn up a cove to line their pockets. But you can explain it to 'em, Jory. Jus' like you is goin' to explain it to us now. If you didn't have any orders to blab on the Barker, why did you do that? The Barker, he never pulled the dirty on you.''

Jory's plucking fingers worked in a regular rhythm, his pale eyes flickered from one to another, resting the whiles on the river, a view from which he always came away with a quick jerk.

''You ain't goin' to spread it 'round as how I turned up the Barker,'' he observed with no conviction at all.

Kevin's expression was one of innocent surprise. ''It's pretty well about now, Jory. News like that has a way of flyin'. It was a close-run thing for me. Nay, it's about the town now, cully. Only you tells us a straight story and the lads maybe will believe it. We wants him what gave them orders more'n we wants you.''

More than ever Jory looked like a cornered rat. His hand dropped from his working mouth and there was a growing bead of saliva on his lip. But he remained obstinately silent.

''You can stay tight in that hole of yours,'' Kevin pointed out. ''But not forever, Jory. And the lads have a long memory for them as they takes a dislike to. You'd best go on the prod and head out of town while you can still walk. Why don't you go to that good friend of yours as got you into this argle—bargle and see what he'll do for you?''

There was another interval of silence. It was plain to all of them that that bit of advice had no attraction for Jory. It led Murray to an inspiration of his own. For the first time he took a vocal part.

''You've a hold on the Captain yourself, Jory.''

At the word ''Captain'' there was a change in

the other. His short upper lip flattened against his big yellow teeth and he drew a hissing breath.

"Aye," Kevin was ready to add to that. "Look here, Jory, this is Lord Farstarr as wants to nabble the Captain. You opens your trap wide enough and the Captain he gets no chance to turn dirty on you. M'lord will see to that!"

"My word on it," promised Murray.

But Jory had retired into stubborn silence. Kevin shook his head.

"Looks like if he can turn up the Captain, why, the Captain can do the like for him! And I ain't goin' to swing, Jory, not for the little matter of pinnin' your dirty hide to the wall. We doesn't lay a famble on you now—you walks out of here and all *we* does is pass word." He glanced out over the river. "Maybe you'll last all of two days—if you's peevy, and lucky. But I wouldn't lay a broad piece on it."

Jory did not raise his eyes from the ground, but he retreated one step at a time until his back was against one of the piles of rotting boards.

"They'll take me apart!" he said dully, his voice hardly above a whisper.

"And you'd be the first to call it right if you was in their stampers," the Jackdaw remarked. "You can go and spill all you know at Bow Street. But there's them there what can swear you into a noose, as you well know, Jory. Better you wag that rotten tongue of yours with us. We'll give you a breathin' space you can use for poundin' away. Nay, the Barker has it right, we don't have to lay finger on you, jus' pass the word loud and clear."

Jory's hands were together, his fingers twiddling in a weird little dance.

"*He'd* finish me."

"If he catches up with you!" Kevin leaped on that. "But you fix him with us and he'll be too busy to cry rope on you. Don't you believe that, cully?"

Jory's head came up. He stared at the Barker's smooth young face, and then looked to Murray, and finally to the Jackdaw. Something he read in all three led him to a decision.

"He's at a farm, back in the moors out of Shornmouth. And that's all I'm sayin'!" With a speed Murray had not expected him to show he whirled about and made for the yard gate. Neither of the others moved to halt him. When he was gone the Jackdaw laughed, slapping his big hand against his thigh.

"D'you see his face? Jory's broke, he's broke to the wide. He'll be on the prod tonight!"

"But not to Shornmouth, I hope," Murray cut in.

The Jackdaw's mirth died away to a chuckle. "No, guv'nor, he ain't goin' near the Cap'n. He's broke to the wide and he knows as how the Cap'n'll find that out. He'll lay low as long as he can, for as long as he's let—with a twist in his neck from tryin' to look over his shoulder."

"We'd better be on the prod too," Kevin said thoughtfully. "But here's some mint sauce for the gravy, Jackdaw." Coins passed from one hand to another before they went back to the street.

"Anytime, gents," the Jackdaw bade them goodbye, "as you needs a little help, just spread the word. I disremember when I've had meself so neat a job as this."

Any satisfaction Murray and Kevin might have felt over the promising conclusion of their day's venture was dissipated when they returned to Starr House and found Edward Stukley waiting for them.

He looked them over with the cold stare of a schoolmaster about to reach for the birch.

"You has been busy, m'lud," he pointedly ignored Kevin.

"To some purpose. Having had no word from you or Trews, we did a little delving on our own."

"Mr. Trews has been in Scotland this past seven night," Stukley replied, " 'cause of an illness in his family. I've not had any talk with him. But the story's out already that the Barker's come to town."

"Come to town maybe," Kevin agreed. "But don't fash yourself about that, Mr. Stukley. He is goin' out again."

"You've laid hand on the end of a rope?" Stukley was on to that instantly.

"Maybe we has us more'n just the end of one. Any rate we goes to see."

Murray sighed wearily as he sat down. "Not just at this moment," he protested forcibly.

17

No Sea Voyage for the Captain

It might once have been a small manor house, that farm on the lost track out of Shornmouth. By the looks of it from the rutted lane only the main section was still in use, and the two small wings were in a state of dilapidation bordering on ruin. It fitted into the curving rise of a hill as if the mound had been hollowed out to receive it. While because of its earth—colored walls it was difficult to determine where the land ceased and the handiwork of man began.

Some bedraggled chickens scratched in the poor-looking farmyard, and in a bit of pasture fronting the lane an old roan farm horse grazed apathetically, a tabby cat sitting unconcernedly on its back watching Murray, Kevin and Stukley with intelligent interest. Pigeons scrabbled for fowl feed. But for this animal and bird life the place might be deserted.

Stukley eyed the scene with manifest suspicion. He was out of his element here and he greeted the unknown with the wariness of one who inevitably fears the worst. In his opinion their expedition had been doomed from the moment they discovered that the house could not be approached except by that front lane. He observed that any visitors would be speedily spied and so could be eluded long before they reached the dwelling.

"We'd be far more conspicuous trying to creep up on our bellies," Murray exploded when they had first become aware of the disadvantages of the terrain. "If Whyte is holed up here he can't make a break without being seen from the lane, even if he strikes up over that hill. It works both for and against him that way. I'll ride up to the house and do the civil, you watch from the gate. We're gentry out to admire the countryside. They expect gentry to be slightly daft in the head about such queer things as scenery, I learned that at Tregarth."

Kevin grinned impishly. "It's good we have a flash cull to play bear leader for us. Best agree, Mr. Stukley. I can't see as how we can find us a better way. If m'lord here flushes Whyte out and sets him a-runnin'—why, all the gain is ours. Me, if I was Whyte's stampers, I'd stay put. A ken like that one," he nodded at the ancient house, "must be as full of good hidey-holes as a cheese. And we can't tear it apart board by board to find 'em all!''

In the end Stukley was forced to agree to the plan Murray had outlined. Lord Farstarr would ride boldly up to the house, play the part of a lost explorer, and try to discover what he could concerning the inhabitants of the place.

The chickens squawked and fled before him and a gander appeared out of nowhere to hiss a challenge. There was a thin trickle of smoke arising from the chimney of the kitchen. Murray had time to dismount and rap upon the door with his crop before he saw any signs of life.

A serving girl, her coarse apron a map of stains which might have been as old as the house, her red hands tugging at the strings of a frowsy cap, swung open the door to stare at him with the slack jaw and dull eyes of the dim witted. She said nothing, as if the very sight of him had struck her dumb. Murray thought there was no use trying his story upon her. He was about to ask for her mistress when some one called from within:

''Mally! Mally! What's to do, you dunderhead? Shut the door. Want you should let in all the cold winds of the world?'' The voice was querulous, but it was not larded with the country idiom and it had a quality of gentility which surjprised Murray.

The girl turned her head slightly, never withdrawing her gaze from Murray, and gabbled some reply in an accent so thick that, coupled with her mumbling tone, he could not make out a word. But the message brought another to the door.

Mally was elbowed aside by her mistress. The woman was slipping into middle age and one of her shoulders was enlarged to the point of deformity, throwing her weight slightly to the left when she moved. Her face was thickly painted, her wealth of inky black hair elaborately curled, plainly a wig. She wore a fine muslin day gown of the first fashion which might be fresh from one of the London dressmakers to the ton, though its diaphanous elegance was grotesque on her bent body, and she shivered continuously in spite of the warmth of the day, drawing a bright crimson shawl tightly about her as she fronted him. As Mally had before her, she appeared transfixed by her sight of Murray. Not, however, to the point of losing her voice.

"Good day, sir," her voice had a harsh break in it, almost like the cackle of the Jackdaw's pet. "What may we do for you?"

Murray had already doffed his hat, now he bowed. "If you can favor me with directions of the road to Shornmouth, ma'am, I shall rest in your debt. I have been exploring the countryside in company with friends, but none of us are familiar with this district and now we fear we have sadly overcast our small knowledge and are entirely lost."

Should he appeal to any sense of hospitality she might have, endeavor to be invited in? That might be a sensible move, but somehow Murray could not make it. There was something here which he could not set name to, but it chilled him, awoke his warning sense, hammered at him to be away instead of farther in. It was as if he teetered on the edge of a web from which there could be no freedom.

The woman was smiling, but it was a malicious, knowing smile, rather than the polite one of good manners. He had an odd impression that she could reach inside his head and sort out every mixed thought there.

"He is gone, you know." She spoke as one making company conversation.

Murray stood very still. She could not have said that! But she was continuing brightly:

"Three of you, plain in sight from the parlor window so I could not mistake." She laughed hoarsely. "Poor little dab of a woman, ain't I? But whenever he steps into too hot water he comes flying back to his dear lady wife. Only this time things are a little too awkward, even for him. What do you hold against him—murder?"

Murray tried to find words, but she swept on, not waiting for a denial or confirmation. She spoke with the surety of one who had long before made her decisions and would hold to them.

"He never explained himself, of course. But this time it was different, all this looking behind him and taking uncommonly to the bottle. He knew he could command a lodging here—but no more." Her raddled face was stiff as she spoke with a venom which convinced Murray that, whoever this woman might be, she did not intend to stand between Captain Whyte and trouble. "Do me this much kindness, sir, accept my assurance that he is not now under this roof."

"You refer to Captain Whyte, ma'am?" Murray asked bluntly.

"Lionel Whyte," she repeated the name musingly. "A singularly apt name, is it not? Enough of the common touch to make it generally accepted, but with that 'y' to suggest gentle birth. With a name such as that, sharp wits, and a carefully cultivated pleasing manner a man can hope to go far. He can con some poor fool into marriage, he can gull other poor fools out of their purses. Was that his offense in your case, sir?"

"I believe I can count myself one of his failures, ma'am."

She nodded. "Yes, even Lionel had to reckon some failures, since he could never be trusted to keep to the line. A man can go far with Lionel's gifts, but I take it that this time he has gone too far." She peered up at Murray with shrewd eyes. "He was frightened when he left here. He can hide it well, but I know him. And I do not recall ever having seen him truly frightened before. Slightly disturbed, yes—but like this, no. It was most amusing to watch. Living so retired as I do, I find a want of amusement hereabouts. But this time I quite enjoyed my dear husband's visit—his manner was so illuminating. I do not think," she paused, "that I shall see Lionel again. I have no wish to intrude upon your affairs, sir, but if you seek Captain Whyte, you'd best look elsewhere."

"Have you any idea in what direction, ma'am?" To Murray that conversation had the fantastic ring of a dream dialogue, but he did not in the least doubt her honesty.

"I would say overseas. He has connections there. Lionel has some odd beliefs, you must understand. He thought that his will was quite paramount. If he bade one be deaf and blind, they were truly so from that moment. When he behaved so, I thought it best to fall in with his humor. He held that all women were imbecilic, you see. An ill-advised attitude. Yes, it is my thought that he will head overseas—probably on one of the smuggling luggers. There are those that harbor from time to time in Shornmouth and they will serve his turn.''

"How long has he been gone?"

"You have missed him by less than an hour, sir. And so you may yet achieve a meeting with him. I should have liked excessively to have it occur here.''

Murray bowed again. "With your permission, ma'am, I'd best be riding on.''

"I wish you all luck, sir, may fortune ride with you!" She swung the door to smartly upon her last word, plainly well pleased with the promise of trouble for the Captain.

Murray joined the others with his news and was slightly surprised that they accepted his story without question. After all, they had not met Mrs. Whyte. However, Stukley at once turned his mount in the direction of Shornmouth.

"True enough she ain't no cause to love Whyte,'' was his comment. "He married her for the goldboys as she had rattlin' 'round in her pa's chest—he was an Indies merchant. Only after the knot was tied it came out that her pa was a careful man, he had those same roundboys tied up so the Captain couldn't lay paw on them all to once. Came in payments durin' the year. So that the Captain, he had to keep the lady under his eyes and come down to collect at times.''

"You know a precious lot about his affairs,'' Kevin noted.

"Ain't I gettin' me rightful fee, a guinea a day *and* expenses for little trips such as this, just to do

that? We can always shake a cove up and tumble
out his secrets—and others too—when we has a
hint or two to start with. The Captain, he's a man
as had talk made about him for years now. Not
that he's ever before set toe over the line of the
law with proof enough so we could take—as you
might say—an active interest in him. But he has
had ogles on him and his doin's steady.''

Kevin snorted. ''If that's so, you've been runnin'
it devilish fine this time. He may be at sea already.
Who do we know in Shornmouth as will put us on
his trail if he ain't?''

Murray had taken out his watch. Now he smiled
to himself, fingering what hung on its fob chain.
He had put the stone ring there as a curiosity, now
it might prove to be the key to a door. If he could
show that in a seaside inn in Shornmouth he might
get the information they needed—or at least it
should serve as an introduction to certain exclusive
circles.

The road which linked the small port with the
inland wound leisurely along and, once they were
out of the farmhouse lane, they set a brisker pace.
Stukley grunted.

''What's this?'' he inquired of the countryside,
''a funeral?''

The black vehicle ahead kept to a sober trot
befitting its hue, but it was not a hearse. Murray
rode forward to have his suspicions confirmed by
the white inscription along its side, the sight of
two small figures bobbing on the backs of the
horses.

''Holgar's!'' At that moment he was struck by
heady inspiration.

Here was the perfect way to enter Shornmouth without remark—if the Holgars would agree. He himself was too well known to Whyte to risk the other sighting him first.

"Holgar!" Murray's shout approached a bellow as he ranged alongside of the van.

As usual Holgar was not in sight. Miss Lucasta turned an affronted face to Murray, and her brothers' heads swung about. Only the cat, serene in its usual seat, paid him no note and yawned rudely in his face. As Murray took off his hat and bowed to Miss Lucasta she brought the van to a stop, her eyes assessing his fashionable dress, his blooded horse, with manifest disapproval.

"Good morning, Miss Holgar."

"Good morning, sir." Her voice was as cool as ever. "I see that you have come into a fortune since our last meeting."

Murray smiled, as he hoped, winningly. "I may still be in the pursuit of it, Miss Holgar. You *are* bound for Shornmouth?"

"Yes. We have had good acceptance there in other years," she returned sharply as if he had in some way challenged the Holgar popularity.

Murray was uncomfortable. How dared he ask bluntly to be allowed to take cover in the Holgar van? To go into a deal of explanation now would not only delay them—but his story sounded so close to preposterous that he could not voice it to such a hostile audience.

Kevin and Stukley came up. Then Murray saw a sudden and vivid change in the prim and colorless Lucasta Holgar. She was actually smiling in welcome. Murray, startled, glanced around in time to see Kevin bow in the saddle, flourishing his hat with the address of a Bond Street Beau.

"Mr. Kevin! You're trading at Shornmouth?"

"Not today, ma'am. We ride on another errand. And how goes matters with Holgar's?"

She retreated behind her prim facade once more. "Well enough in the general way, Mr. Kevin. Father has four new shows, all warranted to make a good stir. The Death of Nelson, The Murder of the Duc d'Enghien, Cleopatra of the Nile, and the Terrible Cave of Swanny Bean," she told them off soberly.

"*Now* what has happened?" Holgar himself came around from the rear of the van. "I thought we might have been set in the ditch once more by some nincompoop who never learned to handle leathers properly."

He caught sight of Kevin and nodded with the ease of old acquaintance. "So it's you, Jack Kevin, trying to talk Cassy into laying out good money on one of those flashy high-steppers of yours? That hare won't start, m'man, she's too knowing to be taken in by your creamtalk." He reached up a hand which bore some paint smears on the fingers and shook hands with Kevin. "Been a good year since we laid eyes on you last. Still hanging about with Strumper?"

"Not now. Holgar's does well by the sight of you."

Holgar shrugged. "We keep bread in our mouths. Why," he caught sight of Murray, "it's the lad who saw us through that ditching. Friend of yours, Jack? I mind now as how he said he was in the show way of business."

"Just now he's on another lay," Kevin was beginning, when Murray cut in, worried at the waste of time.

"Yes, and I have a favor to ask, Mr. Holgar. Will you suffer me and—" He turned to Kevin, "I take it Whyte would be able to recognize you readily?"

"He should." There was a chill in that quiet answer.

"I'd take it as a vast favor on your part, Mr. Holgar," Murray restated his request, "should you allow Kevin and me to ride into Shornmouth in your van. There's a gentleman," his tone underlined that definition, "there who might take it into his head to become invisible should he discover us before we lay eye on him, and it is very necessary that he does *not* so vanish."

Holgar's eyebrows moved upward on his long, mournful countenance. "What kind of a mill you caught up in, Jack?"

"Nothin' on the far side of the law," Kevin's tone was almost as prim as Lucasta's, and Murray bit back a smile. "This here's Ned Stukley o' Bow Street," he beckoned the third member of their party forward. "It's the man we're after who has to explain hisself proper—to all three of us!"

In the end Holgar agreed. The two horses were given into Stukley's charge and it was arranged that he should stable them at the nearest inn while Murray and Kevin stowed away in the cramped interior of the van, to be jolted on toward Shornmouth.

Lucasta's boast that Holgar's entertainment had favor there was born out by the muffled shouts of greeting as the van left the road for the slightly smoother pavement of a street. Holgar nodded with satisfaction at that sound.

"It's good craftsmanship as does it! Some give 'em tawdry, mocked-up things—all paper and trash. But in Holgar's they see the best! Naught can range above our scenes. And we have new ones every year, not the same ones as they has seen before—as well they know."

He twitched the flaps from various boxes and the subdued light present in the van added to the gruesome effectiveness of his carefully wrought miniatures. Kevin whistled.

" 'Tis enough to give one a cold race up the spine to be sure," he commented. "Ain't missed a beheadin' nor a hangin' yet, have you?"

Holgar took that seriously. "There are some too misty in the public mind. 'Tis well not to use stories as are not general knowledge, unless some situation in 'em makes 'em memorable. This is all history, the darker side maybe, but true history. And for those as would refresh their memories as to such events afterwards we have broadsides, two for a penny, the twins sell 'em through the crowd."

Murray watched Kevin a bit curiously. The Barker did not seem at all moved by the various graphic examples of the just ends of criminals, his interest was that of a law-abiding and innocent citizen. So Murray could not forego a sly thrust.

"An excellent series of arguments against a life of crime. Otherwise such an exhibition could scarcely afford gratification to any of delicate sensibilities."

Kevin's expression did not change but Holgar must have sensed the sarcasm. He bristled a little.

"Aye, there are those who would cry down my "Horrors" with words like yours. But there are plenty to crowd to a real hanging, paying out money for a good window seat from which they can see a rogue turned off without having to rub elbows with the riff-raff. There's a lesson to be learned from such as these," he pointed to his small masterpieces. "We are hard on men, but we ain't quite as hard as our grandfathers were. Belike our grandsons will look back with shame on what we do. It's good to be reminded of that once in awhile."

Kevin smiled thinly. "But it all changes very slow, don't it? Ah, we're stoppin'. Come to your pitch, Mr. Holgar?"

Holgar opened the small van door and Murray caught a glimpse of a wall and an unharnessed chaise. They must be in an inn yard. A minute later that guess was confirmed by Holgar.

"This be the Silver Hart. You're not overlooked by the street."

So encouraged, Murray and Kevin left the van, avoiding those already gathering about Holgar's equipage, and made for the inn. The landlord, recognizing in Murray a member of the Quality, showed them to a private parlor, and once the door was closed Kevin spoke:

"Well, we're in Shornmouth. So now how do we flush our pigeon?"

Murray brought out his watch for the second time, snapped loose the fob chain and detached the stone ring.

"If there be any 'free trader' in Shornmouth this is our passport. We should be able to find one in an inn frequented by seamen. Then we have only to outbid Whyte, which should be easy, and he won't be over the channel as he hopes, but right in our hands."

"Sounds peevy enough. But do you comb the inns yourself? A flash cull about these quarters would set word travelin' fast."

"We may have Stukley beat those bushes first. And I have a tale which might help. Wait 'til mine host brings us that homebrewed he so bepraised."

When the landlord returned Murray had his story ready, one he thought, with reason, did credit to his powers of invention. He possessed, he confessed, a wild young brother sent out to tutor in the country. Not being at all bookish, the lad had cut and run.

"My father will be within good reason angry." Murray confided all the signs of honest concern he could summon. "He is already ill advised in this and other matters, should not be quite cast off. I am fearful that he will completely lose his head and make for the channel with some wild taking of going for a sailor in his noodle. He's game as a pebble, but too quick off the mark by far. Keep him tight reined and he'll ever try to bolt. We've traced him here, but I must ask questions of those as have reason to know the channel." he gave the host what he hoped would register as a meaningful glance. "If I can get Kit back with his tutor before it comes to the notice of my father it will save much anxiety all round."

"Lads often turn nonsensical when they be high spirited and crossed, sir," the landlord agreed.

"As to where you can discover those as may help him in such a hare-brained ploy, why if I were you, sir, I'd go to the Star and Compass." He added the directions for reaching that water-front pub.

Stukley arrived just as they prepared to go out. Thus the three of them made their way as inconspicuously as possible to a small place abutting on a wharf. Stukley prowled to the back while Kevin was left in the street, and Murray, his passport in his hand, went inside.

The low room with its noticeable scent of spirits and unwashed humanity was not so far different from the Mermaid, even to the type of men who sat carefully ignoring the newcomer after one startled glance at his entrance.

Murray flipped the pebble on the table where he had chosen to sit alone, tossing it in the air and letting it clink to the wood.

"You was lookin' for someone, guv'nor?" A man slipped onto the stool on the other side of the stained board. Time was running out and Murray came directly to the point.

"I was."

"You comes maybe from down the coast apiece, guv'nor?"

Murray let the stone lie quiet between them. "I come from where this pebble does."

But the man did not look at the stone ring. "Can you lay name as to him you is lookin' for?"

Murray shook his head. "I don't know what name he may be using. But I do know this: he is seeking passage with no questions asked, probably as soon as possible. If he is delivered to me instead,

I'll double the rate he has promised to pay. He has
put himself outside the law, incidentally. In fact
he's in danger of the noose—and not for a matter
of free trading.''

The man raised the tankard he had brought with
him. Over its rim his eyes were steady on Murray.

''You comes with somethin' to back you,'' he
conceded as he put down the empty tankard. ''But
once a cove's money is paid you won't find them
as will split on him.''

''*Has* money passed?''

''Not yet. Was you to be on the Gripe Head
come moonrise you might find what you is a-huntin'
for. But losin' passage money is leavin' honest
men's pockets to let.''

''They won't be to let.'' Murray palmed the
ring. ''Down the coast my word is good. I promise
money past just passage fee.'' He walked out,
wondering just how many hours lay between him
and moonrise now.

18

The Fashioning of an Earl

What hour could be moonrise, mused Murray some hours later, when it was very evident that the moon would not show at all? There was a rising wind, from which they were attempting to shelter against one of the cliffs bordering on a cove. A thick mass of clouds scudded under its shepherding across the sky. As time dragged on, Murray began to suspect that perhaps he had been carefully steered to where he could not interfere, and so left to cool his heels while Whyte disappeared aboard a lugger some distance away. If the Captain had only chosen the smugglers of Tregarth to act his ferrymen! Then the lord of Garth Holme would have had no worries at all. Now he could only depend upon the power of the stone ring and the promise of the stranger he had met at the Star and Compass.

It was his forest training which gave him the first warning. He caught at Kevin's arm in the dark, pressing it lightly, knowing that signal would be passed along to alert Stukley in turn. Then the rattle of a dislodged stone on the shingle somewhere to their right was clear enough to reach the ears of all three. Someone was advancing at a careful pace down the scrap of beach toward the point where they stood in deepest shadow. There was a small splash, a bitten-off oath, the scrape of boot on stone. The newcomer was not discovering his path easy.

The sudden glow of a flash was dazzling, but to see who stood in the dark behind that signal was impossible. For the second time that flash flared. Against the black rise of the cliff it must be plainly visible seaward. Only they could not yet move against the signaler, they must be sure he was the man they wanted.

Breaking waves might cover sounds from the water, but Murray was sure he was able to pick out a thicker shadow riding in on the combers, under the skillful management of men well used to dark shores and night landings. Then a whistle from the sea was answered by a soft hail from the land:

"Here!"

The light moved upward, shone for the third

time, this time illuminating a face Murray had last
seen by candle light. Kevin made recognition in
the same moment and moved forward with Murray.

Whyte was far too intent upon the approaching
skiff to notice them, and Murray's hand closed in
a punishing grip on the wrist above the flare lantern before Whyte realized that he was not alone.
His surprise only immobilized him for a second,
he was so keyed up that his very fears of such a
happening had prepared him to counter it. The
lantern crushed to the shingle and a hard left struck
against Murray's shoulder, bringing a thrill of pain
from his half-healed wound, weakening his hold
upon the struggling man.

Had Murray been alone Whyte might have won
free. But Kevin and Stukley attacked, and together
they brought the frantic captive under control. He
shouted to the waiting skiff for aid. However that
hung off shore. Panting, Murray went down the
beach until the water washed about his ankles.

"Your passenger does not sail tonight," he called.
"But you'll find his passage money on the rock
here." He tossed his own netted purse to the top
of a boulder and the clink of metal in it must have
reassured the oarsmen. At least it seemed to keep
them out of the struggle on the beach.

He splashed back to find Stukley had righted the
lantern and by its glow was examining a limp
figure lying on the sand. Whyte's face, blank and
slack, was turned up to the sky, a thread of blood
trickling from the corner of his gaping mouth. For
a minute Murray was afraid, he looked so very
limp and uncaring.

"Is he—?"

Stukley had rolled the Captain over on his side and was fastening his wrists behind him, looped together with a cord in a manner which showed much familiarity with such restraints.

"He's just sleepin' it off, m'lud. Got him a tap on the nob as will set him to dreamin' for awhile. Only that means as how we has to lug him out o' here. Well," he shrugged, philosophically, "you can't have it both ways in this here world. What you got there, Mr. Lyon?"

Kevin came into the restricted circle of the lantern light, a cloak bag in one hand.

"His, I think. I'll fetch it along and we'll see."

Somehow they got the unconscious Captain up to the road and there laid him out on the ground while Kevin went off to the inn for a horse and trap. Before he returned Whyte had regained his senses. As in the dark he had not been able to identify his captors, he believed that they were revenue officers. His first move was an offer to pay for his release, increasing the sum when neither Murray nor Stukley replied. Then he mentioned that there were those in high places who would come to his assistance and make them, agents of the crown though they might be, smart for their overzealousness.

"There are those in high places who want a word with you right enough," Murray grew impatient enough to counter.

Whyte was silent. Had he recognized his voice, Murray wondered. To make that identification certain he stooped over, under the pretext of examining Whyte's bonds, so that the light revealed his face.

To his amazement Whyte chuckled. "So it's you who've turned me up, Farstarr? I might have suspected. But why risk your neck so freely? If you take me back there'll be questions asked which will lead straight to Royal Street and your very unfortunate cousin."

"It is for the purpose of answering such questions that you are being prevailed upon to return with us," Murray replied. "We want to ask a lot of questions about my unfortunate cousin!"

The rig came down the road and Whyte was stowed in it between Stukley and Murray, while Kevin kept the reins.

"Holgar's giving a performance in the inn yard," Kevin told them. "But it's close to the end. We'd be remarked if we drove in before the crowd scatters. I'll take a long way round and come in from the opposite direction."

"We'd best be off for town as early as possible," Murray cut in. "I take it we can hire a chaise?"

"With enough blunt you can hire anything," was Kevin's return.

Whyte remained dumb, even when his wrists were tied to the bedposts in the inn room shared by Murray and Kevin and he was allowed to recline on the bed in more comfort than enjoyed by his guards. At his first sight of Kevin he had frozen, although the Barker never addressed him or tried to call to mind their former meetings.

The ride back to London was uncomfortable. Whyte sat encased in silence, behind which wall Murray did not doubt that the Captain's wits were turning over a number of plans to free himself from his present embroilment. It was plain that he still nourished hopes of that, and since they did not discuss anything but the most trivial matters before him, he could not guess how much they knew.

They went straight to Starr House, and Murray, before he sat down to a hearty meal, dispatched an urgent message to Trews asking him to join them, hoping that the man of law had returned from Scotland.

An hour later when Whyte faced them in the Book Room, it was with an unscathed aplomb, as if in his narrow hands he still held winning cards to play. Trews, more than a little shaken by the tale which had been poured out to him, and still more by the papers found in the Captain's cloak bag, beat a nervous finger tattoo on the desk, leaving it to the experienced Stukley to open the questioning. The ex-Runner did so with the confidence of a law officer who had his quarry under his hand with no doubt as to the proof of his guilt.

"Captain Whyte, before we hand you over to be charged there's a deal of questions—"

Whyte broke in, his voice soft with his own particular brand of menace.

"So now there's talk of handing over to the law, is there? Here is a man of the law, Mr. Trews, to make plain to all of you that suspicion and proof are two very different matters, and that there is a law of slander in this kingdom. Also, I can certainly not be depended upon to keep silent when I myself am endangered. Ask Lord Farstarr to what purpose his knife was used in a certain room in Royal Street! His lordship had good reason to desire a man dead, and straightway that man is discovered in that state—with his lordship's knife employed to do the business.''

''That cock won't fight,'' Kevin said quietly. ''Since I'm the cove as was the rightful target for such an attack, and I was nowhere near Royal Street. And don't say as how his lordship didn't know that *warn't* me, 'cause we can lay our fambles on Jory, and already we've had a good crack with him. We have only to send out the word and there's them what'll turn him up right and tight for us. Jory ain't popular nowadays. When it comes to a matter of neck-stretchin'—and Jory knows that we have you—do you think he'll keep his clapper-jaws shut? Aye, you probably have that to mind what'll hang Jory, too. But he's the kind of cove as won't hang alone, as you should well know, seein' as how he's played your hands and feet for years.''

Whyte's eyes dropped to his hands, he flexed his fingers, crooking them into claws. Watching him, Kevin laughed.

''Aye, you'd like to hook those about me throat now, wouldn't you? 'Tis your misfortune that you tried to get an honest man to play the dirty. He's been on your trail since the start, ferretin' out all the traps you set to snare us. You mistook two men—him and me!''

''You can't prove murder. Attempted blackmail perhaps, but not murder!'' Whyte was unshaken.

''Perhaps not,'' Stukley agreed. ''But this kind o' blackmail is enough to get you transported. Maybe a slow death overseas is worse'n the rope. We has your papers, we has the testimony of his lordship as to how you made several suggestions to him. We has the sworn word of Mr. Kevin Lyon as to what you asked *him*.''

"A highwayman who dares not come to testify in any court!''

"No,'' Murray said softly. "The Barker is not Kevin Lyon, nor Kevin Lyon the Barker. That can be arranged. There are royal pardons and a pardoned man is free to speak. Kevin Lyon has those who will stand behind him. Also, if your story is true, I do not doubt that you had a hand in forcing him into his trade.''

"That be a true word if there ever was one, m'lud,'' chimed in the ex-Runner. " 'Twas the Captain here as kept Jory lookin' after the lad to know where he was, yet he never did aught to help him to an honest life. We knows a deal of the tale in and out, Captain,'' he spoke directly to Whyte, "don't mistake that!''

"It still provides a nasty blot to beslime the name of Lyon,'' Whyte was outwardly serene, he might have been speaking of some spicy on dit of the town, with which he had no possible connection. "You'll not move, Farstarr, to disinherit yourself and blacken your name. Because if you do bring me to trial, I promise you I'll spread it all out for the snickers of the world. There was a marriage, true enough, but not such as will give any luster to the Lyons of Starr.''

Kevin's face was impassive but he shifted in his chair and Murray guessed that that had struck home. Before he could speak Stukley snorted.

"Lady Starr was Miss Emilia Kelton, and her pa was an officer of the King; killed he was in the American war. So Miss Emilia, she went out for a governess, pore thing, 'cause her pa didn't leave her full in the pocket. She warn't what you've been a hintin', Captain Whyte—only a pore young lady as had misfortunes. An' marryin' with the Earl warn't the least o' them, neither!''

Whyte sat very still but he shot a glance at the ex-Runner which was so venomous that it had the quality of a blow. Kevin had caught his underlip between his teeth. He, too, was staring at Stukley, but with open wonder. This part of the story must be new to him, a surprise for which he was not prepared.

Now Murray took up the argument. For him, for his father, there was only one possible course of action. They would resign all claim to Starr's earldom without bringing the matter to court. Kevin might be a nine-day wonder, the center of a scandal if Whyte could force it so. But with the American branch backing his claim, that would fade. The circle in which he would live in the future was a restricted one, he must not enter it under a cloud.

However, short of disposing of Whyte in some efficient manner, the whispering would begin and grow. The Captain might have no chance legally, but his tongue could clack. There was a poison in that smiling man, showing in every word he spoke. Whyte would have to be silenced—and one way flashed into Murray's mind at that instant. He wondered just how efficient the Captain was with a pistol. A duel was illegal but tolerated—if you could get away with it—accepted by society. Suppose he challenged Whyte.

It did not come to that. For Francis Trews answered first.

"You are mistaken, Whyte." He was now his usual imperturbable self. "Worse scandals than this have been successfully weathered, as well you know. And if the claimant's rights are not challenged in court, much of the uproar is done with. I take it, Farstarr," he spoke now to Murray, "it does not suit your will to fight the claim?"

"If it is just, certainly not!"

"No, the raking up of ill deeds of the past will scarcely afford gratification to any of those concerned. The character of his late lordship was sufficiently well established that any such muddle might only be expected to follow his death. It will afford talk to be sure, but it need not wreck the family as you appear to believe that it will, Whyte."

"Very prettily spoken," returned the Captain softly. "Forget, yes—but does that also imply forgetting in all quarters?"

He was so completely at his ease that Murray's frown deepened. Whyte acted as if he had nothing to fear. Trews must have noted that also, for he asked:

"You expect to walk from this room unhindered?"

"Unhindered and with sufficient funds to reassume an interrupted journey. You have what you want, the truth. Therefore you no longer have any use for me, nor do I have any use for you, since my plans have been so fully undone. But you cannot bring any murder home to me. In fact, though in the eyes of the law my hands may be a little shadowed, they are not really soiled."

"Jory—" Kevin said, but not with much confidence.

"Jory—*if* you find him, *if* you can make him

talk—will only hang himself, and not lay the rope around my neck. I fancy I can be the best judge of Jory's usefulness, since he is a tool of my own. And I am speaking the full truth.''

Murray believed that he was. The very slippery Captain was going to wriggle, eel-like, out of their grip. Kevin broke in:

"You're all certain he's right? I'm the Earl of Starr? But what if I say no?''

"If you're Starr, you're Starr,'' Murray repeated wearily. "We won't take what isn't ours.''

"A very pious sentiment, highly noble,'' Whyte sneered. "Yes, gentlemen, your highwayman is Starr, right and tight. I made sure of that after poor George departed the scene. It was very much to my advantage to do so, and I needed proof which could not be questioned should it be necessary to become embroiled with the law. I can put you in hand with everything needful to back the case.'' His eyes were half closed. He yawned delicately, conveying his weariness of the present company with that gesture. "You will have it all, of course, *after* I am safely at the Hague.''

Murray appealed to Trews and Stukley. "Must it be that way?''

Trews nodded slowly, his expression one of baffled distaste. But the ex-Runner watched the Captain with the bright eyes of a hunting cat. Then the Captain made a suggestion which harked back to Murray's thoughts of a short time before.

"Naturally, if a gentleman considered himself affronted, Farstarr—or should I address you as 'Lyon' now, since the truth is out? If a gentleman suffers an affront he always has one course open to him for action. Or aren't you overseas provincials enough accustomed to the uses of good society to be aware of such niceties of conduct? Having lived so long among savages—of one kind or another—I imagine you do not understand me.''

Murray battened down his temper with rigid control. Why—with the game almost his, escape before him—was Whyte trying to goad him into a meeting? There was a raging animosity in the other's voice, a fire behind that calm facade. He made the shrewdest reply he could have found to force the other into the open:

''What gentlemen do under provocation and what you may do, Whyte, are two separate things. A Lyon fights his equals.''

Whyte moved in a rattlesnake's strike. Murray's eyes watered under the sting of that open hand-slap across the face. The Captain smiled, but the smile was very thin. ''You poor rustic fool, you'll meet me for that!''

However, as always he had made the mistake of judging Murray by his own world and not the one from which the other had sprung. Murray had been tempered in a steeling process the Captain could not imagine in his wildest dreams. He blinked the moisture from his eyes in time to catch Kevin's sleeve as the other jumped to his feet.

''I said that no gentleman will meet with you on equal terms, and I meant that, Whyte. For a cur one uses the whip.'' He reached behind him for the crop he had left on the table upon his return.

Whyte, his lips thinned against his excellent teeth, watched him with narrowed eyes. Believing that the other meant what he said, he snatched up.

the mummy-based candlestick, a deadly club. Murray wrapped the lash about Whyte's wrist in one easy blow. The other screamed, a thin, high howl, and dropped his improvised weapon. Then Kevin tripped him expertly from behind. Murray stood breathing fast. On his cheek the mark of the slap could still be seen. For a second he half raised the crop and then he flung it from him.

"You can't win in that fashion." But he might have been speaking to himself rather than to Whyte.

"He ain't winnin' nohow," Stukley limped forward. "Lionel Whyte, I arrests you in the name of the Crown for murder."

"You can't!" Whyte spat him. "Jory—"

"Jory has been nabbed. And Jory has babbled. Likewise we has proof."

"It was done with Lyon's knife, and he had good cause to kill."

"Was it now?" Stukley's expression was one of mild puzzlement. "Seein' as how this here murder as I have in mind was done before either o' these lads here was breeched, I don't see as how he could."

Had he been striving to create a dramatic pause, he obtained his object. They were all quiet, waiting.

"Them papers as you was carryin' overseas with you, Captain, they tells more'n one tale, if you has hunted down the other pieces, which I has been a-doin' of since his lordship hired me for the same. You was handy with your fambles once, just as Jory was handy with a shiv as didn't nowise belong to him. Pore Miss Emilia, she wouldn't take to your dirty plans either, would she, Captain, that lady what your good friend the Earl married so quiet-like? So you finished her off to get the lad for yourself. Only that went wrong, too.''

Under their astonished gaze Whyte sat very still in the chair into which Kevin had pushed him. A bead of moisture gathered on his lower lip, dripped to his disordered cravat. His eyes had the dull sheen of a sick bird-of-prey.

''You can't prove it!'' Dully he repeated his old boast, but the certainty, the vigor had gone out of it. He had been prepared for one charge, but this other had caught him off guard, and it seemed he could not pull his wits together and use that native sharp intelligence which had always saved him before.

''You made a prime try, Captain,'' Stukley gave credit where it was due. ''It was a close-run thing. But you forgets one thing.'' He leaned across the end of the desk, picking up the candlestick from the floor and using it as a pointer aimed first at Whyte and then himself. ''You forgets Ned Stukley. You didn't never clap ogles on me—likely not to your knowledge, that is. But me, I was with Jem Stimson—me bein' a young lad what he took a shine to, and brought up by hand as it were—and Jem was called in from Bow Street when that pore lady was found cold and stiff in her bed. Jem, he peeked and pried and he was nigh to clappin' hand on *your* shoulder—that bein' a mort of years ago. Talked to me, Jem did, about that case and how he was drawin' a tight net to take you in. But then he was took with a rheum and was gone between two days, coughin' his life out. I had his occurrence book and knew what he knew, but I was just a raw lad only months in the Runners. Before I could get

it all together there was a witness gone, I not bein'
as smart as Jem, and I didn't have no case any
more. By the time I thought as how I could move,
there was them as had a score against me for
another matter, and they saw it settled in a dark
lane one night. Roughed me up proper, they did,
left me to die of it. Only I didn't, you see. By the
time I could crawl about again the trail was doubly
cold. Likewise I warn't no proper Runner any
more—me what had been in the service since I
was younger nor these lads here!

"But, though me leg was crooked," he tapped a
forefinger to his head, "me mind was nowise
bent. I could recall everythin' what happened and I
kept on peekin' and pryin', 'cause that was a big
case and Jem, he'd been sure of you, Captain. But
the lad here," he nodded at Kevin, "was gone, we
both lost track of him, didn't we? And it takes
time, so it does, to hunt along a cold trace and lay
a peevy one like you under the wraps, Captain.
But time I had, plenty of it. Look here—"

From the inner breast pocket of his brown coat
he brought some slips of paper. "There be a
statement, sworn to all legal and tight, made by
Molly Hawkins. You disremember Molly Hawkins,
do you, Captain? She took over the lad when his
mother was gone.

"She's dead, but 'fore that she talked. There's
them still livin' as will talk also, now that you're
laid up by the heels. Those papers as you was
carryin' sews it all tight. As Mr. Trews has said,
the old earl, he had no good name, and nobody is
goin' to raise an eyebrow too high over no antic of

his'n. This lad won't have to worry too much about side-looks.''

"Except,'' Kevin pointed out with a certain detachment, "he was my father.''

Murray faced him quickly. "There're Lyons and Lyons. One rotten apple doesn't poison the tree.''

Kevin shrugged. "He's naught to me. I never set ogle on him that I know of. What I am is me own makin'.''

"A highwayman!'' sneered Whyte.

"The Barker!'' cut back Kevin. "A bridle-cull as is second to none!''

"That had best be forgotten and quickly,'' Trews warned. "I take it, Stukley, you have this fellow to rights?'' He regarded Whyte as frostily as if the Captain had already been tried and condemned.

"It's been a long time, but I have, sir. I gives you your new Lord Starr, but me, I takes this gallows-fruit here, and is pleased to do so!''

For Murray the question of Starr's true heir was done and settled, though Trews proceeded cautiously, investigating the evidence three times over. The American, or so he thought of himself once again, shucked off the viscount as he would liked to have shucked off a tight, fashionable coat for the freedom of forest buckskin. Only Kevin would have none of that. Murray must stay, at least until Fitzhugh Lyon returned to England and the last bit of legal work was done.

It was later that Murray had a taste of Kevin's own brand of justice. He came into Starr House fresh from an interview with Trews to seek out his cousin.

"And why did you do that?" he demanded at the end of his recital of the afternoon's disclosures.

Kevin grinned. "As once you said, there's Lyons and Lyons. Maybe I've got to prove it right and tight as how I ain't the same breed as me pa. But it's just a matter of play and pay. Lord, ain't I now got pockets so crammed with roundboys I ain't never goin' to see their bare bottoms again? Our great-grandfather never did right by you accordin' to the accounts Trews has dug up. He saw as how your pa didn't get the money he should have had from his grandmother's leavin's. So you're only to take what is yours by rights."

Murray pulled at the cravat which still tended to fret his throat in moments of excitement. "It'll be enough to set up the company again, you know that. Pay all debts and give us good capital. Once this cursed embargo is off, why we'll have clear sailing for good!"

"You threw away a bigger fortune," the new Earl of Starr reminded him.

"We never really had it. Somehow I had that thought in the back of my mind from the first day I saw Trews in Baltimore."

Kevin stretched. In his well-cut clothing, with his fashionably barbered head, he was the picture of a proper young gentleman. And the self-confidence of the Barker who had been at the top of his chosen "lay" blended well into the carriage of Lord Starr.

"Lyons and Lyons," he repeated. "Somehow I thinks as how we is goin' to go a right sight better from now on. No more pistols and—" he shot a mischievous side-glance at Murray, then rubbed his arm in reminiscence, "no more knives!"

Murray laughed. "Naturally not—unless they are needed!" His native distrust of the future made him add that rider in the way of warning any listening Fate.